China Girl

Douglas Owen

Science Fiction and Fantasy Publications

CHINA GIRL
DOUGLAS OWEN

Science Fiction and Fantasy Publications

https://scififantasypublications.com
A division of DAOwen Publications

China Girl / Douglas Owen

ISBN - 978-1-928094-72-2
EISBN - 978-1-928094-70-8

This is a work of fiction. Names, characters, places, and incidents either are the product of the author's imagination or are used fictitiously, and any resemblance to actual persons, living or dead, businesses, companies, events, or locales is entirely coincidental.

Jacket Art commissioned by MMT Productions

10 9 8 7 6 5 4 3 2

For my Dad

January 9th, 2033 – Gabriella

Snow fogs the sky, a silken sheet shimmering in the wind. Piles of it litter the ground. Plows have yet to clear the roads or sidewalks. But it makes no difference. Gabriella floats through it in a cannabis-induced haze. Three joints of Electric Blue course through her system, dulling out the snow filling her boots. She pulls her coat tighter and smiles, not a care in the world.

Gabriella laughs, remembering Josh stroking her arm, whispering his request to accompany her home, though living just a few blocks from the Pot Land shop has its advantages. She declined the offer, not wanting to have his hairy ass in her hands while he pumped himself into her. But still, once he did satisfy the emptiness inside. No, it's better to be alone tonight and enjoy the buzz.

She glances at the houses on Taunton Road. Light from one building breaks through the snow only to be masked by the limbs of a tall bush. Small spots of light glisten and reflect off particles in the wind as she walks toward her basement apartment.

Gabriella shivers as the cold stabs, threatening to disperse the evening's two-hundred-dollar euphoria purchase. Wind masks all sound. Even busy Yonge Street is all but closed to traffic. Her phone buzzes and vibrates. Another warning of the storm raging across the

GTA blazes across the screen and through her numbed mind. Gabriella stuffs the device back into a pocket.

She stops, rests a hand against the light pole, and lifts up her left foot. The heel is gone.

"Fuck," she mutters, letting out an exasperated breath. She shivers as the bite of the cold hits her for the first time since leaving the pot shop. Her buzz wanes. The wind whips around her head, lifting loose hair. She pulls up the collar of the coat to protect the shaven sides of her scalp.

Headlights flood the street as a cargo van turns down the un-plowed road. The slow pace allows it to push through the drifts. White paint against white roads. Black windows hiding the occupants.

Gabriella stares at her ruined boot. The van pulls up beside her, the door slides open. Two hooded men in black jump out. Hands wrap around her arms, steel-like. A stab of pain hits her neck. A needle punctures skin and fire swarms through her. Muscles go numb and lax. The euphoria scatters. Legs give out, but two hands grab her before she falls. The world darkens.

More hands grasp her around the legs. Vision blurring, Gabriella screams, but nothing comes out. She struggles to move her arms and legs, but they dangle like a rag doll's. The van's side door is open. Her head lulls back, and an upside-down cavernous maw of darkness encompasses her. Acrid cigarette smoke fills her nostrils, and yellow tobacco-stained teeth that look like salt on the rim of a Margareta glass smile at her as the light turns dark.

The power light flashes on the dash. The only twelve more kilometers of charge left before I'm walking. With the snow as high as it is, there's no way I want to do that. Fucking winter. I'd replace the car's battery, but they want over ten thousand for a new one. Plus they'll charge disposal fees for removal of the old one because the environmental zealots in City Hall demand to feed the ever-increasing budget.

I stop before a bright orange holographic banner with the words "Police Barrier - Do Not Cross" projected in a marquee. The red and blue lights in the back of my car reflect off the glistening snow behind me. Better turn them off before they suck the last of the juice from the battery.

A knock on the window brings me out of the melancholy. A quick press of the button and cold January air steals all the heat out of the car.

"Roberts," Shan says, brushing snow off his new Sergeant stripes. The man looks as miserable as I feel. His pencil-thin mustache is peppered with white from frozen moisture. He's swimming in an over-sized police-issued coat. A black band still covers the top of his shield from the funeral yesterday. His teeth chatter. He's not used to this climate, even after twenty years.

The temperature gauge on the dash says -22°C. Bitter cold in Toronto. The wind swirls around the car's cab.

I release my seatbelt. "Bad one?"

"Yes and no." He waves at the road beyond the barrier. "Nothing except the heel of a boot."

A bootheel? I'm here for something as mundane as that? I turn the car off. "So why call me in?"

"Eyewitness says a girl was taken."

I press a button, the lights in the car go dark. The window automatically rolls up when I open the door. The wind catches my coat. I scramble to hold the edges together and button up at the same time. Winter sucks.

"Kidnapping? Who's the vic?"

Shan shakes his head. "No name. We're canvassing the area to find more information."

I thread the last button through its hole, but winter takes one last bite from my skin to make those little bumps swell up across my stomach. The station house will be warm, but I'll need a good couple of hours to thaw. I push my phone, and it releases from the dashboard. With one hand on the Jesus handle, I pull myself fully into the cold grasp of winter. The wind snaps against my neck before I can raise my collar for protection.

Shan walks with me through the police barrier but hangs back. Not much to the scene. The heel of a boot. A woman's clutch, open and empty. Nothing else. I stand back from the immediate area to let the forensic team recover things.

"Roberts, over here," Shan says. He stands beside one of the investigators, motioning me over.

I hike up my collar a little more. The shadow of a beard scrapes against the rough material of my coat. "What you have there, Shan?"

"Little blood under the snow," he says.

A few strides in his direction, and there they are—three small dots under the snow. I meet the gaze of the investigator who found them. Her dark brown hair twirls around in the wind covering part of her face. She wears glasses as if surgery to correct her vision is something beneath her. Thin lips are pursed together while she brushes away the covering snow off her find. Once revealed, she tweezers up one drop at a time and puts each into their own zip bag. Her ID tag is obscured. I hate that. Now I have to wait until someone says her name.

"Run an analysis to ensure the blood is from the same person," I say.

She lifts the bags and gazes at three spots. Her one eye is different than the other. Little lines of scar tissue disrupt the otherwise perfect skin at the corner of the lid. Her left iris is more bluish in color than the right. Text runs across her glasses. She's an augy. Should have noticed that sooner from her ability to spot the blood.

"Already have." She pulls out a marker and scribbles something on one bag. "Female." The same pen dances on another bag. "Same here. Same woman." She holds up the last bag. "Male."

She puts the bags into her side pocket and smiles at me. Her gaze captivates me until the weight of my wedding ring brings me around. Look away—no need to take in those high cheekbones and angular face. I break the uncomfortably long stare and look to the sky.

"Anything else you find?"

She takes in a long breath and lets it out. "No. We're lucky to have found this." With a turn, she motions up the street. "Plows were along here a few minutes before the report came in." She stands up, her long legs putting her at eye level with me. "Besides, the wind did a good job of scrubbing everything before we got here."

Shan touches my arm. "I'll make sure everything is scanned. You're not dressed for the weather, might as well head back."

He's a good man. I can trust him. "Thanks, but it's not the cold..."

"It's the humidity," the woman says before Shan can finish the pun. "I'll do a full analysis and upload it to your storage, Bruce."

How does she know me? I glance at her again. There's a little upward curve touching the side of her lip. Dwelling on such matters can drive a man insane. Instead, I nod and go back to the car. Maybe the house is the best place for me.

The car lights come on just as the battery drops. I turn off the automatic sensor that controls them, and daytime runners give me just enough light to find my parking space. The car jerks slightly as the wheels turn into the spot. The city can pay for the charge today.

The garage heaters are blasting out warm air, but it's still cold in the underground. Slush drops off the car adding to the already slippery floor. It almost takes me out, even with grips on the bottom of my boots.

The metal handle of the charging plug clings to my flesh like a long-lost lover. Swear I'm going to leave part of my hand on it. But at least the car will be fully charged in two hours.

I take the elevator to the main lobby, flashing my badge to get past the metal detectors without a hassle. The elevator call screen wants my phone to scan the certificate in case I try to access floors I'm not cleared for. All I want is to go to the fifteenth, and my desk. I hit the button on the screen, and it changes to the letter E. The elevator with that designation is already letting people on. I squeeze in with a muffled sorry.

The elevator stops a few times, leaving a few of us to stare mindlessly at the door. I catch a glimpse of an Asian woman. She's easily the tallest I've seen in a while. Her hair is pulled back in a tight bun, and an oversized coat covers her body. She catches my gaze in the door's reflection. There's no emotion, just a hard stare. My collar tightens, and a lump fills my throat as I look away.

A polite ding announces my floor. The doors open and I step out with four other people, but pay them no heed, heading right to my desk.

There's a five-level pyramid of shoe heels decorates the top of my desk. I sit down and open a drawer. Shoe heels are piled inside to the brim. As if cops have nothing better to do with their time but pull jokes on one another.

A uniform drops a folder on my desk as he passes. It's got to be another joke. I open the thing. Pictures of boots without heels adorn the inside of the envelope, each with a printout describing an elaborate past: from walking behind the elderly waiting to trip them, to loitering without a wearer. All have the heels removed in the photos.

"Funny." I let my voice carry. "If you put as much care into your work as you do with the jokes, you'd be able to find the criminal with no problem."

They laugh.

My phone vibrates. Helen's name flashes on the screen. I don't know if she's home or at work. The fight last night had me sleeping on the couch. She left this morning without saying goodbye. It seems to be the norm in our relationship now.

"Detective Roberts," I say.

"Bring home bread." The tone is flat, but there's a doctor being paged in the background before the line goes dead.

Great, she's still mad.

Not sure why things always revolve around me doing something that makes her mad. Lately, we argue about everything. It's like I can't move without pissing her off. Now I have to get bread. What type of bread? If I get it wrong, she'll crawl up one side of me and down the other.

Regular white bread will have to do. She once said it has less gluten.

"Roberts!"

Captain Braden Max stands at the door to his office. His voice split the air perfectly.

I walk toward him. "Yes, Cap?"

He hates the short form of his title. Rather we call him Brad or Captain Max. Right now, I'm not in a placating mood.

Cap steps aside for me to enter his office. One step into his office, and I see her sitting there, back to me.

I can tell it's her. She sits perfectly straight. The bun on the back of her head is wound tight, and no hair is out of place. Her coat is off. Epaulets sit on her shoulders with two, thick solid gold bars. A captain.

"You caught the heel case," Cap says. It's a statement, not a question. "There's more to it than just one missing girl."

He walks to his desk and sits, motioning me to the chair beside our mystery guest. She focuses on the captain as I settle into my seat.

"Captain Max." She tilts her head slightly. "I here only as courtesy. Interpol not interested in Toronto Police. They not take part in investigate lost woman. We autonomous, work with no interference." Her accent cuts as sharp as her figure.

Cap taps a folder on his desk with one finger. His head tilts to the side, and a look of defiance crosses his face. "Captain Ling, Canada does not have a policing agreement with Interpol. If you want to investigate anything on our soil, it will be done with one of our officers. Especially if it involves a Canadian citizen."

"Case far beyond borders of you country, Captain." She pushes her sleeve up a centimeter. I catch a glimpse of the new wrist phones everyone is talking about. Small, out of the way, and fast. They say the reception is clear and the power immense. She taps a button, and an image comes to life around her wrist, floating a few millimeters above the skin. "Total been twelve abduction and twelve murder in GTA area. They start in Hong Kong and branch to Vancouver, US, Mexico, South America. If we no find soon, they reach across Europe. They target women and make money selling sensory data of sex act. It in report — on desk."

Cap opens the folder and scans the contents. An eyebrow arches as he flips the pages. Our Interpol visitor doesn't blink. I keep glancing between the two. Someone is going to break. Cap turns another page in the report.

"You missed something in your file," Cap mumbles.

Our guest leans forward. "I miss nothing."

"It says you need to follow the guidelines set forth by the country you investigate in if they do not use Interpol. We don't."

She leans back. "It my discretion."

The corner of Cap's mouth creeps up. "Actually, it's up to my discretion, and I opt to have my man here shadow you. Understand?"

Not a flicker of emotion passes her face. She doesn't frown or swear. No disappointment or relief. Just an unending stare.

"Very well. I expect man keep with me."

Cap nods at me. "Okay, then Roberts is your liaison."

"Can keep up?" Interpol's stare pierces through me.

"You don't need to worry about me."

She squints, and tilts her head a little. "Yes, do."

"Roberts can take care of himself. I assure you."

Her eyes don't leave me. "I not want you assurance or man. I work alone. This"–she looks me up and down–"officer not look well to keep up anyone. What make you better than others in department? Or better, what make you special?"

I glance at Cap. "Nothing, I'm just a cop."

"Just cop," she echoes. "Spoke like true American." She turns her attention back to Cap. "He can keep up, he can stay. He lag, I leave him."

"Fair enough." Cap reaches out his hand.

She stands and gives a slight bow, ignoring his outstretched offer.

My phone goes off in my pocket. I pull it out and see the caller's name just as Cap closes his office door behind me. The kid's school. What the fuck is wrong now. I take a deep breath and accept it.

I start walking to my desk. "Hello?"

"Mr. Roberts?" A woman's voice, possibly in her late forties or near it. There's tension in her tone. No image transmission. Not a good sign.

"That's me."

"Lilly-Grace Pham from Markville Secondary School. Your daughter is here in my office. I need to see you concerning an issue."

I look at the time. 10:15 a.m. What the hell could Sarah have done now? I sit at my desk, resting an elbow on it and put my head in a hand. "I'm at work. Have you called her mother?"

"Yes, I've called her mother." There's a deep breath at her end. "She told me to call you."

I fixate on the bread. She wants me to pick up bread on the way home. Breathe, one in and one out. Take control of the situation. You're at work. She's at work. Who can pull off a visit on short notice? "What's the problem?"

"We need to talk. In person."

The car probably doesn't have enough charge in it yet; better delay so I don't get stuck. "I can be there in about an hour."

"Fine. I'll keep her in the office."

A quick thumb tap and the call ends—another day in paradise. I need to get to the lab and then Markham. This and escort an Interpol officer around town. Not the best of situations when investigating a reported kidnapping.

A chair rolls up beside me. Phil, the detective whose desk is behind mine, leans back. He has a problem with personal space, in that he doesn't believe in it. That and he wears some weird vanilla aftershave that aggravates my sinuses.

"Who's the hottie you got paired with?"

"Interpol," I say, just as the room goes quiet.

We both look up as everyone else in the room does; even the women stare. Captain Ling walks toward me. Her uniform no longer hides everything. Long black hair, now braided into a ponytail, swings to the small of her back. There is a slight blue tint near the middle giving just enough contrast to be noticed but not enough to take away from the color. Almond eyes with near-black irises penetrate my soul as her gaze lands on me. A smile crosses perfect lips and disappears just as quick. The pants suit picks up a little shimmer from the lights and the jacket opens to reveal a slim build. Her gait is like a predator. Measured and fluid paces bring her to the side of my desk.

"Show what have," she demands.

Phil groans and wheels back to his desk, mind going somewhere only he knows.

January 10th, 2033 - 49ERs

Gabriella blinks to clear the cobwebs from her mind. Light seeps through the rough band of fabric that obscures her sight. She tries to brush it away with a hand. Bindings keep them firm above her head. She attempts to still her breath but the stink of cigarettes assaults every sense.

Laughter and male voices speaking Chinese surround her. She shakes her head and twists to get away from the soft touch of fingers against her bare breasts.

A slap stings her face. She comes back to the present. Rough fingers grasp her jaw. Others force their way between her tight lips. She bites hard. A man screams. Blood fills her mouth as she clenches. Quick, panicked words fly around her. A fist hammers her stomach. Gabriella releases her hold in a grunted exhale of air. Tears well up and wet the blindfold. Heated breath caresses her ear as whiskers tickle. It's foul with old fish and beer.

"You no bite and keep teeth."

Again, fingers touch her face. She freezes as her lips are pulled back, and metal touches her front teeth. It clinks several times against the enamel.

"You almost ready. Soon you have push-push fun."

The group of men laugh.

I allow Interpol to see how tall I am. The few centimeters are not much, but I use it to my advantage. Phil whimpers as he tries not to laugh. The others lose interest and return to work.

"Let me get you a chair." I swing the nearest one around.

She reaches behind her neck and slips the long ponytail to her front. The light scent of ginger floats past my nose. I pull up my chair and sit.

"Our database is modeled on a double verification protocol." I set my phone down and place a hand flat beside it on the desk. The desktop goes black as an outline glows under both the phone and hand. "Roberts, Bruce. Badge nine-five-seven-three. Authenticate."

Interpol nods, eyes not even watching what I'm doing. The same way my daughter Sarah does when I explain things to her.

"If you put your phone on the desk and hand beside it, I'll log you into the system."

She watches me for a second, then removes the phone from her wrist. It goes on the desk flat next to her hand. I tap a few commands, and light encircles both. It shrinks to an outline. The one under the phone turns red. The words, Unrecognized Device , flash under it. She picks up her cell and runs through the menu it displays in the air.

"Did not have on legacy." Her tone is flat, and she places the phone back on the desk.

The desk scans her hand and connects to the device. She snatches her phone away and puts it back on again like the removal of it pained her. I start to pull up the keyboard and stop as she speaks softly into her cell. It's quick and in Chinese, but she mutters, "In English. Code name China Girl."

Information displays on the desktop. Diagrams, images, text. It's so fast I can't keep up with it. The whole transfer takes a minute, and the desk display shows 50 gigs of data.

I tap the new folder titled China Girl, and it opens. "Some legacy connection. How fast can your phone transmit?"

Inside the folder is a list of schematics, reports, images, and history files. A piece of tech called a halo with multiple cranial points of contact is laid out. Micro circuitry beyond any I've seen. Storage slots for high capacity micro flash drives. I flip through them and come to a report. Halfway through, I push back and stare at Ling.

"Is this for real?"

Interpol nods. Still no emotion. "Halo record tactile experience and store on flash drives. Multiple copies made for sale on black market. Girls are killed." She flips through the system and comes to a chart. "The TRIAD behind it, but even Hong Kong Police have hard time finding witness. Here organization structure. 49ers take Blue Lanterns and initiate them. They wear halo while rape girl and then kill. No record of killer but hands on girl throat."

She reaches out and flips the report to another section with an embedded media file. A girl, no more than 19, lays on her back, hands tied above her head. Shoulder length hair is matted on one side revealing a small nose with soft freckles, full lips with bite marks, and bruising on the side of her face. The anguish and shame etched on her face makes my heart ache. Her breasts are in full view as the video plays. Bloodstains and red, angry skin rashes mark her body. A man pants and others edging him on in Chinese. He must be cumming. The woman cries as his hands take hold of her throat and tighten their grip. She bucks and fights. Two minutes in, and the life goes out of her eyes. Cheers erupt as the image pulls back, showing the now-dead girl spread eagle on a bed, limbs tied apart. Contusions frame her legs and lower body—blood around her pubic area.

I look away to see Interpol, unfocused eyes welling with moisture but still focus at the screen. Finally, emotion.

"God, how can anyone even think of doing such a thing?" I reach out to close the image. Interpol grabs my wrist, her fingers tighten. Pain lances up my arm. She pulls my hand back.

"Take good look," she hisses. "This what we are against." She blows up the picture of the girl's face. "She not ask for this. Her life. What they do is devil work. Remember her face."

"What makes you think this is what we have here?" I pull up the org chart for the TRIAD.

Interpol taps on the chart and a holographic image of a man's head appears. Stats print out beside it. The image rotates, showing a short bowl-type haircut. A pencil-thin scar runs down the left side of his face near the ear. The corner of the man's mouth twitches up, and reveal heavily stained teeth under the gums.

"This Bojing Wang. He 426 of Triad."

"426. Never did understand why the Triad numbered their members." I study the face.

"Each member of Triad level have number assigned. Chinese numerology based on Yi Jing. English mean Boo of Changes or some-time Classic of Changes. 426 for Red Pole, the enforcer." She looks at the face and her thin eyebrows draw together, lips remain in a straight line. Her nostrils flare a little. "And name Mie Ling."

Of course, she has a name. I should probably start using it. But there's something about the way she stares at this man's image. The facial structure is so different between the two of them, but she keeps analyzing him as if trying to burn his face into her mind.

"Mie, is there something I should know?"

She takes a shuddering breath and visibly relaxes. Her fist uncurls. Red grooves lay where her fingernails were pressed against flesh, but the lines disappear quickly. She straightens up. "No." Flat, informative, and a lie.

Mie reaches out and turns off the image, then swipes through the folder until one particular item comes to view. A few commands and an image of the halo floats in the air in front of me.

It's a simple enough device, more in tune with what earmuffs look like. The semi-circular band-type that fit over your ears and circle around the back of your head. Only this one is a little thicker with metal and plastic about it. A few more commands and several text areas appear with pointers to sections of the device. They are first in Chinese until the system translates. From receptors to translation ports to interface ports, the list of components rolls down.

"Device sit on the head and record you." She points at several key areas of the device. "This part pleasure, this part pain. They use first to record and monitor initiation. Make sure the Blue Lantern feel no remorse for killing. It make their ranks pure of thought." Mie points to the micro drive ports. "Then they distribute recording to rich men wanting thrill, or women wanting know what it like to be man inside woman."

"I'm surprised we haven't encountered this tech here." I open a new interface and initiate a search based on the criteria before me. The amount of data that streams out surprises me. "I take that back. Seems we have."

The department's gang squad already has one of the devices, but they've no idea how to turn it on. The thing uses standard flash drives available to anyone through tech stores. Still, the storage capacity throws me for a loop. Three petabytes each. And it needs two.

"Each device need sync with wearer. Can show people how done."

I shoot an internal message to a friend at the gang squad. His reply comes immediately. He's on his way, a reflection of the amount of information they're lacking.

"A friend is coming up to learn how to sync the device." I lean back, stretch a little. Mie levels a glazed-eyed look at me. I straighten up. "It's early. Once you show them the device, I need to take off for an hour. Personal time."

"Much work to do, no time to take." Mie stands. "Thought you bad for partner. I get new one."

She takes a step toward the Captain's office. I reach out and grab her arm. The muscles there are firm and unyielding though the limb is slight. Her other hand comes around and grabs my wrist, thumb pressing against the soft meat of the underside between the bones. My fingers go numb. I have no grip. She twists my hand away and around, pulling me off the chair and onto my knees.

"My body," she says in that even tone. "I choose who touch."

Nerve endings in my shoulder erupt as she twists.

"Understand?" She applies a little more pressure in the hold.

"Understand," I manage to get out, trying not to show the effect her grip has on me.

She releases my wrist. The feeling comes back to my hand as I stand and massage it.

"It's just... Cap won't assign anyone else to you because I caught the missing girl case. I'm your partner while you're here." I rub at my wrist and sit down. A bluish bruise the same size as her thumb starts to form.

I lower my voice to a whisper and glance at Phil. His head is down while he bites a fingernail. "Besides, you could get Phil."

She glances at him and sits down. I turn my head to see his shocked expression. His eyes must have been on another part of her anatomy when she looked at him.

" Shi, " Mie says. A scan of the room and she takes a deep breath. "Where we go?"

Ron, from gang's, enters just in time to cut off the thought. He's followed by three of his group, two carrying small evidence boxes. They beeline right to my desk. The boxes are set down, and he reaches out a hand.

"Thanks for this, Bruce."

"No problem." I shake his hand. "Let me introduce Mie Ling from Interpol." I motion to Mie, who stands. She only gives a slight nod, taking everyone in. Like a predator, she scans Ron from top to bottom, looking for weakness in his lean form and grey hair.

Ron is one of the older detectives at the station. Probably should have taken his pensioned by now but stayed on the force to ride out his time with the desk. It's not that he's out of shape, just pushing sixty. He wears his grey hair close-cropped with heavy eyebrows over blue eyes. Jeans with a white shirt top off his look. His hand is out to Mie and hangs there. She doesn't reach to take. The scene stretches out before she finally gives him a quick shake. Ron's eyebrows rise at the touch.

"Your hand—"

"Yes." Mie nods but doesn't say anything else.

"I'd love to talk with you about it if possible." Ron stares at her. "Just the hand?"

Mie doesn't answer. Her gaze darts between Ron and me, then a quick one to Phil, who is still absorbed in cleaning his fingernails.

"Sorry, I'm overstepping." Ron turns to me. "So, what can you tell me about this?"

He holds a unit with a little red stain on the white plastic cover. Just like evidence will have when locked away for a trial in the future, it's in a clear plastic bag. A little tuft of hair sticks to the inside near the back.

With her left hand, Mie reaches out and takes the device. Ron cannot take his eyes off of Mie's other hand for some reason. She turns the device around and examines it in detail before putting it on the desk.

"Damaged. This one not working."

Ron pulls another one out of the same box. Unlike the first, it appears to be new—no stains or hair attached to it. Mie takes the new unit and nods while examining it. She places it on my desk's inductive charger. Power flows between the two devices.

"You not charge it." The readout shows the device's power level at 0%. The words CHARGING glow green under it. The level increases at a fast pace. "Ready in minute. Small battery. Good for hour."

Ron asks a few technical questions that go above my head. Mie spills out answers but what I guess is only basic information, no voluntary details. I just watch the charge number climb until it hits 100%. Something about the unit fascinates me — a soft glow around the edges or the way my gaze slides off the surface. The appearance of the unit takes out-of-reality to a world of imagination as the two banter back and forth on what makes it tick. I swear, it starts to turn a little bluish as the light from my desk shifts underneath it. For the briefest moment, it no longer rests in my sight, and I long to have it back. A yearning aches deep inside me, stirring a need to have the glistening material supply what I want, but am not getting from my marriage.

"Roberts." Mie's voice breaks the link. "Device calibrate for you."

I glance at her. The China Girl is in her hands. The call of the headset pulls me to stand and take it from her, but that doesn't feel like the right thing to do—a piece of illegal tech. Instead, she gives a quick nod. It hits me, what she said.

"Calibrated to me?"

Ron reaches out and takes the headset. "How can that be, Mie?"

"Appears this one not calibrated before charge." Mie indicates the side of the device. "When charged full, it try sync one interested and take person. Roberts that one." She looks in the box and pulls out microdrives connected with a plastic link. "This recorded experience." Mie slides the drives into the opening at the back of the device and hands it over to me.

I take the device. "What do I do with it?" The casing is warm to the touch, like most devices when they are rapid-charged.

"Put on."

"If you need help..." Ron pantomimes putting earmuffs on.

I roll my eyes. "Not that." I slide the device into place on my head. "Just, how does this–"

The world goes black. No light. I'm plunged into the darkness beyond simple night. A tingle spreads from the back of my scalp to my forehead, and lights slowly come on. I'm standing in a room surrounded by seven others. Stale cigarette smoke hangs in the air. My mouth is on fire.

"Have another hot pepper, Po," a man says behind me while a hand slaps my back. I'm turned around to face the man. He's very familiar, though older than the image shown to me. It's Red Pole. 426. He smiles. Tea stained teeth fill his mouth, and there's a gap between some of them. The lower ones are pushed together, reminding me of pieces of shattered safety glass. His breath carries a fish smell. Thoughts of the ocean and home fill my memory. A young woman crying. A slap across my face brings me back. "You still with us, Po?"

"Yes, very much so," I say back in Chinese. But I don't know how to speak the language. How can I be speaking it to them?

"Good. You become a 49er today. Come, we have something special for you."

Hands slap my back and push me toward the other side of a room. Many others wait there, blocking me from seeing what is behind them. They all smile and slap my naked shoulders. I scratch at my genitals and glance down. When did I remove my clothes? My penis is erect at the thought of having sex. It starts to push other thoughts away.

"Remember, you must choke her at the end,"426 whispers in my ear. "If you don't, your little pecker will never rise again."

My erection wavers at the thought, but I keep walking.

The last of the men give way to a bed. A young girl, no more than sixteen, is laid spread-eagle on the mattress. A blindfold is tied around her head, obscuring much of what I can see of her face. Small breasts with large pink nipples on a slender body. Saliva fills my mouth. I climb onto the bed, hand touching the hair between her legs and rubbing.

A chant raises. "Fuck her! Fuck her!"

The blindfold is wet. Her body jerks back and forth as she tries to get away from me. I slip a finger into her. Tight. It comes back with a little red on it. She's a virgin. The crowd starts to cheer at the sight.

I mount her, pushing my dick into her as she cries out in pain. It only takes two thrusts until I cum. A great wave passes over my body. Shame floods me. They didn't know I was a virgin as well. Or did they? I keep thrusting, not letting them know my shame.

"You must kill her," 426 whispers in my ear as he whips off the girl's blindfold.

Tears stream from her face as I thrust again and again. My left-hand fumbles until it's around her neck, then the right. I squeeze. Lightly at first, then build up more and more pressure. A cry escapes her lips as she thrashes about, gasping for breath. My loins are hyper-sensitive as my body approaches another orgasm. This one, I play up, thrusting faster and faster.

"I'm cumming!" I scream. My hand is on the girl's throat now while the other is on a breast. Soft. Nice. Such a waste. I cum again. My body jerks, and I squeeze both hands as hard as I can. A simple snap slaps my ears.

January 10th, 2033 - Red Pole

Bojing sits on the side of the bed. Cigarette smoke rolls from his mouth, stinging his eyes. The nicotine is part of the pleasure. The sheets on the bed are soft, just like the mattress. Everything in the West is soft. Even the smoke runs smooth down the throat. He puts the butt to his lips and draws deep into his throat. It is the best thing after sex besides Snake Wine.

Caucasian girls are not like the others from home. Western women take too many lovers before marriage. Not the same as Chinese. But the skin. He reaches out and touches the body next to him in the bed. Pale eyes stare at the ceiling as he runs a hand over the belly and cups a breast. No hand slaps his away. No heart beats under the flesh. No breath moves the chest. The purple marks around the neck tell a tale of a violent death, and he enjoyed the bucking as he took her life.

He stands, walks to the large window in the hotel room, and stares at the downtown core of Toronto. Why did they choose this city? The question runs through his head every time he travels to the West. Cities of soft people. Sheep. He itches the rash under his pubic hair. Sex is good in the West. Girls are easy to lure to the room. The 49ers make sure he has a pick. The recruits do not have that luxury. Blue Lanterns have no choice but to take whichever ones he picks for them.

One last puff of the cigarette, and he walks back to the bed. He squelches the burning butt in a water glass, and he reaches out to the soft blonde hair. With a light touch, he pushes her head to the side, not wanting to see the unblinking eyes. Maybe one last time before he calls the men to take her away. He mounts the body, rubbing himself against the soft flesh until he is hard. She is dry and aggravates his rash, and no longer fights for her life, but it does not register as he pushes himself into the corpse.

***

My head thunders as if being rolled in a dryer. The light hurts my eyes as it pulses down from the fluorescent tubes overhead. The lumpy couch of the break room across the office is not comfortable. How did I get here? I lift an arm.

"He's awake," Phil says in the distance.

Feet approach. Each step a hammer in the din. It hits me—the image of the young girl pleading for life. Bile rises from my stomach. I roll to my side, retching out nothing but fluid.

"Fuck!" Phil says.

Soft, strong fingers grip my shoulders and steady me. I retch again—some splashes on my hand.

"You take Halo off before over." She's not mad, but there is a concern in her voice. Nice to know she's human. "It make you dizzy. Shen jing gan rao tong bu ti. Sorry, no English words."

My empty stomach aches. I remember being in a fight as a kid. The local bully knocked me down and kept punching my gut. This feels worse. Shame floods me. I couldn't have... My breath ratchets in and out at the thought of what I experienced. What I did. No, what I relived through someone else's eyes.

My breathing slows, becoming easier. Gasps turn into pants. Pants turn into deep breaths. Numbness around my mouth starts to fade. Mie helps me sit up on the couch. The world spins.

"He's going to spew again," Phil says.

"No, he not." Mie pulls a few tissues from a box and pats at my forehead. As her hand moves down to my chin, allowing me to see the discoloration of two fingers against the tone of her face. It is odd.

"How long was I out?"

"Two hours," Phil volunteers.

Crap, Sarah's school. "I need to get out of here for a bit."

"You have lab report," Mie says.

Phil jerks a thumb at Mie. "You're not leaving me here with her."

"It's my kid. Got to get her from the school."

Mie stands. "I go with."

"No need." I start to stand. The world spins. My ass is back on the couch before anything can happen.

"I help. Keep you aware." She taps the side of her head. "Brain scramble from halo."

I relent. Phil helps her lift me off the couch. I stand, albeit on wobbly legs. There's no way to un-see what I saw or remove the memory of raping and killing an innocent woman – even if it wasn't me.

The cold rips through my hand as I pull the charging plug out of the car. The gauge reads 97%. Good enough for a few days if I don't go too far. The garage door rolls down with a rattle. It stops the knifing-cold but not the bite of winter. I hit the release, and the doors unlock. Mie watches me get in before she climbs into the passenger side, paying close attention to my movements, calculating how reliable I am in this current state. I don't blame her. The Halo was on me for only a few seconds, but long enough to watch a lifetime of disregard for human life. The horror I experienced adds certainty to the world we live in. Something dangerous is out there, and it needs to be stopped.

I snap the phone into its holder, and I scan my thumb to start the car. The dash lights up.

Mie pulls her seatbelt on. She looks at everything in my old vehicle. Mileage, charge, battery condition, radio. The nav system comes to life and blinks the appointment with Sarah's principal with an overdue alert. Maybe we'll make it before the school closes; maybe we'll get screwed in traffic. Who knows? A glance in the rearview and the girl's face floats there before me, then it is gone. I wipe my eyes, quickly dial Sarah's cell, but it goes right to voicemail.

"You see something?" Mie asks.

I put the car into reverse. "No, nothing."

"Times image float in mind for some hours. I know word"–she stares off into the distance–"ghost, I think."

I back out of the spot and throw the car into drive. "Sounds right."

The roads are slick. Traffic is good through the city into Markham, but the highway is jammed. I take the city route to save what the nav system says is ten minutes. Not much of a savings, but enough. Mie watches people and other cars. I hold my thoughts close. There is no tension, just nothing to say. I keep us going, pushing the stupid speed limit to its fullest as I drive.

"What did he mean by both hands?" I ask Mie when we reach the half-way point.

She returns to the car from some faraway place. "Hands?"

"Yes, when you and Ron shook hands, he asked about yours." I push past a changing light. "He asked if it was just one or both."

She holds up her right hand. The skin looks the same as her face. Same tint, light bone structure, but it moves with a predetermined grace that tells me something is just not right with it. She holds the other up with it. They are identical. I mean perfect mirror images of each other without any error that I can see from a quick glance. My hands have subtle differences. The hair, creases, freckles. They are not perfect matches for each other. Hers are. From the fingernail length to the small dot on the webbing between the first finger and thumb. It just looks wrong.

She puts her hands down. "Nothing."

"Don't nothing me, Interpol. Tell me. Hands are not perfect, but both of yours are." I race another light.

"I no speak of it." She turns to look out the window. "Never."

"Well, if we're going to be partners, I have to know if they will be a problem. We need to rely on each other."

"I rely on none."

The hammer of the artery in her neck tells me otherwise. It pulses to supply blood to her brain faster than someone at rest should need. She's lying.

"Come on, Interpol. Tell me something so I know you're not just wires and a brain."

The pulsing stops. It's like her heart is no longer beating. She turns her head to me and glares. The hammer has hit the nail, and maybe I've taken it too far. I go to say something, but she stops me.

"I tell you later."

And with that, she looks out the window again, cutting off any further questions.

I let the car drive in silence, wondering what Sarah has done to be in trouble again. She's my problem child. The biggest joy in my life and the biggest heartache. She is also the one thing that keeps Julie and me together. But to what end? I want us to be a family, but we're being pulled apart somehow.

The GPS announces our arrival at the school. I take over control of the vehicle, weaving into a visitor parking spot with cars crowded on either side. Thankfully, it stopped snowing a while ago, and the white stuff no longer piles up.

"You don't need to come in if you don't want to."

"I follow you," she says dryly, already opening the door. "Partner." The word lingers in her mouth like an afterthought, but it's well appreciated.

The wind grabs at my door, threatening to take it away from me, but I hold on tight. Mie has no trouble with hers. I pull up my collar and push the door shut. Winter is returning to what my father used to call "a little chilly." Snow whips through the air from drifts separating the parking lot from the road. The town needs to find a better way to remove snow besides spring. I aim for the building's main entrance and push through the small drifts.

Mie's long ponytail rides in air currents until she reaches back and pulls it around in front, tucking it into her coat.

We push through snowdrifts until we make it to the front door. A guard sits between the outer and inner doors to the school. Just in front of him stands a metal detector array to scan the kids as they come in. The man's stomach hides the front of his pants like an apron. Thinning grey hair spews out from under a baseball cap with a part at the sides just above the ears. The haircut screams comb-over. He watches us approach, hand halfway to a steaming cup on the small table beside him, half-eaten sandwich sitting beside it.

Behind him, kids mill about in groups as they make their way through the halls to class. Their eyes glance at cell phones and wall clocks as if wishing the final bell to sound the end of school.

Above the door, an LED display reads the school is in lockdown until 3 pm, another hour away. A stiff reminder of their American counterparts whose violence against others has made them famous. The youth have no appreciation for life. The violence of gangs spreads through the school district faster than police can end it. Education is nothing like when I went to school.

The guard watches as I pull the door. Magnetic locks hold it in place, not giving me the satisfaction of making it rattle. He looks at his watch, at the door, and then at a monitor to the side. He shakes his head and presses a button on the table. The intercom comes to life beside the door.

"We're in lockdown for another hour," he says, his voice coming through a speaker hidden somewhere in the doorway. "Come back then."

"I have an appointment with Mrs. Pham." I indicate my wrist. "She's expecting me."

The guard looks over to the monitor again. "What's your name?"

"Bruce Roberts." I reach into my coat to grab ID.

The guard stands, hand going to a sidearm on his hip, other stretched out in a stop sign. I glance down to see my service weapon peeking out in the cold. He's reacting to a perceived threat. I don't want him to overreact.

"Hold on, I'm just getting my ID," I say when a thump hits the door. Mie has her ID out and pressed against the pane.

The guard steps forward like a cat approaching an unknown person after being in the wild for years. He squints at the badge and reads the information on the picture above it. "Interpol?" he grunts. "Why would Interpol be interested in some brat?"

I put my badge and ID against the glass. He comes over, eyes widening as he reads. "My brat."

"Hold on," he mutters more to himself, though his voice does make it through the crack between the doors.

A buzz erupts with a sharp smack of metal being released from a death grip. I pull the door, and it moves out of the way. Mie enters, and I follow. As the door closes behind us, the metal clangs into place as the heavy magnet seals us in.

Alarms go off as we pass through the metal detector. Mie frowns as I step forward.

"Sorry, I'll need to wand you," the guard says, holding up a small detection device. He runs the thing over my body. It bleeps at my sidearm, wrist, waist, and right knee. He points to the last as if the subtle gesture tells me what to do. "Lift your pant leg, please."

I reach down and haul the pant leg up, showing a ten-centimeter scar running beside my kneecap. "Metal knee."

He accepts the answer and steps to Mie. She takes one pace back and right under the metal detectors. They scream at her presence. "No scan." Her hands are up.

"Interpol, it's just to verify you're only carrying the one issued weapon into the school. They need to make sure nothing is left."

"No scan," she says again, voice wavering a little.

"It's standard practice, officer," the guard rolls out, beckoning her forward. "Your partner did it without issue."

She steps forward, still unsure, but the guard starts his scan. The baton lights up all over her body. She frowns. The guard stares at her in wonderment and an unanswered question in his eyes.

"There has to be a mistake." He runs the wand over her again, and it repeats the light show. He steps to the monitor and hits a few buttons.

Mie takes a deep breath. "No mistake." She walks over to him, her back to me. There's a metallic click akin to a latch or snap, and the guard's eyes grow wide.

"Jesus!"

Another click. Mie bends slightly, then straightens up.

"You know." She places a hand on his. "This not for sharing."

The guard nods, eyes wide. "Sorry."

"You no do." She steps back, one hand twisting the other at the wrist as a click is audible. "We go in now?"

The guard nods as he pushes another button on the table. The doors to the inside of the school open. I step through and stop. "The office is which way?"

The guard motions with a hand. "To the left, just a little down the corridor."

"Thanks."

We enter the main foyer as a bell rings out. Students speed up their steps and start to disappear into classrooms. It's the last period. I head left to a sign jutting out into the hall, announcing the location of the office.

"What was that all about?" I ask.

Mie keeps walking, face flat and without expression. I don't think I'll get an answer out of her.

Ten paces and I'm in front of a reinforced metal door with a wire mesh-filled glass in the center. A tap pad beside the door handle glows red, indicating it's locked. I strike the pad with my hand and wait.

Mie stands at the other side of the hall staring at the bulletin board as it rolls through a display of upcoming events and news. The CP channel runs on one side, showing a new weather system approaching the Greater Toronto Area, destined to hit in a few hours. I should have been a weatherman—an imperfect science. Everyone would still hate me, but less people would want to kill me.

Her head shakes, and she turns, eyes focusing on me watching the same news.

"It wrong." She steps toward me. "We need leave soon. Storm come now."

A buzz from the door pulls me away from the moment.

"Office," a woman's voice announces.

"Bruce Roberts to see Principal Pham."

A few seconds pass, and the buzz sounds out again. "Enter."

I pull the handle, and the door opens. A large room with multiple desks behind a three-meter long counter holds men and women poking away at keyboards. Some are talking, but most appear busy recording who knows what. A bank of flat screens decorates one wall with images of classrooms swapping out with one another. More than anything, the room smells of shattered dreams and depression. Only those who work here or are facing disciplinary actions are allowed into this room with their guardians. Not something a troubled teenager should be facing.

The wall where the door is has multiple chairs against it, all bolted into place. Two young girls sit whispering to one another. A boy slouches at the other end. He glances at me, then his eyes move to Mie and stop. At maybe sixteen, his hormones are probably causing his body to crave sex. His olive eyes dart over my partner's figure, memorizing it for some time in the future.

A gray-haired woman looks up from her typing and pushes her bulk out of the chair. Her waddling gate brings her to the counter, and she flips open an actual book.

"Mr. Roberts?" she asks.

"Yes, here to see Principal Pham."

"She'll be with you in a moment." The woman starts to turn.

"What is all this about?" I ask.

She takes in my look and returns to the book. "Principal Pham didn't tell you?"

"No, why?"

"Not my place to tell you." She closes the book, her eyes traveling down until it hits the badge I've hooked into my belt along with my sidearm. With a beckoning hand, she leans forward. "But, you may want to be ready to take your daughter home after the meeting."

"What? Where's my daughter?"

She pushes away from the counter and points to a door to the right. It has a sliding bar locking it in place. "In isolation, where all the trouble students go."

January 10th, 2033 – Initiation

The skinny kid stands naked, hands in front of his groin. Florescent lights spill across his eighteen-year-old body as Bojing closes the door behind him. The boy is not ready. The halo unit still sits on the small table, charge light showing full. This is the right of passage. Today they will strip away a Blue Lantern to reveal the 49er inside. He reaches out and slaps the young man's back.

"It is almost time. Are you ready?" Bojing asks.

"Yes, sir. I'm ready," the boy says.

The kid's body shakes as a tremor runs through it. It could be the cold, but Bojing has witnessed hundreds of initiations. This one will mark something different, for the kid is related to him. Blood of his blood runs through the veins of the youngest initiate for twenty years.

Bojing picks up the halo and turns it around in his hands.

"It is elegant, you know." The unit pulses, waiting for a finger to touch the activation sensor. "Our initiations used to be simple. More religious than they are now. A small altar dedicated to the general Guan Yu. Back then, you would be called upon to sacrifice an animal. Drink blood and wine, very similar to what will happen today. But the difference is you need to prove yourself in blood."

The boy turns to Bojing. "And who is the girl?"

"An animal, nothing more." Bojing smiles. He looks to the paper on the table. The words are messy as if written by a shaking hand—the oath of a 49er. Bojing places the Halo on the table and raises his left hand with three fingers held straight. "When you read the words, raise your fingers as such." He turns, eyes running up and down the boy as if he can see the thoughts running through the mind. "The oath must be spoken aloud for all present to hear. Remember to take off the halo after the sacrifice."

"Uncle..." The boy blushes.

Bojing takes a step toward the initiate, his right hand darting out quick to strike the face before him. "Never call me that."

The switch from shy to humble happens immediately. Head bows. Eyes squint shut. Bojing watches a tear form and fall to the floor.

"They must not know our relation." He places a hand on a shaking shoulder. "Nephew, if they knew, you would be sent to another group. I cannot help you if they do that." His hand drops. "You'll be pleased. It's your initiation, and a surprise is waiting for you in the other room." He hands the paper of vows to the boy. "You have it memorized?"

"Yes. I'll do you proud."

"Then remember, the device turns on, and you can no longer look at the faces of those around you. Have control. But above all, enjoy this moment and the sacrifice."

I want to reach out and slap the smug smile from the woman's face—my little girl in a small isolation room. Criminals get bigger cells during solitary. How dare they do such a thing. We're not barbarians. The middle ages are long gone. With a hot face, I watch as the woman closes the book and waddles back to her desk a little more than two meters away. The monitor wall flashes red as one image expands to take up all the displays. A kid, maybe sixteen or seventeen from the look of his classmates. He's tall with short blonde hair and a light complexion. A teacher is sprawled and the tall blonde boy is stalking toward him. His frame a mass of muscle. He's too large to be in a class of kids, or maybe too angry.

The volume comes up—the other kids back away from the scene before them. A picture of the kid is enlarged with a readout of name, age, psych eval—all pertinent information to assess the situation. But no one is doing anything but watching the monitors.

I glance at the door behind which my baby sits waiting, then to the monitors. A split-second runs past as I point to the monitors.

"Where is this?" I use my cop voice, demanding an answer.

"Our internal security has been dispatched," a man near the monitor says. "ETA ten minutes."

I do a quick scan of the psych evaluation. "That teacher doesn't have ten minutes. You, show me that classroom now."

The man, mid-forties at least, with short hair and wire-frame glasses, glances over at the woman who attended to me earlier. She shakes her head.

"Don't look to her for permission." I bang my fist on the counter. "Show me now, or I'll press charges against you for obstructing justice." I turn to the woman. "And you'll be in the cell right next to him for the same thing."

Her visage becomes defiant.

"It's a crime to impede the police when they are attempting to render assistance." I point to the door of the isolation room. "And I suggest you get my daughter out of there before I get back."

I nod to Mie and pull open the door. She enters the back of the classroom in time with my entrance from the front. The teen still straddles the teacher, raining down bloody fists on him. In five paces, I'm at the kid with a cuff around his wrist, pulling his arm back. He only realizes it after trying to slam the a fist into the teacher.

The kid struggles. Tries to break free. It takes both my hands to pull the cuffed wrist behind his back. Mie grabs the other arm with one hand and yanks it around with no effort. A popping sound comes from the kid's body, and his left shoulder droops. Mie's dislocated it. The kid screams in rage and pain.

Mie pushes down on the kid's shoulder. "I have him. Check teacher."

A quick glance tells me all I need to know. The man is dead. Where his face used to be is just bloody pulp. His nose is crushed in, and both eye sockets shattered to the point of bone jutting out. The back of his skull is flattened by the force of the blows, and gray matter decorates the floor. No coming back from this one.

The kid struggles and screams, "I'm not useless." Spittle escapes from his mouth along with the words. He's still struggling to get to the dead man, but Mie holds him tight. Kids stand there with phones out, taking pictures. All of them are focusing on how we treat the perp instead of what he's done to the man. The internet is going to be screaming about this in a few seconds. They always focus on the bad. The kid will be the vic soon, not the person he murdered. And why would they not think that way? There's nothing we can do for the teacher – someone forced to endure hours on end in a classroom, browbeaten until he conforms and teaches math and spelling a new way every time a new government is elected.

A uniformed school rent-a-cop bursts into the room, his shirt hastily tucked into pants in a weak attempt to hold back the girth of his belly. Sweat drips from his forehead, and he bends with a hand propped on a knee to help him from falling to the ground in exhaustion.

"What's... Going... On... Here?" he gasps.

Mie pulls the kid to his feet.

I stare at the middle-aged guard. If he showed up before us, he'd be on the floor next to the teacher. No way he's effective against any violence.

"Keep the kids from leaving the room," I say to the guard. It could have been the words. Maybe it was the way I said them. The kids start rushing to the door, leaving all their personal items behind.

The guard pushes himself up and then slumps back down. "We know who's in the class. They won't get far with the lockdown."

"That's not the point. You need to secure their phones before someone deletes the information or footage."

His glare at me speaks volumes. He's out of shape, and now I've told him to do more. "I'm not a cop."

"No, but you're security. Do your job and secure their phones." I turn back to the kid. His face has changed. He no longer looks like a punk, but more a child of maybe fifteen. A small scratching of teenage whiskers shows on his chin. One side of his head is shaved down, and the hair on top spills over it and across his face. I pick up his wallet and search for ID. "James Fav…"

The kid on the ID is smiling. A cruel look at what happiness once was. His last name has at least twelve consonants in it and almost as many vowels. A test for any linguist. Not going to happen. I toss the wallet to the rest of the junk Mie pulled out of his pockets.

A Japanese woman walks into the room, her wizened face a mass of wrinkles and regret. An air of importance belies the stature of an old and diminutive frame. A frown wrinkles her face, and if she tipped the scales at seventy pounds soaking wet, I'd give up. Gray-streaked hair clings to her skull as the bun holding it back is pulled so tight it might tear away from the flesh by the roots. The thing that strikes my mind is the thudding of her shoes against the floor as she walks. It's as if the ground must give way to her feet as they hit the ground. A clunking of heel to floor. How she does this with flats, I'll never figure out.

"Ladies and gentlemen, you will stay in this room and put…" Her voice drops to nothing as her dark eyes focus on the corpse. A hand comes up to her chest, and she takes a breath. But the loss of composure lasts only a split second. Those black eyes dart from Mie to me. Lips press into a pencil-thin line. "Phones on the desk in front of you." The kids don't move. She takes in a breath. "Now." It's a command, more like the voice as described in the novel Dune . All those in attendance take their phones out and place them on the closest desk.

She watches them. Her lips move slightly as if counting both the bodies and the phones at the same time. As the last phone hits a desk, she nods. "Library, all of you. That little room near the gym where books with paper in them rest. No one goes home until the police have talked to them."

Some grumble, others make their way to the door without a word.

None stay behind as the woman walks toward Mie with a striking glint of hate in her eyes.

"What happened here?" Her voice is steady, but a drip of shock quivers in the underlying tone. Death is not something she is trained to deal with, but I am.

"This is a crime scene. You need to take a step back while we secure everything." I stand and haul the kid to his feet.

"I'm the principal here, and I will–"

"You will sit, or I cuff you to chair." Mie glares causing the principal to look away. She sits down in a chair at the front of the room, far from the body, and takes out a tablet. Probably making notes or playing a game. I'm not too interested in what she's doing as long as she's far away from me.

The kid whimpers as I pull him to his feet. His whole upper body must be sore from Mei twisting his arm. I'll need to remember that if we want to question him, but this is an open and shut case. He killed the teacher, and we witnessed it. Blood on his clothes tells the story well. It doesn't hurt that his hands are scraped and bleeding, cuts from the bone fragments of the teacher's face.

I sit the kid at the front of the class but far away from Principal Pham. A few steps bring me beside the body. Mie uses her fancy phone to record the evidence. She speaks Chinese to it in a soft voice. Easier for her, I guess. It's her native language, so there's no need for her to translate before speaking.

Principal Pham clears her throat. "Can you cover him?"

I glance up and then dismiss her comment. Some people need to step back when police are working.

The pool of blood under the head of the vic grows darker as it congeals. "Any idea how long the kid hit him before he died?"

"Minute maybe, two at most." Mie reaches out to move the head.

"Don't get your prints on it." I fish around in a pocket and pull out a glove. "Here."

She takes the glove and uses it to keep her fingerprints off the body. The head moves easily to the side as she examines the flattened back of the skull. "Blood drying. Brain drying." She rocks back and sits on her haunches. It's a delicate way of sitting, and something I'll never achieve with the ease she uses. "Two minute." She nods.

"Damn." If only we could have saved him. Such a waste of life, being killed while teaching kids. I pull the kid closer to the body, making him look at the mess. If it scares him, there's no proof of such, but at least here's something burned into his brain.

Sirens wail outside, just loud enough to make it through the sound deadening walls. Principal Pham stands up and makes her way to the door. Her arms are crossed behind, giving me a clear view of the tablet and my daughter's file. Crap, another thing to remember to do today. Bet she's still locked in the room.

A commotion erupts in the halls as the period bell rings and kids move between classes. The back door of the room opens, and a few students enter and stop. I go over to the door and usher the kids out, telling them to stand to the side, then return. Pham is doing the same at the front.

A man pokes his head in the door and looks over the principal. "Lilly-Grace, what's going on?"

Blood drains from his cheeks as his gaze takes in the body. I rush forward, blocking the view.

"Please step back from the door," I order.

The man has his cell out, aiming it at the corpse. I raise a hand and block the shot. He tries to aim a picture around me, but I put my hand around the phone, blocking the lens.

"Get your hand off my phone," he huffs.

"You'll be charged with obstruction if you keep this up." I push against him, forcing his body out the door.

"Roberts," Mie says.

I glance at Mie. She's standing beside the kid who is sitting, rocking back and forth. He's mumbling to himself, but it's so soft nothing makes sense. Something about a star. A few steps take me close to him.

"I'm a China star. You can't do this to me," the kid mumbles.

I catch the words a little, but nothing sinks in.

Two medics push open the door and rush toward the corpse. They slow down as they catch sight of the grey matter on the floor.

"Call it," one says to the other.

There's a squelch as the other medic radios in and waits for confirmation of death.

I turn back to the kid. "James?"

He keeps rocking in place. Two simple sentences come out as he rocks. "I'm a China star. You can't do this to me."

It clicks somehow—the connection between his words and the device. We'll need to search his locker.

"Your phone." I want it. Need to look at it.

"I'm a China star. You can't do this to me."

His gaze is far off and pointed at nothing. He's snapped. Not a medical term, just what we call it when someone is disassociated from reality.

"Yes, you're a star. Do you have images to show me?" I have my voice level, even soft. We need to get through to him and find out what is happening at the school. There's more to this case than a few missing girls. His words link it all. I figure we've stumbled onto some underground economy taking advantage of teenagers.

"James, where's your phone?" Again, I speak soft and level. Try to convince him nothing is wrong.

His eyes focus for a second and dip down to his pocket. The clue. He's got one on him, as if that would surprise me.

His lower lip trembles a little. "My pocket."

I reach out. "Is it okay if I take it out for you?"

He recoils a little but nods when I don't make a move. I reach and touch the left front pocket.

A smile crosses his face. "I'm a China star."

I slip the phone up and out. It's a fancy clear one you can fold or twist any way you want. Not hard to operate, but still more complicated than the solid one I have. I pry the sides out and the top-up. The device powers on with text and a picture of a girl on a bed, face almost obscured—breasts standing out like only a teenager's can. I try to swipe to get into the phone, but it's locked.

"Facial lock?" I ask James.

He nods, leans forward. "And my dick image will unlock it." Laughter escapes him.

I point the phone's front camera at his face, hoping the image is close enough. It is. The lock screen disappears, and the phone's home screen is there for me to see. The top dock shows alerts with an icon saying more to see. I pull down the menu, scan through his class list and alerts. App updates come scrolling down and then the calls he's missed. In the chaos, one number comes up that I recognize. Heat builds in my face, and I stare at it. Only five minutes ago, this punk received a call from my little girl.

January 10th, 2033 - The Show

Bojing waits with all the others of his Triad cell. As the Red Pole in Ontario, he stands next to the bed with the black 49ers mask as his only clothing. Twenty other members stand a respectful distance away from the bed, but he wants to be upfront—the place of honor. Blood will be the pinnacle of this initiation, and he's looking forward to his nephew becoming a man.

The girl struggles against the bindings. Red mars the skin around her wrists and ankles. The cold air in the room teases goosebumps, and nipples on both the woman and the watching men harden. She is beautiful. Even with the fear welling up in her, the structure of the cheeks and eyes stand out. He wants so desperately to remove the gag and hear her scream.

Large eyes dart from one masked face to another as the girl struggles against the bindings. She is young, maybe seventeen at the most, but even so, tattoos adorn her otherwise pale complexion. A heart is drawn over her left ribs, writing under the right breast. Chinese characters adorn one of her forearms. The words make no sense to Bojing. Girl, Boy, Love, Ever. Stupid Westerners, they try to use our language on their bodies only to make themselves look like fools.

He wants to piss on her. Show disrespect. His language adorns her skin. How dare she do such. But it is not the time. Now is the time for his nephew to shine.

Bojing glances at the others. Their China Girl sets hang from their necks as they wait for the initiate to enter. A small broadcast box sits by the bed, ready to take the signals of the experience and send it to all witnessing the initiation. He glances at the clock. It's taking too long.

The members do not talk. They know better. A few shuffle from foot to foot. A few have lost their excitement, no longer staring at the woman on the bed with anticipation. The cold negatively effects them after such a long wait. And it's been twenty minutes. Where is the boy?

Bojing stares at the door willing his nephew to enter. It is customary to allow up to five minutes. Being naked in front of others, exposing yourself, letting them into your experience with the device, it is not something taken lightly. And his nephew is a gentle soul than those usually allowed into the 49ers. He needed pushing at all the stages. It almost exposed their relationship. But he will learn.

The door opens as if on cue. His nephew stands there, hands by his side, just as Bojing instructed him. Don't show hesitation or fear. Clear your mind. Come and mount the animal. And as you climax, crush her throat. It is simple. It is easy. It must be done.

Members around the bed don their sets, eyes rolling back. He does the same, giving in to the show.

I put the phone on the desk. My hands shake as they come together in front of me. James smiles. Mie comes over, picks up the phone, and glances at the screen, then puts it down. The medics lift the body onto the gurney, cover the head with plastic, and pull a sheet over it. At least there will be no blood in the hall.

The bigger of the two medics approaches me. "I'll need your card."

He extends his hand. The black glove he wears has a small piece of brain on it. He probably doesn't notice. I stare at it for a second and try to calm my internal voice. A scream fights to get out. To take the smiling kid and demand answers. Not about the case, but why my daughter is calling him. For his credit, the medic waits for the card.

"Bruce?" Mie says.

Her voice is enough to break the spell. I reach into my breast pocket and pull out my card. The medic takes it and slides the thing into a pocket at the foot of the stretcher. A surreal aspect to how it all unravels tugs at me. The medics push the stretcher out the door. Pictures click as they exit, and phones in eager hands stretch into the room as the rent-a-cop comes back in. He jerks a thumb toward the door.

"You want me to do something about that?"

I glance at the door. "Yeah, clear them while backup comes, will ya?"

"Sure," he says, nodding as if he thinks I'm joking. "I'll get right on that."

It's enough to get my anger up. "That's right, you'll get on it. I want nothing leaking until the rest of the team shows up. Now move."

He gives me a sidelong look but spins and heads to the door. I glance at my watch, wondering when the rest of the rent-a-cops will be here, and when I'll get to my daughter. When I'll be able to question James alone, and ask him about my daughter. Better hurry up just in case time runs out.

"We need to call his parents," Lilly-Grace says. "They need to be present during any questioning when charges are brought up against him."

"I never said I was charging him with anything. Until I do..." I pull the chair around facing the kid. "Anyway, he's almost eighteen. He can make his own decisions. Can't you, James?"

James is still smiling, but there's something in the background when his parents are mentioned. A dread, if anything. I've seen that slight wince on others. He's afraid of them. Hard to believe any kid is afraid of their parents these days. I take it as bait to get him talking.

His eyes are glassy, so I snap my fingers. "James, you with us?"

He lifts his head, and the smile widens. "I'm a star. They told me."

"James, I want to know if we should contact your parents." It's simple, get them to think you're helping them. If they're afraid, be the shield. Get on their good side, and they'll eventually tell you everything. I pull out my phone and set it to record. "Do you want us to contact your parents?"

The fear is there again. A little brighter than before, but he does not drop the smile. "No."

I raise an eyebrow. "Good, I don't want you to get in trouble."

He nods. "Dad doesn't understand. Him and Mom are longers."

I smile. The slang longers is not lost on me. Couples together for longer than ten years are usually referred to using that term. With the Canadian divorce rate over eighty percent, people just don't stay together anymore. "I wouldn't want my parents around if I got in trouble. They've been married for forty years."

The trick is to build up a sense of false security with the perp. Let them see the common ground—false hope. I look up to Mie. "Can you get a can of soda?"

She gives me an understanding nod.

"You want a pop?" I ask James.

"Sure, ginger." He smiles. "I like the fizz it gives."

"Two gingers, Mie." I hand over my credit card for the machine. Hope there's room on it. "Should just be able to tap it."

A hand touches mine. Fingers probe around my wedding ring. James examines my ring.

"How long," James asks.

"We've been longers for a few years." I lift my hand. The band glints in the light. Simple gold band. Nothing but light scratches on the surface. So unlike the relationship.

"One day, I'll get a girl and be a longer." His eyes stare far away for a second. "Raise a kid. But I want to be a long-time star as well. Can't do both. One or the other, they said." His eyes stare into the distance as if in another reality.

"Really?" It's time to dig. "One or the other? Why?"

"Girls don't like sharing their man." He still stares off into the distance. "Not unless they're into the China as well."

He's mentioned China before. Could he mean China Girl? "Been a lot of girls?"

"Twenty-two." His smile broadens even more. "I'm the best there is."

"Man, must be nice being with that many." I sit back a little, try to hold my anger at the kid, hoping he's not sleeping with Sarah. Mie comes in with the pop and hands me both cans. "Here." I put one in front of him. He scoops it up and levers the tab to open the top. I follow his lead. "Nothing like ginger ale."

He raises the can in a mock toast. "That's for sure."

I only take a sip while he gulps half the can. With a belch, he puts the thing down. "Fizzes the nose."

It does. It hasn't changed a bit since they first made it. "Some families on the islands make it themselves." I take another sip, trying to lull him into giving more information. "A lot stronger. They use real ginger."

"I'm going to the islands in three months. They promised. They want their star with them."

"Really? They must be rich to afford to take you."

His smile almost disappears. "No, they want me to work down there for a year. Have to give up school." The smile comes back again. "But I'm a star."

"Really? How much of a star? I haven't heard about you except for today."

He leans forward conspiratorially. "Want to see?"

I nod. He stands. Mie comes up behind him, but a quick glance at her and she stops. James slips his pants and underwear down. I didn't see that coming.

The wind slams against the car, caking the side with snow. It took an hour to get the kid's pants back on, report to the relief crew, and spring my daughter from her jail cell in the school. Principal Pham and I exchanged a lot of words, but Sarah, my daughter, is mixed up with a bad crowd and trying to make a name for herself — not in a good way.

Mie sits in the front passenger seat, and Sarah is in the back. I glance down at the dash. Battery power is at 40%. The cold is killing the car. I need to get home. Hell, Sarah and I have to get home. I'll make Julie deal with this one somehow. All I want to do is kill that James kid. I have images of him touching Sarah with his... Christ! He must have had an operation on his penis while he was young. No one has one that long. It reached his knee and almost as thick as my forearm.

The crew will search his locker, then search his home. I swear he was talking about a China Girl rig. It makes sense. And if that's right, it's also child porn to be in possession of those recordings. This case is blowing up.

Heat streams out of the vents. Just a bit at first, but every second brings the warmth up. It'll kill the charge faster, but I don't care. Better to be warm than freezing. I glance at Sarah in the rearview. She's staring out the side window, headphones on. Thank god they hold the sound. I don't want to hear the thrash punk she listens to.

"The child, she... how you say... wild?" Mie keeps her gaze out the front of the car.

"Yes, wild." I clench the wheel as wind threatens to take us into another lane. "Good kid, really. Just this last year, she's grown away from us. Not sure why. We get her everything she wants that we can afford. Even those fucking headphones. Six hundred. And that's with a discount." I take a deep breath.

"Maybe not getting everything better." Mie uncovers her phone, swipes, types, and lets the sleeve drop back in seconds. "Many distractions. Not focus." She makes a blinders sign with her hands. The cold and wind caused her to redden; the stark difference between the pale skin on her hands against her rosy face stands out. Her hands are the same color they've always been.

"What's different about your hands?" I ask.

She tucks them under her coat. "Nothing."

"At the precinct, Ron asked you about your hands, and you said both. Both what?"

"Nothing."

"Look, if we're going to be partnered up for this, you need to come clean. You said you'd tell me later. So, what is it?"

She turns her face to me, glaring. A click sounds with a soft pop of a sealed wine bottle having the cork pulled. She lifts one arm out. It ends just after the elbow–a prosthetic.

"Shit!" The car swerves. I battle it back under control.

"You want to know." Her voice is cold and without emotion.

"Other even longer. Young when happen. Candidate for special surgery. Father with money." She holds up her stump of an arm. The limb slides into the folds with a sucking sound, and she twists it. A click and the limb's back on. She holds her hand up and moves the fingers. "Had for long time."

"I'm sorry. I didn't know." I'm an idiot, that's what I should say. No feelings for others. Just a clod looking for a place to open his mouth and pushing for information I didn't need.

"No. You need know." She holds out her other arm and pulls back the coat sleeve. A definite line is mid-way up her upper arm. "Half me, half not." She pulls the sleeve back. "Legs same."

I bite the surprise back.

"Thirteen. Triad take me. Pressure father for money. He give. They think not fast. 49ers use me for initiation but not kill. Ropes tight, stop blood. Hospital take. Father fix." Her flat voice is totally removed of emotion from the incident. "Take two year to become me." She turns to face me as I stop at a light. "Each I hunt. Take manhood and"–she takes her open hand and squeezes it into a fist–"they not do it again."

A honk from behind makes my knees come apart just enough to hit the accelerator. It is not imaginable what she went through, but every guy has been kicked in the nut sack at least once in their life. The fact she crushed the guys who did this to her is poetic justice. It's just not something a guy wants to imagine. I glance in the rearview mirror, and Sarah is staring in Mie's direction, mouth open, eyes wide, leaning forward just a little. Guess her music finished just in time to see the show.

I make the last turn into the parking garage. The scanner reads my plate and opens the tolling doors for us to drive in. We go down three levels, and I park in my designated spot. I unlock the charger and latch it in place. This is going to be a heavy month for electricity. Makes me wish we were back to burning gas.

Snow drips from the wheel wells and sloshes to the cement floor. Small rivulets of dirty water run into a grate to be collected for recycling. I reach out a foot and kick a tire. Slushy snow drops with a plop from the car. Sarah takes her sweet time getting out. Probably queuing up more music, like usual.

Mie stands at the rear of the car and looks around. There's not much noise. It's still early. Going to have to clock in when I get upstairs. Maybe Julie's at work. No, not this week. She's working the graveyard shift. Maybe she'll be asleep. We need to be quiet.

"You hungry?" I ask Mie.

Sarah finally stumbles out of the car. "I'm hungry. Can we have take out or something?"

Fuck. More money to burn that we don't have.

Mie glances at me. "I cook."

Sarah pumps her arm up and down. "Hell yeah! I'm in."

I turn to Sarah. "Mie's our guest. She doesn't need to cook for us."

"It okay. I enjoy cook. Make great... how you say... lung soup."

Sarah stops dancing in place. "Yuck!"

"You'll eat what's put in front of you." I smile at Mie, who gives me a wink. We probably don't have the ingredients, but she shows me the whole thing was a jest. "Well, if you want to make something, I'll eat it."

The elevator takes forever. One is out, the other's going down, and this one stops at every other floor for the old lady who can't remember which one she lives on. It isn't ours. She keeps riding up after we depart.

Sarah, Julie, and I live in the ninth unit on floor twenty-five. It's a corner one with three bedrooms and a large living/dining room. The kitchen, though small, has everything we need. It does take most of our income to stay here, but being this close to our work makes the rent worth it–only thirty minutes for either of us.

Julie would've gotten home between eight and nine, after her twelve-hour shift. Give her another hour to change and message me about Sarah, and her head would have hit the pillow around ten this morning. It's just after two. Hopefully, she'll still be asleep. If we keep it quiet, she'll stay asleep when I take Mie to whatever hotel she's staying at. Christ.

I reach into my pocket for keys and pull out the right one. "Julie is probably asleep, so let's keep it quiet for now."

Mie nods, and Sarah ignores me, her headphones on and music playing. I open the door.

Sarah doesn't even look up as she kicks off her shoes and heads to her room. Our bedroom door is closed, blocking out most of the noise we'll generate. I take Mie's coat and hang it up in the closet with mine.

"Kitchen there?" Mie points.

I nod my head, and she shuffles off too fast for me to stop. It only takes me a second to catch up to her, and she already has flour out.

"Where did you find that?"

She just smiles. "Kitchen same everywhere. You have bigger than mine in China." She pulls out a bowl and mixes flour and salt into it. Two eggs follow along with water. She makes a dough and sets it aside. "You have chicken?"

I grab some out of the fridge, and she cuts it up into strips. Before I know it, she has our wok out and places the chicken in it with other spices. As this all comes together, the dough is cut up and stretched. She folds it and cuts homemade noodles.

"Father rich from street food." She puts the noodles into a pot of water. "He make fortune with noodle and chicken. Need set table."

I head to Sarah's room and knock on the door. It takes a second, but if she has her headphones on she won't be able to hear the knock. I open the door.

She's lying on her bed, wearing her damn headphones, TV going with no sound. I step toward the bed.

"Stop," Mie whispers in my ear.

I just about jump.

"She have China Girl on."

January 10th, 2033
– Clearing the Air

A crid burning tobacco fills the small office. The room is almost dark, with one light shining on a complex keyboard with Chinese characters. All Cantonese. Bojing switches between holding down the shift key to the alt to none. A very complicated way of writing. The method is slow, but it is the only way to send messages using their own code of numbers and letters. He lets the smoke from his cigarette curl up around his face. It sometimes stings his eyes, but he doesn't care. The pain makes him feel alive.

A light tap interrupts his typing. He flicks the ash from the smoke onto the side of his desk.

"Come," he says with deliberate calm.

The door opens, and one of the 49ers pushes an eighteen-year-old naked man into the room. He immediately stumbles to the ground before the desk. One hand is bandaged with red blots of blood seeping through. The other sports fingers twisted in obscene angles. Dirt covers the once average looking man, his lips cracked, and one cheek bulging out, obviously broken. When the man looks up, his mouth forms the word Uncle, but no sound comes out. Teeth stumps show pink and red from grinding.

The 49er puts a foot against the man's back and pushes again, forcing the now crippled ex-member to the ground. He goes to kick him, but Bojing holds up a hand. The man stops and shakes his head before retreating through the door, closing it as he leaves.

Bojing stands, clears his throat, and walks around his desk to stand in front of the prone man who once claimed to be his nephew. He takes a chair from the wall and unfolds it. With more gentleness than he's ever shown before, he bends and helps the young man to the seat. He produces a small kerchief and wipes the dirt from the other's brow, showing no emotion as beads of blood discolor the white cloth.

His nephew shivers. He coughs up blood. It decorates the ground with a light splatter. Some hits Bojing's shoes, but he does not clean it away.

With a pull on the cigarette, Bojing inhales smoke. He pulls the stub from his mouth and butts it out on the desk. Looking at his nephew, he fishes in his pocket for the pack and pulls out another cancer stick.

He flicks a lighter and touches the flame to a cigarette, and places the smoldering cig between the trembling lips of his nephew.

"One thing," Bojing says. "You only had to do one thing. Keep your mind clear and fuck the girl. Even if you couldn't kill her, you needed to fuck her." He leaned against his desk. "But instead, you thought of fucking Gin-Jong." He spits the name out in disgust. "Why?"

His nephew takes a small drag on the cigarette and coughs again. "I... I don't... I don't know."

"Bull shit!" Bojing reaches out and slaps him. "Why?"

Tears roll down his nephew's face, and he looks away in shame. "I don't like women."

Bojing sighs. "You should have told me."

The man cries in anguish. Shame spills out. "Father forced me to come. He wanted me to be like you, his famous brother. The one high in the seat. Enough to make it in another country." The cigarette dangles from his mouth, the filter soaked with spit. "He said I could be famous like Bojing—"

Bojing reaches out and slaps his nephew again. "I am Red Pole here. Or four-two-six. You do not use my name."

He turns his head back to look up at Bojing. Slobber colored by blood runs in a string from his mount and down his front. "I want Gin-

Jong. He excites me. I thought if I could just get hard. Hard enough to enter her. The initiation could be successful..."

The air thickens in the room. The one-man staring in disgust at the other. Hatred for what happened and what will happen floods the older one. He lifts a hand. "I could no more strike my hand off than fuck someone I hate. Now it ends."

He grabs his nephew by the throat, lifting him to his feet and slamming him into the wall. Bojing shoves hard. Bones snap. He pushes one more time. The last of the neck bones shatter.

Bojing leans forward and whispers, "I love you, nephew. This is why I do this. It is fast. No more torture. The end of your pain."

Eyes widen. An open mouth gasps for air.

His naked body slides down the wall. Blank eyes stay locked on Bojing. His rear touches the floor, urine gushes from the body. One shoulder slumps, pulling the torso down. A single eye now stares up as lungs try desperately to pull air through a collapsed windpipe. The orb loses focus, starved of oxygen. Flatulence fills the room.

Bojing steps back, pulls out a cigarette, and lights it.

Sarah looks asleep. Her room, a fusion of pink and purple wallpaper, gives an eerie glow to her skin. The headphones rest just over her ears, but a thick cord is plugged into the socket. I follow the cable with my gaze, and it ends in her phone, plugged into the USB type X while the unit sits on the charging plate.

I've seen her like this many times, thinking she's napping, and haven't connected the dots until now. She twitches. Her cheeks flush. The throws of the experience run through her body. I can only imagine what they might be. She's my little girl.

This needs to end.

I take a step, but Mie's hand on my shoulder stops me.

"You remember when stop? It hurt. She younger. No filter."

"I have to do something. Who knows what she's living in there." I reach out to remove the headphones from her, but Mie squeezes my shoulder.

"Turn off phone." She indicates with a nod. "It better remove unit power. Remove unit takes away. Remove player stops."

I grab the cell phone. It has a clear body that I can see my hand through, though slightly out of focus. The power drops. I think it is slow at discharging, but the heat coming off it almost burns. It's eating up juice faster than the rapid charger can supply. I pull the USB free.

A groan. Her hand comes up and touches her head. She feels the headset, and the other comes up as well to check the cord. Her left eye opens. Sarah sits up.

"Hey! That's mine!"

"No, it's illegal technology," I say.

"You bought that phone for me." She grabs for it.

I lift the phone and reach out my other hand to snatch the headphones. She goes to grab them. To protect them. Too late. They slide off her head and out of her reach. I toss them to Mie.

"Modified." She turns them in her hands. "Leads in phones and strap. Good job. Still, you see connections. Sewing not perfect." Mie lifts her head. "Made in America mod."

Sarah weeps. Her head is forward, hands up to it. My heart breaks. She's not really a bad kid, just makes bad choices like all teenagers. I go down on a knee. "Hey, it's okay."

I try to hug her, but she twists to get my hands to release her shoulders.

"It's mine," she whimpers just above a whisper.

"It's bad for you." I look up to Mie, who shrugs. "The tech it uses is untested. It could cause all sorts of problems."

"But it's mine." Her hands drop. Tears flow down, taking black eye shadow with them in streaks.

I take her hands. "I don't want anything bad to happen to my baby." She tugs at her hands, but I hold them tight. "The rig goes to evidence. You'll need—"

Her eyes widen. "No!"

She breaks away from me, dives at the rig in Mie's hands. Mie steps aside. Sarah lands on the floor in a lump. "I want it back!"

A door slams. Julie is staring in the room, eyes dark from little sleep. Her head swivels to take in the scene. Flannel pajamas flow over her shoulders and spill about her. Not her sexiest look, but we must have woken her from a dead sleep. She stares at Mie for a second before bending over to take Sarah into her arms.

"Get out," she says. "I'll take care of this."

Mie heads out, but I stand there like a fool being made fun of by the Queen. "I need to ask her some questions. This device is linked to a criminal organization."

Julie lifts her head and stares at me. "Not now."

Ice somehow fills my body. Simply cold. Her words have such an effect on me. I step around both of the women in my life and indicate for Mie to follow me. Outside is warmer than how I feel with that glare on me. I get out of the cold room.

The noodles slide down my throat, leaving a trail of flavor behind them. They're so different from what I'm used to. The sauce clings to the crunchy vegetables. My stomach accepts the nourishment greedily.

Mie sits on one side of the table, her back to the wall. My back is to the balcony, the cold air held back by thin windows. We both look up as Julie stalks into the room. She's been with Sarah for half an hour and is dragging her feet. Her eyes are half-opened at best, hair in a bit of a rat's nest, and she moves at a lumbering pace. Zombies would think she's one of their own.

I get up, go to the kitchen, grab a large bowl, and fill it with the noodles, chicken, and veg. The coffee maker is there, so in goes a pod while I shove a cup under the drip.

The coffee finishes drizzling into the cup. I add a dash of cream to make it drinkable for her.

I return to the dining area just as she is becoming aware of my new partner. The two stare at each other from either side of the table like cats ready to mark their territory. Wind blasts against the windows as a storm kicks up. I put down the noodle dish in front of my wife with the coffee. She curls both hands around the mug, lifts the steaming liquid, and takes two gulps. She lowers the cup and, for the first time, looks across the table at Mie.

"Who are you?"

"Mie Ling," Mie says. "Work with Bruce."

"Cop?"

"Yes."

Julie leans back in her chair. "You made this?" She lifts the fork. Noodles drape down from the utensil.

"Yes."

Julie drops the fork. "I hate noodles."

Mie nods, stands, and walks to the door. I follow her. "You don't have to go—"

"Yes, I go." She glances at Julie, who has not yet moved from the table. "You need talk. Fix what wrong."

"I can give you a lift to your hotel."

"No. I get cab." She puts a hand on my arm. "You talk. Fix. See tomorrow."

She slips on her boots and leans to the side. "Nice meeting," she says to Julie, who just waves an arm in the air.

Mie frowns, the first real emotion she's shown me. Her voice is soft. "Tomorrow, we talk. Today, try solve." She nods toward Julie.

A quick turn, and she opens the door but stops before leaving. "I text you hotel in morning." And she leaves.

I stand there, watching the stairway door close. Nothing comes to mind about the strange way Julie acted toward Mie. There has to be a reason for her being so rude to a stranger. Maybe the lack of sleep or Sarah's meltdown.

She's eating the noodles as I sit at the table.

"Good noodles," Julie says.

I want to talk about so many things. Our daughter and her behavior at school. The danger that is happening and how Sarah could be connected to it. All I can ask is, "Why?"

"I don't know. Where did she buy them?"

"No, why did you treat Mie like that?"

Julie puts the fork down and pushes the bowl away. She presses her fingers against her eyes. "I'm tired. You and Sarah woke me from a dead sleep." She drops her hand and stares at me. "Why the hell did you make so much noise?"

I let my thoughts swim through the few minutes with Sarah on the bed, her face flushed. Several seconds tick away before I reach over and pick up her phone and headset. "This."

Julie glances down. "Her cell and headset?"

It takes a second for me to pull back some of the fake leather in the band to expose the leads. Julie watches, eyes growing wide.

"It's called China Girl. A technology being used by the Asian market and gangs." I turn on the cell phone and start the app. The usual message comes up about the program being from a third party and not recommended. I hit the accept.

It takes a few seconds for the app to initialize, then the phone starts to heat up with the energy usage.

"Put the headset on."

Julie reaches out then hesitates. "Is this some sort of trick?"

I take a deep breath. "No." It's the softest I've spoken in a long time. Softer than when I spoke to Sarah during her rant. Softer than I did the last time I said goodnight to Julie. The sound of someone beaten down and numb to the spite directed at them.

Julie takes the headset and places them on the conventional way. I reach out and move the band a little more to the back of her head. Once they are on correctly, I engage the program.

The phone goes from warm to hot. Julie lifts an eyebrow, and I mouth the words, "Close your eyes." She does, and the system takes her on a ride.

Five seconds. Ten. Fifteen. Her brow furrows. Twenty. Thirty. She starts to twitch. The power runs out on the phone, and Julie snaps her eyes open.

"What the hell!" She pulls off the offending tech.

I raise an eyebrow. "What did you see?"

"It was Sarah." She rubs her forehead. "She had some headset on, like this one but no earpieces."

"And?"

"I was her... or seeing and feeling everything through her eyes. She watched herself in a mirror until some guy came up behind her. Young guy, maybe seventeen. He started to feel me... I mean her... up. When his hands went into her pants, the feed stopped, and I opened my eyes."

"Some guy?"

"Yeah." She describes James.

"I know the kid. We have him locked up." I turn off Sarah's phone.

"On what?"

"Murder. He killed a teacher in school today."

Julie sits back and bites her nail for a second. "Destroy the recording."

"No!" Sarah screams.

We both look up. Sarah stands in the hall just a step before the bathroom. She looks tired. Not the same as Julie, just worn out. She stomps to the table and grabs the phone before I can do anything. Her face goes pale.

"You played with my phone!"

"Sarah, it's no longer your phone." I reach out and take it from her. The device gives off heat and almost burns my hand. The app has killed the battery. A quick boot and the "show" starts running again. It's a third of the way through but drains the last of the power and shuts down.

Her eyelids quiver—lower lip trembles. I've never seen her like this. Sarah drops to her knees and cries the tears of a lost soul.

Julie is out of her chair and hugging our daughter. She makes shushing sounds to help out, but nothing is working. Gibberish comes out of Sarah – first time – special – only once. It dawns on me. My little girl is growing up. She's a woman, and someone has defiled her.

The star.

Blood pounds in my ears. I get up and walk to the hall and into my daughter's room, her phone still in my hand. It has to be somewhere. Her computer. The lifeblood of a teenager. I grab her school bag from the floor and upturn it. The small device tumbles onto the bed.

With the computer cube in hand, I stalk into the living room. Julie is still calming Sarah on the floor. I sit on the couch and place the cube on the coffee table. A small desktop unfolds, and a quick tap of the cube turns it on—the screen projects into the air and keyboard on the tabletop. My admin password is accepted, and I search the storage for large files. Multiple show up.

I filter the search, making the connection from the file on the phone: two-hundred plus tera-bytes with an extension of CG. Twelve show up. Each has a name on it. I run down them and see a pattern in the date and time. The files show a creation date over the last three weeks, but they all came in two days ago. It's an evolution in porn. Worse, it's child porn.

An icon blinks in the corner of the screen. I open it – file transmitting.

Someone sends a file through the sharing site I told her never to use. The download is painstakingly slow, though it is actually very fast. Three minutes later and a new icon shows up. I take the title and throw it into the search field of the browser. One hit. A discussion forum. China Girl. Under New Releases. Five stars. Snuff. Sex. I select the link.

January 11th, 2033 - Loose Ends

Bojing sits back on his haunches and lights a cigarette. The smoke curls in the air, dissipating before him. The remains of his actions from the prior day no longer decorate the floor. He's not stripped the meat off a human body in a number of years, and it was nice to know he could still do it. The pigs will destroy the bones while the meat can go into their feed. He smiles. The slaughterhouse they purchased for their operation works well.

He thinks of the last profit and loss statement for a few seconds. It will do. He stands. Ammonia destroys DNA.

A knock, and his door opens. A small teenaged girl enters, her black straight hair falls on diminutive shoulders. She hands him a file, and he flips through it. She leaves, closing the door behind her. The report shows an additional sixty kilos of raw food consumed by the animals.

Outside, a pig-squeal breaks the silence. Another slaughter. More practice for the recruits. Sadness threatens to take away the elation of death. His nephew would've been the next to slaughter the pigs. The others would have taken him into the back, shown him how to disembowel with a knife. Hang the meat. Put the victim's bones into the slop. He would then get prepared to pick the next girl. But no. He had to show the side of him that needed killing.

An email comes in—coded, like all the others before it. Bojing opens the document and supplies the correct cipher. A simple message. Is it done? The signature displays a number. Most would think it a telephone number, but Bojing pulls out his cell and starts the app. A special one the clan developed. He enters the digits. The face of 438 stares back at him. The heavyset eyes with a thick brow over them are hard to ignore. The man's pug nose shows black hair in need of a trim. Brown stained teeth peek through a mouth held open to breathe.

"426, is your line secure? Are you alone?"

Bojing checks the connection and nods. "Alone and secure, 438."

The man nods. Bojing cannot help but notice the receding gray hairline. This is the man I am told to fear?

"I have reports. The last record. It is poor."

Bojing bows. "An oversight now fixed. The initiative was not well suited for the 49ers."

438 nods. "I have not sampled it, but as you say, it is done. I have no need to follow up."

Bojing bows again. "I request a stipend for the family."

The heavy caterpillar brow furrows. "Really? Highly unusual."

"I understand." He takes a deep breath. This is the only thing he can do for his brother. "They petitioned me directly. It's my fault he failed. I will pay for my failure." Bojing lifts his hand and places a knife against the left little finger.

438 raises one side of the caterpillar brow. Ten seconds pass with silence before the older one speaks. "That is not necessary." He reaches out, and something scrapes against the wood of his desk. "I will make the necessary arrangements. Stipend as initiate or member?"

Bojing swallows. "Member, 438. Gratitude." He lowers the knife. As his hand stops by his side, a small droplet of blood trickles down the finger, threatening to fall, then finally releases. The tumble is slow, but Bojing dares not move. His breath stays in his chest. The blood hammers against the ground so loud he almost flinches. Show no emotion. Keep it casual as if you are just making a normal request.

438 scribbles something on the paper and nods. "It is done. I ask, do you wish to divert some of your stipends from this month to support the family?"

It's something of a trap, but Bojing pretends to ignore it. "Five percent. It is my fault for accepting the boy, and I will pay it from my own pocket."

"Generous. But something tells me the western culture of the North is rubbing off on you, 426."

"I do wish to return." A tremble runs through his body. The home of his birth. Where he can enjoy life without hiding. Make the police turn a blind eye. "How long do you need me here?"

"Long enough, but not that much longer." 438 sits back in his chair, steepling his fingers together. "You're missed here. You control the 49ers well, and they follow you. Soon, my friend. Soon you will be by our side."

Bojing bows deeply. "I await your orders."

438 nods once again. "The order is sent. We have one bid for a substantial sum. He wants someone young, the high school star with his girlfriend once again, but done specially for his exotic taste."

Mie Ling sits in the hot seat, one arm resting on my desk. Her hair looks a little more relaxed. Instead of the ponytail, it is loose, long and shimmering in the light of the squad room. A heavy coat drapes over the back of the chair but does not hide the professional pantsuit she wears. I try to ignore the knowledge of her arms and legs being artificial constructs that are not flesh and blood but fail miserably.

To lighten the mood, I sneak up on her, intending to surprise, but just as I get near, she stands and takes two steps forward before turning. She stands in a column of light filtering through a window. The clear sky allows for as much sun as possible, the reason I picked that desk.

A slight frown on her face, she points at my desk to a scrap piece of paper with the words "Not surprised" written on it.

"How?" I ask. "There's so much noise in here."

A smile threatens her face but gives up in total humiliation. "You do not know? How you pick desk and not know all around?" She directs me to sit in the hot seat. "Look forward."

I sit in the chair and stare forward. She points. I follow the finger.

Across the room, a mirror on the wall reflects in another, and it, in turn, reflects in another. The juxtaposition is almost perfect to see the squad room door, though like it is a million kilometers away. If a perp could use them, they could tell who's coming and going.

"You must have good eyesight," I say.

She attempts a smile again, partially succeeds, then lets her face fall back into the placid look. I change seats and sit at the desk.

She pulls up a chair beside me. "You find anything?"

"Nothing." I sluff my coat onto the back of the chair and slump. "Stayed up half the night talking with her. It's hard to realize she's old enough to be in a relationship, let alone involved in... You know, that thing. I don't know where I went wrong. She has it in her mind that adults are the bad guys. I'm not, really. Bad, that is. I just want my little girl back."

"You good father."

"I hope so." I put my elbow on the chair arm and my head against my fist. "There has to be a way to get through to her. Let her know how much I care and that what she's doing is not the life I want her to have."

"Child raised by strong hand learn respect. Respect make child be better adult. Better adult be better for people. Get further, they say. But not true. Bad get further."

"Is that Confucius?"

"No, father." She puts her phone on the desk, and it links to the system. Information downloads to my desk. "More come through Interpol in morning."

I point to the time displayed on the desk. She shakes her head. "Some wake early." She swipes folders and opens a few files. "This man, Bojing Wang. We need find evidence, in Canada. Triad and 49ers grow. He 426. Red Pole. Enforcer. He to make power here to get..." She stumbles over an English idiom. "Hold for foot."

"You mean foothold."

"Foothold. Yes, that word." She flips through one of the files. "Last arrest in China, but he get off. Police refuse information. Seal file."

"Then how did you get it?"

She looks at me sideways, then back to the desk. I reach out and tap open the translation function—Steams of Chinese change into English.

Pages unfold. I start to read. There are identification numbers, rape, murder, embezzlement, theft, and a myriad of other charges, none of which stuck. Witnesses disappeared or failed to confirm, changing their story during the trial. I always thought criminals were caught in China, but this tells a very different tale.

The file becomes a listing of physical traits and capabilities, from the small replacement of a self-amputated little toe to an ability to break a four-centimeter slab of concrete. Bojing is a weapon. He is a monster that shows no fear, no remorse, no emotion. He uses people like The Star, and indirectly, my little girl.

"How do we crack him?"

We sit in my car on the 404, heading north to the courthouse. The heater blasts against the window, trying to keep the ice from building up. Wipers slosh back and forth every few seconds. Mie taps on the terminal, and the appointment time on my phone flashes. We're needed. The prosecutor's asking for more information. James Favolopolus. The Star. The teacher killer.

It appears the kid's father is a big executive in one of those tech firms in Markham. I can't keep up with all the companies that have sprouted up. This one has survived for at least three years, so it's considered an oldtimer. Most close the doors just before the first year, getting bottomed out by China when one of their companies buys each one of their models and produces it for half the price. And the justice system operates the same as the ones in the past. Money is the way to make yourself innocent.

"I'm getting tired of this traffic," I say.

"You need teach people to drive," Mie says.

I tap a button on the dash. The lights flash front and back. Blue and red tells people the police are here. Some slow, others move over like they're supposed to. The lane opens up, and I press the accelerator down a little more to get us over forty. I put both hands firmly on the wheel and hope no idiot jumps into the lane in front of me.

We make it to the Mulock exit, but it's jammed. There's no way people can get out of our path, and the shoulder is piled high with snow. Even when the light turns green, only a few get out of our lane to allow us to sneak a little closer to the intersection. And when we get there, the road is full of cars and trucks trying to get into Newmarket.

"Need more road. China make lot roads for move people. People move, better economy."

"Tell that to the politicians. They only tax cars and trucks. Bikers get all the perks as we build the roads from vehicle taxes." I clamp up. My political views are what has kept me from climbing higher than a simple detective—no need to dump it on someone from another country.

"Most round eye country do same."

I glance over.

Mie smiles at me this time, like we've made a connection. I let a corner of my mouth go up and hit the brakes as some old woman noses out into the lane people have cleared for us. I pitch up the siren, but she seems not to see us.

"She's going to kill someone. Run her plates." I hit the horn as well. The more noise there is, the more she may notice.

A hand exits her window and waves. Then the middle finger goes up in defiance.

"Shelly, Mary," Mie reads. "Age seventy-five. Home address–"

"I don't need her whole bio. Where's she from?"

"Canada."

I glance over. "Smart answer, Mie, really smart."

"She have override in car."

It takes just a second to decide. "Hit the override and put her back into her own lane, will you."

The old woman's car slowly moves back into the other lane. She's fighting the wheel, trying to retake control as I scream past. Once a few hundred meters apart, we'll be out of range, so I talk Mie through submitting a summons for interfering with an emergency vehicle and a request for her to be re-tested. The driver will love that. But her actions call for hard choices, and keeping someone off the streets who interferes like she did is the best part of the job. It's the law to pull over, and she didn't. Traffic is slow. I cross over to the oncoming side, where it's lighter. People pull to the side to let us go. The need to be at the hearing is just enough justification for the action. We're not moving much faster, but it's better than the stand-still on the other side.

At the intersection of Leslie and Mulock, an accident has the west lanes going around it. This is the tie-up. I push the car into the West-bound lanes and keep the siren going – will have to turn it off before the courthouse.

When we approach intersections, I slow us down, make sure the coast is clear, and rush through. Years ago, as a teenager, I wanted to do just this. It was one of the reasons for becoming a cop. Little did I know back then that most of the work of a cop is talking to people. Not many car chases. Only one, really. But I did take the course on pursuit. A net cannon hidden under the front left fender can incapacitate any vehicle. I'm itching to try it out one day.

Yonge Street comes up fast as traffic pulls to the side to let us go. That's one thing I have to admire. Most Canadians do understand the need to move over during an emergency. I take the street up to Eagle and turn into the parking lot. Whoever thought of the layout of this thing really needs to get their head examined.

The courthouse stands on a slight rise from the road. Not much, about two meters elevated. Parking is at the side of the building farthest away from the entrance. In the winter, like today, it's a long walk through snow that's shoveled just enough to make it legal. We cops have a closer entrance.

Three spots are open in the police parking spaces. I pick one, not the closest, but not the farthest either. It's not cool to take the closest space when you have good legs.

Wind blows, and a snow squall forms. It all but tears the door from my grasp. Mie picks her way, holding her coat tight against the chilling wind. I take three steps, and ice takes my feet from under me. My ass buffers my fall. Mie is there with her hand out. I take it, trying to recover some of my dignity.

We walk to the police entrance.

I drop my cuffs into the bin next to my glock and walk through the metal detector. The old tech still works to save us from a lot of problems, but it is not infallible. No beep. The bin is passed back to me, and I start putting things back into place.

Mie stares at the bin, eyes growing a little wide. A few items come out of her pockets, along with a gun I've never seen before. A long sleek barrel and gleaming handle stand out against the gray plastic they sit in. The uniform's eyes don't come off it as he pushes the container over the desk. Mie halts just before the metal detector and looks at him.

"Detector will—"

The guy actually smiles with a nod. "You need to step through now."

Mie steps forward.

The detector has a stroke. Four lights glare, and an alarm goes off. I cover my ears as it happens.

"Christ! Can you turn that thing off?" I ask.

One of the uniforms, a girl no older than twenty-five, comes forward with a wand and display. She makes a motion for Mie to hold out her arms and spread her legs a little. As she does, the officer starts waving the wand across her body.

"It'll light up on both arms and legs," I say, stepping forward.

The cop steps aside as I come between the two women. I reach out and put a hand on Mie's arms, dropping them to her side.

"I need to scan her." The officer steps beside me. "We're not allowed to let anyone enter until they're scanned."

Right out of the academy, I bet, by the book, no bending. She steps back.

"I'll vouch, but you need to know for the report on the light show." I nod to Mie, making my voice soft. "They need to see at least one to make sure."

It takes a lot for someone to show what they have or what's been taken from them. Even people in wheelchairs don't want to lose their legs due to amputation and go to great lengths to hide the scars. Mie is just like that. It took a lot for her to show me her arm yesterday, and even then, if Brandon hadn't spotted it, she probably wouldn't have.

A little color flashes across Mie's cheek. A click sounds, and the slight pop of air breaking a seal. She holds out her left arm for inspection.

The uniform stares for a second, then sees the connections inside the arm's cup and the metal ring on Mie's stump.

"Sorry, I didn't mean to..." She's flustered, not knowing what to say.

"You right," Mie says softly. "Must protect." She slides the arm back in place, and the click echoes as if it's the only sound in the world.

I reached out, take her arm, and walked toward the elevator with only a quick stop to scoop up her belongings, along with the impressive gun.

We walk in silence, neither wanting to address what happened. At the elevator, I hit the call button and stare at the numbers as they count down. Doors open after a ding, and we get in. I press the main floor. Thank God, no music breaks the silence.

Two floors count past before the doors open, and we both walk out into a zoo of reporters. Lights flare as voices call out.

I spy James through the crowd with another man beside him. They're talking to each other, and people yell questions at them. Behind them stands Bojing Wang.

January 11th, 2033 - The One

Bojing Wang frowns at the now blank screen of his cell phone. He wants to throw it against the wall. Remove any evidence of what 438 told him to do. The boy produces, and his product sells. He brings the girls and talks them into submitting without a care, just to get a copy of it for their personal viewing. They've made millions off the impressions. Now that old man wants to throw it all away because of some Jing Fang. They expect results and tie his hands.

He takes out a cigarette and lights it. The smoke coils around his tongue, and he sucks in the acrid fumes. One day he will retire and quit this life, but until that time, it is the only way he knows how to make money. He opens the contact list on the phone and scrolls down to a number he doesn't want to call. This will be hard. A call he does not look forward to. Maybe they are out. Maybe he can just leave a message. Maybe he can put it off just a little longer.

It's ridiculous that this has stirred up his emotions. The kid is just a tool that needs to be silenced, and it falls on him to protect the organization.

He hits the contact, and the phone connects the number.

"Hello?" It's a man, the star's father. His voice shakes as if mad.

"Wang here," Bojing says, his rusty English is finally getting some use.

"Mr. Wang!" Relief floods the man's voice. "Good to hear from you. I would talk but–"

"Your son arrested." Bojing takes a long drag of his cigarette. "I know and will deal with it. He is part of our clan."

"Your clan?"

"Yes, our clan." Bojing takes another drag. "He very special to us. I take care this today."

"We have a lawyer on retainer in my firm, and he—"

"Is no good enough." Bojing stares at the glowing tip of the cigarette. "We got better lawyer. One know better than you lawyer."

"I appreciate that, but our lawyer—"

"Mr. Favolopulos, I say we take care of it. You understand?" He slams his hand on the desk. "You show up at courthouse in two hour, and you no bring lawyer." Another drag. "We make sure no problem. We handle. Tell son to shut up." With that, he disconnects the phone. The call to the lawyer will be easier. The perfect one who can get the kid out without watchdogs or bail. Now it's time to pull the strings of the justice system in this country.

The prosecutor stands behind the group with the kid. I want to ask him why James is not in cuffs and a jail cell, but hesitate to see if Mie is following me. She isn't. Instead, she stands by the elevator, eyes wide and face pale. A slight shaking makes her head vibrate. She needs help. I take a step close to her, pushing some of the press trying to get a picture of the Star out of my way.

"Mie!" I wave a hand in front of her face to get her attention. "Mie! Snap out of it."

Her eyes focus on me. Something isn't right. I grip her arm, above the prosthetic, and make our way to the prosecutor.

"Lost your chance there, old man," James calls out, eyes staring at me through the throng. "Is that the chick cop? She tore ligaments in my arm. I'm suing the police. Brutality!"

Bojing gives the punk a little shove from behind. A man, I assume to be the father, pulls the kid away through the crowd.

"I'm not only a star, but I'm going to be rich!" he yells at us.

I ignore him, keep pushing Mie toward the man who might supply answers to why the kid is out of jail and free. Someone screwed the pooch here, and it wasn't us. We completed everything we needed to for this case, even if we were not at the hearing, and that leaves one person responsible for the kid's release.

"Damn it, Roberts, where were you and Ling when the call came in?" the prosecutor, William Louis III, asks. I remember his name finally. He's someone who has his sights on politics if he can earn a position higher up in the ranks—a real slime.

"If you haven't noticed, there's a blizzard outside," I say. Mie stands beside me; the color returns to her face. "We raced up from Toronto. You remember where I work."

"I told your office to get you up here as soon as you got in. Now I have to explain why you weren't here on time for the judge and suck up to pull this case back in a few days." He sighs, rubs the back of his neck.

I'm floored at the statement. "A few days? What do you mean a few days?"

"They brought in a real snapper of a lawyer. He cited passages about how the arrest went down. The film from the school—"

"Film from the school?" I ask.

"Yes, Roberts. The film from the school was released to the defendant's lawyer this morning, and he played the part where you wrestled him to the ground without saying anything. It didn't help that your Interpol partner here almost snapped his arm off. Excessive force. The whole court heard the pop!" He reaches up and runs his fingers through his hair.

"What the hell?" I put my hands on my hips. "The pop was not that loud."

"All I know is that pop made everyone in the courtroom flinch."

He opens his briefcase and balances it with one hand. "I have a copy of it. Tried to get it taken out of evidence, but the judge said we could have recovered it just like the defense did. Our fault." He pulls out a memory card. "Here. All the docs they hit us with are on that. You'll need to bone up when their lawyer hits us with a civil suit for police brutality."

Shit. Civil suit. Having that on my record will be hard to handle. Means I'll have to suck up for anything. Civil suits have ruined many a cop's careers, let alone long-timers like me. I'll be blackballed from getting any promotion. We'll need a copy from the school to make sure this one is not doctored. Call in a few of the kids as witnesses. Maybe even the principal.

William is shoving paperwork and the card into my hands, looking at me as if I've just gone stupid. I take them. Shove it all into a pocket.

"Don't lose any of that. There are some forms printed on the card for you to fill out. I want another statement by tomorrow morning." He closes his case and finally looks at me. I mean, really looks at me. "Hell, Roberts. It's not the end of the world. The civil suit will go away once the kid is behind bars. Till then, just keep your nose clean."

My return smile doesn't work, just like Mie's when I try to explain something funny. She isn't much of a smiler. It's the job—all the negative energy.

"I'll try to remember that," I force out.

He claps me on the shoulder. "Good. Just get the forms done and forwarded to my office. I'll take care of the rest. Talk to your union rep as well. They'll have resources for you. Take care, Roberts." And with that, he makes his way down the hall through the throng of people.

I back up to the wall and slowly slide down it. Mie comes over and sits on her haunches beside me. Her hands shake, which is something I didn't think possible with prosthetics. We sit in silence. No one pays us much attention. It's like we're invisible to those around us.

"He the one," Mie says.

It doesn't take long to realize what she means. There are things a man can do to a woman that just never heal. It's why I never worked in sex crimes. I couldn't stomach it. The one day I did for cross-training had me shaking the whole time. Kept seeing Sarah's face on all the vics. Every teen hooker we arrested forced me to wonder if my daughter could end up like that. It wasn't for me.

Mie is living through a private little hell. Bojing must be the man who raped her so many years ago. She shouldn't have to put up with that.

No one has the right to force someone to live with that type of horror.

We stay where we are. I wait for a sign that it's okay to move. It takes five minutes before her hands stop shaking. Another ten and she's breathing without trembling on the exhale. She brushes the hair from her face, and the facade of a rock-hard woman returns. She's not an android. Just a broken little girl coming out of the shadows of her past.

"We need follow Bojing," she says, voice a little unsteady but gaining strength.

"They're gone already." I stand and reach down a hand. To my surprise, she takes it. I'm under no illusion she could crush my hand, but instead, her touch is light, and she only uses me to steady herself.

"Thank you." She wipes at her face. There's no smudge of mascara. I don't think she even wears any. "You have drones at precinct?"

"Hoverbots. Totally independent from human instructions."

"We need to track that man. He 426. We get him and cut head off snake in Canada. Maybe find missing girls."

I put my hand in my pocket. Touch my daughter's phone. "I forgot." I pull it out. "A file came in last night with the name Virginia. I don't understand how they're getting this stuff out there, but Cyber Crimes will need to close down the site."

"No." She puts a hand on mine that is holding the phone. "We need track."

I stare at the cup, trying to force it to cool down. The black liquid inside keeps steaming as if just boiled.

Paperwork scatters across my desk, screaming for attention. Both Mie and I are trying to get through all the requisition forms to have a hoverbot assigned to Bojing Wang. With all the hoops we need to jump through, even with Mie's access, it seems like the request will be a few days out. It's not like we don't have enough of the little facial recognition drones sitting in storage waiting to be used. I push another one to the completed pile. Mie pushes it back.

"Three copy," she says.

"I don't understand why we have so much to fill out." I lean back and stretch. "I'm hungry. Want anything?"

"Wonton soup." She drops another set of forms on the finished pile. Her stack of completed paperwork is bigger than mine, even with the language barrier.

"I'll see what they have downstairs."

Working in Downtown Toronto has its perks. There's a ton of food outlets all within spitting distance. Torontonians have a love of diversity. A Chinese Food outlet is next to the coffee shop where I grabbed my partially full cup.

I pick up a soup along with some honey pork and rice. The chef cuts the strip of meat on a round cutting block with a large butcher knife. His skill is something to behold. One step brings me to the cash register. I reach into my pocket for my phone just as someone reaches over and pays the lady. She doesn't smile, just takes the cash and reaches out with change.

"No, you keep," a soft man's voice says behind me. There's a little grumble in the tone along with the smell of cigarettes.

The woman bows, closes the cash drawer, and steps to the side, ignoring me.

I start to turn around. "Thanks, but I can pay for my own..."

Bojing smiles at me. The thin scar running from his left ear is an off blue color from the cold outside. "Police need not pay for food." He winks. "Many thing not pay for if done right."

My stomach freezes. Not from his voice. The softness of his tone is clear and pleasant. There's something about the way he says it. Certain inflections and a nod of his head. An unspoken suggestion of something.

"I'm afraid you have me at a disadvantage, Mr..." I reach out a hand.

He stares at it for a second before taking it in his. "I Bojing Wang. Import-export specialist with Woo Tang Shipping. Glad to meet you, Detective Roberts."

His handshake is as slippery as a snake. A dry hand with little pressure until a little squeeze happens just before he lets go. The stench of cigarettes covers him, and I can smell it on his breath.

"You know me, but I don't know you." I hold off the desire to wipe my hand against my jacket.

"Oh, we know each." He gives me a wink. "Chinese girls very pretty, don't you think?" His smile shows off tobacco-stained and crooked teeth of someone needing an orthodontist. "North girls lose looks young."

"I don't understand your reference, Mr. Wang." I put a hand in my pocket and activate the record function on my cell.

He tilts his head to the left. "You have a pretty daughter, Detective Roberts."

My blood turns to ice. "How do you know–"

"I know many things." He pulls his left hand out of his pocket, along with a pack of cigarettes. A quick flick of his wrist and one slides out a little. The small finger on that hand is missing. "I know you have wife who not happy."

"How do you know about my wife?" My voice rises a little.

He lights the cigarette, takes a deep drag, and continues. "Life can be hard for cop in Toronto. Though you live Markham with the ones who live here for while."

"You can't smoke in here." I wave my hand a little. "Laws about smoking in public places can be a little harsh."

He only smiles. "You could be well off. Comfortable. It take very little to get."

Bojing reaches into his coat with his right hand. I stiffen. My Glock is under my left arm, but if he pulls something out before I have time to get at it. He holds out an envelope.

"For you," he says.

I glance at the envelope. It's thick with cash. No one uses hard currency anymore. Well, almost no one. Criminals and tax cheats use it. Hard to track what isn't recorded in some database. But the banks have to report large deposits to the government. That's what keeps cash in the hands of criminals.

"I don't understand what this is for." If I can get him to say something incriminating, we can tie a knot in the case and get it running the way we want. But until he says it directly, I'm not touching the envelope.

"To make things easier." He nods at it and extends his hand a little more.

Playing dumb is not something I do easily, and taking it to this extreme is difficult for me. Staring at the envelope, the thickness is obvious. There must be quite a stack inside it. I place a hand on his shoulder. This makes him uncomfortable. He glances down as if I'm poking him. He looks back at me, the smile wavering a little on his face.

"Look, friend. I'm flattered you want to offer me whatever is in the envelope, but this place is not where you want to do it." I glance around a little. "There are cameras everywhere outside, and some of them are focused on us. Besides that, the people who own this place may not be watching us directly, but they are listening." I need to get him to say something incriminating.

He takes the envelope back and puts it in his coat pocket. "You are careful. I understand." Bojing turns but stops halfway facing the door. "Your family nice, Detective. Much nicer to care for when one has money." He turns and takes two steps before stopping again. "Be mindful of family. For they cannot be replaced."

I rush toward him. A bribe attempt is one thing, but threatening my family is another. He could say it was not meant to be a threat, so instead of taking him in, I just want to slam his smug face into the door before he leaves. But two young Chinese men wearing dark glasses enter as he steps out. Each takes one of my arms and pulls me back into the shop. Electricity jolts through me. Taser. My legs give out. A shriek erupts behind me. A woman. Probably the shop owner. I try to yell out to her. Get her to leave through the back. Nothing works. Another current of electricity runs through my body. Maybe they want to make a point. The thugs have me against the counter. One smells of fish and the other of cigarettes. The smoker smiles and exposes yellow and crooked teeth.

The woman in the back screams something in Chinese. Wish I knew what it was. A gunshot goes off. The two thugs laugh. More electricity shoots through my body. I hold on, not wanting to lose my bladder control.

One thug screams. It's high pitched. The glasses fall from his face. Eyes bulge out. Wide to the point of confusion. Lips squish together.

"Dong?" one thug says, looking at the pain on his buddy's face.

As the one sinks to the ground, a hand grabs the hair of the second man. He's jerked back then forward, and down. His forehead hits the counter. I slump to the ground alongside him. My legs don't work, and the world grows dark. Or is it someone in front of me? I can make out dark hair. The scent of jasmine fills my senses, and I reach out a hand. It encounters something soft, warm, and definitely female. The hand is softly moved away as the world goes dark.

January 13th, 2033 – Bribe

Bojing stares up at the courthouse, cigarette smoke spills from his mouth only to be whipped away by the wind. He holds the smoke tight with his thin lips.

The sun makes the cold more palatable. They said it would be warm, but four months of the year is not a lot of warmth when the rest of the days he puts up with this shit.

He takes the cigarette out of his mouth and starts to throw it into the snow. The sound of a throat clearing catches his attention, and a big cop in the smoker's shelter shakes his head and points to a tall mushroom looking piece of metal. Small slits decorate the head, and wisps of smoke curling up from them.

Cops should know their place. In this country, they always show up at the time you don't want them and have little respect for those with true power.

Bojing smiles and nods. He sticks the last part of the cigarette into a slot and bows his head to the cop, who just nods and returns to his phone. 8784. Toronto Police. He'll need to remember that badge.

A mountain of work waits for him at the office. Tedious without enjoyment. He pulls out his phone and scans the news feed headlines. The weather is more interesting. There's not a single sign of any body parts being found in the area they use as a dump. He smiles. The disposal team does a good job, especially since their lives depended on it.

Sirens blare down the street in front of a small take, right next to the precinct. The muscle should arrive soon, and send the pesky cop in an ambulance on his way to the hospital. Bojing decides to wait a little longer for his men to come to him. No telling what story they'll use to explain why they took so long.

Bojing's phone vibrates. A message. He opens it, and the cryptic code used to communicate in the open is displayed. A second is all it takes for him to decipher it. Captured. Injured. His men were stopped while carrying out the plan. Something, or someone, interrupted it.

"Dou ta ma de!" he swears under his breath. Fuck both of them. He needs to find out what happened.

Bojing puts the phone into his pocket, looks to the cop who's speaking into a shoulder mic, and walks into the howling wind. As he passes the cop, the slight sound of a squelchy voice says, "...both of them by herself. Don't say anything, but Interpol is one..."

Interpol. He heard the female police refered to like that. The familiarity of the woman comes to his mind, and he hesitates for just a second. But the thought passes as he puts the connections together. She was his initiation. Just ten years ago, he used her body. It awoke his memories of the event. The tying down of the legs with such force that blood didn't circulate to them. The bindings just over the elbows that made the arms go purple. But he had strangled her. How could she be alive?

He decides to look into it.

With that, he lengthens his stride to make up the distance to the small take out store.

Pain stirs my consciousness. Fingers pry an eyelid open, and the light shines into it. Pressure constricts the bicep of my arm. I manage to close one eye as the other is forced open and subjected to the same light. In the distance, a voice comments on pupils being responsive.

A warm hand touches my shoulder with a little more force than one would expect from something so small.

"Roberts," a voice calls out in an Asian accent. "Roberts."

I try to raise my hand to my head, but it's blocked.

"Don't move. Medics checking." I put a name to the voice. Mie.

"What happened..." I manage to get out through the haze of my thoughts.

"You take long. Maybe mistake order. I come down, and you in fight."

I open one eye and glance at her. Genuine concern etches on her face—more than I've seen before.

"Two... jiro tou ... beat you. I stop them."

Memory starts to come back to the surface of my thoughts. A headache erupts behind my eyes. Bones and muscles complain of the injuries they sustained in the assault.

"I held my own."

Mie shakes her head. "No. They kicking you."

Great, this is going to get around the squad, and there'll be no end to the pranks being pulled.

"We're taking him to the hospital," a man says. "Concussion. Bruises. We'll record the injuries for the court."

Mie nods. "I go with."

"We're only allowed to—"

The sound of a round being chambered deadens the air. She places a hand on my chest. "I go with."

The medic swallows a ball of something. "Sure. Just make sure that thing doesn't go off."

Another medic, this one an overweight woman, probably in her forties, wheels in a gurney. She presses a few levers, and it drops to less than a foot off the ground.

"No, no gurney. I'll walk out of here."

"No brave. Just stubborn," Mie says, waving the gurney away. "I keep close if falls. We try make walk out."

The first medic helps me to a sitting position as my head spins out of control. I get them to wait for it to slow before trying to pull me to my feet. It's not fun trying to walk as the world spins around you. But I do make it to the ambulance, and the gurney is slid in with me. I sit on it as Mie takes the space beside me. One last thing for the squad to talk about and my family to worry about.

"No more alone," she says.

"What?"

"No more alone," she says again. "We go together on all thing."

"Okay, but it doesn't mean we're a couple."

She stares at me for a second, then a slight smile hits her eyes. "No, just partner."

I talk them out of making me use the gurney to get into emerg, but I can't get them to bypass the wheelchair. Something about perception: I can't take an ambulance to the hospital and walk into it expecting to get taken seriously. That's not something I was worried about, but it bothers the medics to no end. I decide not to push the argument and sit in the chair. Mie walks in with me, and I'm in a bed within a few minutes. Being a cop injured while on duty tends to make nurses rush you through the red tape.

After about a half-hour, Julie rushes in. Concern glistens in her eyes —more than I expected, knowing how rocky the last few days have been.

The doctor follows her in and takes the lead on the questions while examining me. Julie takes my hand while he fills out the chart. Gotta give it to her. She's not talking over the Doc and asking me questions, just holding my hand and giving it a squeeze.

After I finish telling them what happened, Mie fills in what she saw. She doesn't tell him about subduing the two thugs, thankfully. Just the facts about what went on. It appears she saw a lot.

Julie glances at her and nods as if the beating creates a bond between them that transgresses last night's rift. This is new for my wife. Little miracles are accepted in our line of work. Take them when they come.

The doc gives me something for the headache before ordering a nurse to do a head CT. Not sure what that entails, but I think glowing in the dark could be one of them. I'm not disappointed. Everyone shuffles out, and a strange machine is brought in to spin around my head.

The doc lets Julie and Mie in again and goes back to staring at his tablet.

"A little swelling but not much to worry about." He puts the tablet down and starts feeling around my head. "Bump here. You've had a concussion before? Seems like a rough patch of scar tissue back here."

"King Ball accident," I say.

"King ball?" the doc questions.

"Yeah, old game. Football on a basketball court. Get the football through the basketball hoop to score, and anything goes. Tackled into a hardwood bench a few times as a kid." Except for one of the scars which came from an arrest ten years ago.

He takes the answer with a nod and makes a few more notes on his tablet. "I'll want you to be here overnight. Need to ensure nothing happens to your head."

I glance at Julie, then Mie. "I'm in the middle of an investigation—"

"That can wait," Julie says.

"Nothing do now. They make sure you good. Start again tomorrow."

"Looks like you're out-voted. You can be discharged tomorrow. For now, I'll want you to rest a little." The doc clips a monitor on my finger, I think it reads blood oxygen or something, then leaves the room.

Mie looks uncomfortably at Julie for a second and nods. "I leave. You talk." She says the last part at me, nodding to Julie before she goes.

Julie sits there, gaze following Mie as she leaves the room. After a few seconds of dead silence, my wife turns to me. "You said being a detective would be fewer problems than a beat cop. No chance of injury."

"It is. But with every investigation, there's a chance of something happening." I wiggle a bit to get more comfortable in the bed but still hold her hand. "This is one of them."

"Should I be worried?"

"Probably not," I lie. "If anything, the bad guys should worry. Mie is good at her job. In fact, one of the best I've met. Great instincts and an incredible partner."

"Sounds like you admire her. What is she, like, twenty-five?"

It's a slight, and I'm tired of hearing them. "Why do you always do that?"

"Do what?"

"Go negative like that. It's like you never want someone to just be a good person or great at their job."

"I'm not negative."

"Yes, you are." I take a deep breath. "When I got the promotion all you thought about was the time I would need to be at the office. What about the fact I got a promotion above all the others? More money but longer hours. It's a trade-off. But at least if I'm working on the weekends, I'm just doing that. Not driving around like a target."

It's the old argument we've had for years. Julie wanted me home to take care of our child a lot more, but also wanted me to be successful. Bring home a bigger paycheck. But that means more time at the office, which she didn't like at all. Hell, I didn't like it either, but sacrifices need to be made to get ahead of the rest of the world.

"When I brought Mie home with me, all you could think about was why. Why not? I just started working with her as a partner on a case. Instead of looking at the negative, think of the positive. It's high profile and could lead to a possible promotion."

"One that will have you at work even more than now?"

I stop at that. Me being out of the home and at work is what kept her from getting further ahead in nursing. Everything focused on me. Her own career suffered due to sacrifices never asked but always taken.

Julie could have been a head nurse. Hell, she has the brains for it, just not the time. Unable to work overtime takes a lot of advancement out of the picture. If she only had a few extra shifts here and there, we'd have been able to buy that house. But then again, the commute would have killed me. Over an hour each way.

"Sometimes a promotion means less time at the office," I say.

"Sure, it does." She pulls her hand away from mine. "You'd be more responsible for things and spend all your waking moments pondering over what everyone else is doing." She takes a deep breath and stands. "We wanted... No, we needed you home more than you think. How hard do you think it is to raise a child on the spectrum when they keep asking where their father is?"

"You never said anything—"

"You should have asked." She walks to the machine, reading my oxygen level and frowning. "Every day, you came home and told me about your day. Every day I listened and waited. If I had gone back to work just a few months..."

"What?" Her unspoken words hit me. Something about her career or something. "Finish your thought."

She hesitates. Not sure what to say or even if she should have let the cat out. But then there's something that crosses her mind, and she turns back to me. Instead of accusation, there's sadness.

"You remember Melody Bateman?"

"You two went to school together. Yes."

"Well, she aborted just about the same time I got pregnant with Sarah."

"You never told me that."

"Didn't come up." She turns back to the machine. "Anyway, she got the promotion to head nurse for the floor we worked on. After a year, she went to a new floor, and the hospital paid for her schooling to get her practitioner's license. She now makes almost double I do and works less hours."

I'm not sure where this is going. "Are you upset we had Sarah?"

She turns to me. A little tear makes its way down her cheek. "No. I love her. She's the only real good thing to come of our marriage."

"That's not–"

"Fair? Right, it's not. But that's how I feel. We rent an apartment. Hell, it's not even a condo, for Christ's sake. When's the last time we went on vacation? Together?"

I tried to think but couldn't remember. Maybe up North, but then again, it could've been before we were married.

"See? That's what I'm talking about. We've been living paycheck to paycheck with nothing to show for it. I want to get away, get out of here to unwind, and I need to do it more than anything now."

My head reels. This is it. Finally, the reason for all the animosity in our lives. She's tired of not getting ahead. Wants more out of life. Somehow, I already knew this. But with all that's happened in the world, there's nothing we can do but keep trying to live. I want to go over to her. Hold her. Tell her everything will be okay. But I'm stuck on a bed with orders to rest. I'm not resting now, so I sweep my feet off the bed and stand. A few steps and the sensor pops off my finger to start a little dance of its own. A slight beeping comes from its machine to alert me. It's no longer attached.

Julie turns as I put my arms around her. She slumps forward and cries.

"Damn you, Bruce." Her hands ball into fists gripping my hospital gown.

I hold her like that. Seconds turn into minutes, and I still hold her. She's crying hard. Sobs that start out light and move to shoulder heaving cries and back down to light whimpers. But still, tears run from her eyes. It must be a strange sight for a nurse enters the room and then quickly turns off the alarm before heading out the door in a rush.

After a few minutes, I stroke Julie's hair like I used to when we dated. A couple of shushing noises helps to calm her down a little more, and she lets go of my gown. Her arms encircle my chest, and I keep stroking her back.

Finally, she drops her arms, all spent out. The front of my gown is wet with tears, and my ass is cold from the draft. The headache is back, but I don't want to hurt the moment by getting something for it. And Julie starts to smile through red eyes. The grin turns into a halted gaff and then a full laugh. I look around to see what she's having fun with, but nothing is around us.

"What?" I ask.

She points down at my crotch. Tented, a soldier stands out with all the excitement in the world. Very much at attention. Now I know why my ass was getting the cold breeze – my dick is pushing the gown away from my body.

"I'm sorry," I say, reflexively pushing my member down with a hand. I think of ice for a second. Maybe Lilly-Grace Pham or someone else to take it away, but it just stands out there. I sit on the edge of the bed and hide it between my legs.

"At least that's still working." She steps forward and sits on the bed beside me. Her head drops lightly to my shoulder. "What the hell happened to us, Bruce?"

I take a deep breath. "Life."

Her hand finds mine. "We do have a good life, don't we?"

Yeah. A child making recordings of her boyfriend screwing her. Fine life.

"Sure, we do." Maybe if I keep repeating it, I'll start to believe it.

"I'm sorry how I treated your new partner." She glances up at me. "Maybe you should ask her over for dinner on the weekend."

"Saturday or Sunday?" It doesn't matter. We'll have tomorrow at least to set it all up.

"Sunday, I have both off and won't pick up a shift. I think it's time we got ourselves back into a life we'll enjoy."

"I should be out of here tomorrow. Wrap a few things up at the office and come home early. Any idea what we should make?"

"No noodles."

I let out a little smirk. "No noodles."

"Bruce," Julie says.

"Yes?"

"What the hell are we going to do with Sarah?"

January 12th, 2033 - Missing You

The girl stumbles down the walkway between the houses. She stops, pulls at something under her long coat, and then continues her pinballing walk. Misted breath floats behind her as she walks in a seemingly drunken haze. Dirty blonde hair hangs down the girl's shoulders. A scarf decorates her neck.

A street light flickers in the brightness of the full moon. Light from one lone security flood bounces off the hard snow, illuminating the girl before defusing in the storm. It and the full moon give a better view than just the light would, but tonight is the only one they can use for their purpose. Bojing sits forward in the chair and watches from the white van parked a dozen meters outside of the apartment building.

He breathes in, and the cigarette glows in his mouth. Smoke curls up, and the sound of tobacco going from frozen to burning fills the air. Just a little closer.

The engine roars to life. The girl stops on the path. Freezing air turns her breath into a mist that billows from her mouth only to disappear as the air around it steals the heat.

"Turn that off!" Bojing hisses, slapping the arm of the driver as he peaks through the dark tinted glass in the back of the van.

The man in the driver's seat turns off the engine. "Sir, it's cold. You need warmth. And if the van gets too cold, it won't start."

Bojing turns his gaze that has stared down Triad monsters to glare at the 49er. Years of horror-filled experience bore into the driver's eyes.

The driver bows his head in supplication. "Sorry, sir. I await your orders."

Bojing turns back to the window. The girl still stands there, at least ten meters away. Too far to grab her. Damn driver. He'll need to deal with the imbecile when they get back to the warehouse. If anything goes wrong with the grab, Bojing will take it out on him.

A man next to Bojing tries to look through the window. "What's she doing?"

"What all white women do. She's deciding if it was a good idea to walk home drunk."

"What if she pukes in the van?"

Bojing smiles. "We get someone to lick it up."

The girl walks forward a few paces and stops. She puts her hands on knees and stoops forward. Liquid spills from her mouth as her stomach rejects its contents.

"She's really drunk," the man says.

"Yes, and stupid." Bojing snuffs out his cigarette and pulls a long binding made of hemp from his coat pocket. He smiles, thinking of how much this little girl will struggle and the distraction her disappearance will be to her father.

I've always hated sleeping in a new bed. Something about them not being what I'm used to. Even with the pill the nurse gave me, I still lay staring at the ceiling for over an hour. Julie refuses to leave. Seems she's decided we've mended the proverbial fence in our relationship.

Warm breath ruffles my chest as Julie stirs. It has to be early; the light of the full moon spills into the room from the window. I look at the hall. The digital clock on the wall reads way too early to get up, but I'm wide awake.

Sarah is alone at the apartment. We need to check up on her, but my cell is in the locker across the room with my clothes. I'll need to wake Julie.

There's an art to waking up your wife. One of my friend's makes the bed shake. Another kisses his wife's neck. I usually bring coffee, but that's not going to work today. And she's curled up against me. I give a slight rub on her arm and a glassy eye pries open.

"What time is it?" Her voice is groggy.

"Early. Just after five." I force my aching body toward the edge of the bed. The bathroom calls my name.

Julie scratches her head, spilling long hair into a mess. "I know the nurses here."

"You want coffee? Bet there's a machine down the hall." I enter the bathroom. Cold floor bites at the bottoms of my feet. "I'll get it in a sec."

"Never mind," she says through the door. "I'll get us something from the nurse's station."

I finish off and flush. The water swirls and disappears. It tells me I'm okay, no headache, no dizziness. Well, just a little, but I'm not dizzy from watching the water circle around the bowl. Same with the water in the sink. No issues as it pours through my fingers and swirls into the drain. God, I need a shower. A quick hand through my hair confirms a bump in full tender mode on the back of the head. Damn, that's going to be sore for a while.

The door swings open as I head back toward the bed. Shan sticks his head into the room. He's in uniform, and the black swatch is no longer over his shield.

"You okay, Bruce?" There's real concern in his voice. It's not fake, I can tell. The guy is happy to see me up and walking around.

I better not tell him about the headache. "What the heck are you doing here?"

"They've got us watching your room. I pulled the night shift." He steps a little more into the doorway. "You did it for me once, remember?"

He'd caught a bullet during a raid. One of the reasons we actually talk. "Yeah, but you don't owe me anything. We all watch each other's backs."

His smile widened. "That we do. Still, I'm watching yours."

Julie walks to the door with two mugs in her hands. Real mugs, not those foam or paper cups usually given to patients.

Shan nods and takes up his post, watching the people in the corridor as well as at the desk while they go through their morning routine.

I reach out a hand as Julie comes to me. The mug is warm and filled to the brim. I sit on the edge of the bed and blow away steam before taking a sip. The blend is aromatic and strong. I sip a little bit at a time to keep from burning the roof of my mouth.

"When do you think I'll be able to get out of here?" I ask.

"Probably in an hour." Julie sits in the one chair the room has. "Doctors usually cycle off around seven. We can see if someone will discharge you early. If not, it won't be until nine."

"Long delay."

"They have a lot of patients and need to look over all the charts. Not easy when you're assigned so many. At least nurses have a few extra hands on each floor. Sometimes a doctor oversees the same number of patients that the nursing staff has." She takes a sip. "But we usually handle the majority of the issues, like filling out the forms without talking to the docs."

We sip in silence, absorbed in our own thoughts. The room's light brightens as the morning chases the moon into hiding. But at six, Julie corners the doctor who comes to see me.

It takes only a few minutes for the woman to discharge me. Maybe I'll even get to work without taking a sick day.

My clothes are not as fresh as I'd like, and the socks smell, leaving a lot to be desired. Julie hints I should shower, but who wants to put on dirty clothes after cleaning up? I decline, saying I'll shower at home. Maybe we can do a little more making up, knowing Sarah should be at school by the time we get back.

I say goodbye to Shan, shaking his hand and telling him I owe him. He just smiles and says he hopes to never collect on that. It makes me smile as we agree that it would be a good debt to be owed. Safe is safe as far as I'm concerned.

It's still cold out. Julie parked her SUV in the paid parking because her pass doesn't work on their gates. We pay, wincing at the cost—over a hundred for twelve hours. There's no wind this morning, but the cold still bites through our clothing. One of the good things about electric vehicles is they pump out heat almost immediately.

I let her drive, though she does offer me the keys. At least we'll be on the road before the majority of the traffic starts. Nothing like Toronto during rush hour... or should I say rush hours . Traffic is heavy from six to nine. It'll be nice to be home at a decent time.

Someone from the department brought my car home for me. It sits parked in my spot. Not sure who I owe for that, but it's not going unnoticed. The parking garage is well lit and not as biting cold as outside. Julie takes my hand as we walk to the elevators and take one up. She keeps my hand in hers while I juggle keys to open the door.

Lights are on in the apartment, like someone left in a rush. Julie looks in the kitchen and swears under her breath. Probably something Sarah didn't do. I don't want to take the chance of being the focus of the rage that may come out of my wife. Instead, I head toward the bathroom and leave the door open a crack, something that never happens with a teenage girl in the house. Good thing she's at school now.

The shower pours out hot water. I adjust the temperature and step in. Warm wetness washes away some of the pain from sore muscles, and I take inventory. Neck, sore. Left leg, sore. It could have been worse. At least Mie was able to get in the middle of things.

It takes a while, but the water finally chases away the cold from my bones. I finish off cleaning just as the door to the bathroom opens wide. Julie walks in and shucks off her clothes. It's a good thing the kid's at school.

I feel like a teenager again—the hell with the sore muscles. Sex will trump everything. And it did. Julie and I lay in each other's arms, making up for a lot of things we said to each other. It's the act of love. Once performed with a partner you really care about, nothing can overcome it. You go into a whole new world with them. And your knowledge of what they like, coupled with their knowledge of what you like, sends the experience to a new level.

We both lay in bed, bodies wanting to sleep but not wanting to give into it. Legs and arms intertwined. Soft parts touching soft parts. Neither wanting to move for fear of what could happen. I don't want to go back to the way our lives have been for the last two years. She probably doesn't either. So we stay the way we are, enjoying the warmth of each other's body. Time passes without meaning. The sun tries to add warmth to the world as it makes a show of climbing into the sky.

My cell vibrated a few minutes ago, and Julie's is vibrating away on the bedside table. If it's important, the caller will leave a message or try again. That's how I look at it. Hell, I'm taking a sick day.

Both our cells go off at the same time, which is unusual. Not sure what is going on. I reach over and fumble at the two phones, seeing the number displayed on Julie's is the same as the one on mine. Strange, very strange.

I thumb on the accept. "Hello?"

"Mr. Roberts?"

I know that voice from somewhere. It's more smug than the last time. Lilly-Grace Pham.

"Yes, who am I speaking to?"

"Principal Lilly-Grace Pham," she says, letting her name draw out. "I've been trying to reach you all morning." She sighs.

"Sorry, been occupied. Just got out of the hospital."

"Nothing serious, I hope."

The inflection, in her words, stabs at me. I ignore it. "How can I help you, Principal Pham?"

"Your daughter. Where is she?"

Of all the things Sarah does, she doesn't skip school. Her grades aren't great, but all her friends are there.

"At your school, in class."

Julie sits up. I swing out of bed.

"No, she's not. She hasn't shown up for the first or second period. Do you not know where she is?"

"She's not there?" I ask, starting to pace.

Julie gets out of bed and grabs her phone. "Bruce, what's going on?"

I turn to walk out of the room, but Julie grabs my arm. Her eyebrows hunch up together and raise in the middle. Her mouth is slightly open, and a quiver rushes through the lower lip.

With a hand over the receiver on the phone, I whisper, "I don't know, but we'll find out."

"Mr. Roberts, I need to log your daughter as absent without permission. The truancy officer will be given her picture in case he comes across her."

"Bruce, tell me what's going on!" Julie's hand squeezes my arm hard.

"Tracker," I say. It doesn't register on her face, but then understanding shows up. Julie rushes out of the room. I turn back to my phone. "I'm investigating what happened. I will report to you when I find out."

"No need. She's marked absent. With her record, if one more issue comes up, she'll be expelled from the school."

The line goes dead.

"Bitch."

Not my finest statement, but it does match. I walk out of the bedroom and head for the computer in the living room. Julie is already there, a blanket wrapped around herself to either keep warm or to ward off any further advances. I become aware of my nudity and the coolness of the air. Better get something on as well.

I come back to the living room only to see Julie staring at a map on the screen. A dot blinks above our building, then it goes out. A second goes by, and the dot appears on another building, then another. How the hell can Sarah be in two buildings at once? Then there are five flashing dots, all displaying Sarah's chip number. This shouldn't be happening. I lift my cell and hit the number for the company tracking her cell.

The rep who answers couldn't be more than fifteen from the sound of his voice. I imagine a pimply face with braces. In the background, several other voices are talking. Probably parents wanting more information. I give my customer number, go through the mother's maiden name check, and read off Sarah's tracking ID. He taps out a lot of keys, more than I said, and is silent.

"Do you see what I'm talking about?" I ask the rep.

"Mr. Roberts, I see an issue with the—"

"With the impenetrable security system that we pay a lot of money for? I see it too. Which one is my daughter?"

The line is silent. He's probably using the mute. Six more blips show up on the map.

"Hello, Mr. Roberts?" A new voice, not the kid's.

"Yes," I say. I'm annoyed. He probably hears it.

"Justin Lawrence, IT security. Where's your daughter? Is she with you?"

I want to explode. It takes a lot to keep from screaming at him that we wouldn't be calling if we knew where Sarah was. "That's why we have the tracker on her. To find out where she is when we don't know. But we're seeing..."

"Twenty-three," Julie says.

"Twenty-three blips with our daughter's ID number on them. This system is supposed to be foolproof."

He stays calm. Even and light breathing is a technique used even in our shop. Puts most people at ease. But not me.

"Yes, we are tracking them now. You'll notice some show-up, and then they are removed. We're deleting the ones that cannot be valid and trying to identify the technology being used. It may take a little more time."

"Time? We don't have time. My daughter could be in trouble. She probably is. And your system is failing to help us like the advertisements claim." Frantic typing echoes in the background.

"Of course, we'll be investigating why this is happening. We're not seeing anyone intruding on the code. Just these anomalies coming up."

My head spins. He calls them anomalies. "Have you reported this to the police yet?"

Dead air hovers on the line for a few seconds. "No. This is an internal code issue. Nothing for the police to—"

"Like hell. My daughter is missing, and your system is not working. If you don't report it, I will."

"Mr. Roberts, there's no need to involve the police. Your daughter is probably just at scho-"

"She's not at school. They alerted me about her not being there."
My voice is almost a shout now. "Fix it. Now."

I end the call. Julie is staring at the screen. Thirty dots showing our
daughter from Markham to Stouffville. This needs to be reported to the
police, but unless we can report her missing for more than two hours,
their hands are tied, regardless of who I am. I could talk them into
taking a report of the tracker issue, but other than that, nothing.

"What do we do?" A tear races down Julie's cheek.

What can you tell your wife concerning her missing child and the
police procedure for reporting it? Nothing will suffice to calm her except
the return of her child. But why is she missing now?

I run a hand through my hair. There's got to be something I can say
—some way of pleasing her, taking away the concern. And I can use it
on myself. Where's my baby girl?

My phone vibrates.

A text. No number. I open it. A single line.

4 Cardico Drive. One Hour. Come alone if want daughter.

January 12th, 2033 - My Little Girl

Favoring his left leg, Bojing limps into his office trailing cigarette smoke. Scowling, he spits the butt out of his mouth and rubs at his tender lips. He almost steps on the burning nib of the butt that even a beggar wouldn't find worth picking up. Without pause, he leans against the desk, opens another pack, and pulls his last cigarette from it. He spins the wheel of the old lighter and takes a long drag before tossing the empty package into the garbage.

"Fuck!"

The word disappears into the sound dampening walls. He was clumsy in the snatch. And again, as they tied her up. The little insect. One hand rubs the ballooning knee as the other fumbles in the desk's drawers. He put it somewhere.

Only the empty wrapper from his last cigarette carton greets him. He closes the drawer—another thing to do. He looks at his desk. A note on the screen shows "Buy cigarettes" to remind him of the purchase.

Bojing finds a small octagonal jar. The ointment inside is the only good thing he has going for him now. He puts it on the desk. The red printing on the lid tells him he's right. A label, all in Chinese writing, faces him. The image of a tiger walking is the only clue to what is in the jar. He unscrews it, and the scent of heated menthol floats up. He scoops a generous portion of the salve and rubs it on his troubled knee. Relief floods angry nerves, but the swelling appears to have increased since he came into his office.

The door opens. A young 49er enters, face blank. Good, they realize if they say something wrong they will not live to talk about it again . Respect is what he needs to control the group. If any of them decided to take him on, it could be disastrous for the organization.

"Ping, what do you want?" Bojing asks.

"Sir. There was a message sent to 438 on the progress. I thought you would like to read it."

Bojing holds out his hand, the one without the tiger balm on it, and takes the report.

To 438 - Status report. It is with honor we send this to you on our capture of Sarah Roberts. She will be instrumental in securing the cooperation of the detective in charge.

Bojing looks up from the paper to Ping. "Did you send this?"

The young man's eyes don't move from the spot he stares at on the wall behind Bojing. "Sir. No. Yang sent the message."

"Who gave him permission?"

Ping flinches a little, but he keeps staring ahead. "Sir. It was Ling."

"Bring me Ling. Immediately."

"Sir." Ping spins on his heels and leaves the office.

Ling dares send a message without my permission. I will have words with him about this transgression.

His knee throbs some more before it settles down. He tried to ignore it, but the pain makes him realize there's more damage done than the tiger balm will help repair. Too much, maybe. He opens the middle drawer and pulls out a cleaver. The edge glistens in the light, and he loses himself in it.

A knock on the door takes him out of the trance.

"Come."

Ping opens the door with Ling following close behind. Both stop before the desk and stand there straight, staring at the wall.

"Close the door." Bojing turns the paper containing the message, so it is readable to the two men. The door closes, and Ling's forehead shines from sweat.

"Sir. Ling for you." Ping steps back.

Bojing lets himself smile inside, but outside he keeps his face placid and unreadable. He snubs out the last cigarette he brought from home and wonders how long it will take before his craving makes him hunt for more.

Ling swallows but stands before Bojing with his back straight. Seconds pass and turn into a minute. Bojing waits for two minutes before he puts the cleaver down on the desk and pushes the paper a little closer to Ling.

"This message. You approved it?"

Ling gives a slight bow. "Sir. Yes."

"Did you send it personally?"

"Sir. No, I asked Yang to send it." Again, a slight bow.

"Protocol was established that all communications with sensitive information be sent by me through my secure terminal."

Ling swallows. "Sir. I watched as Yang encrypted the message myself."

"Using what cipher?"

He bows once more. "Our standard... Sir."

"The standard can be broken." Bojing pushes away from the desk. "You have jeopardized our organization and dishonored your group."

"Sir." Ling bows.

"You will take this cleaver and give it to Yang. He is to remove two fingers from your left hand for breaking the protocol."

Ling bows. "Sir."

"And he is to remove one finger from his left hand for doing this as well."

"Sir." Ling bows and steps forward. "I will remove my fingers."

"No," Bojing says. "You will have Yang do it."

The man glances down at the cleaver, then at Bojing. The insult of one member removing the fingers of another will stain him for years to come. He reaches out to take the cleaver, but Bojing grabs his wrist with a lightning-fast hand.

"Ping will go with you and gather the others. They will witness this. Ping will report back to me, and you will personally deliver the fingers to me."

Yang bows, deeper this time.

"Tell them, the next time it will be the balls of the person who goes against protocol."

"Sir."

He lets go. The man picks up the cleaver and leaves with Ping in tow.

Bojing picks up a burner phone. Now I need to send a much different message.

The bang on the door takes my attention away from the phone. Julie almost jumps from the sound. She puts her hand to her heart.

The knocks repeat, harder. I head for the hall closet and my gun safe. A fingerprint lock scans my thumb and opens with a click. The .45 is loaded, and I thumb back the hammer.

One tap of the door viewer and I see Mie standing outside, about to hit the door again with one upraised fist. I pull it open.

"You left hospital." She walks in, hooks her coat on the chair by the door, and stoops to pull off her shoes.

I ease the .45's hammer back into place, click on the safety, and set the gun on a side table. "Sarah's missing."

"Bruce was okay enough to come home," Julie quickly explains. "But the school called when we got here. She never went to her first class. We're frantic trying to find her."

Mie pulls out a file from a small sachet. She opens it to the report, two pictures of young Asian men almost sneering at the camera are there with their rap sheets. Not much. Just a few things about speeding and disorderly conduct.

"Not much here," I say.

She pulls out another, thicker file and hands it to me. "This from China."

I open it. The clipped photos show the same two faces again. The problem is the writing is in Chinese. "This might work for you, but I can't read it."

"Simple. Lot of crime. Robbery. Rape. Murder, though dismissed."

Julie looks over my shoulder. "Nice people we let into Canada, right? But how does that help us?"

Mie tilts her head. It reminds me of a curious cocker spaniel. Her eyes go from Julie to me.

"She means Sarah. She's worried about our daughter, and so am I." I flip some pages. "Why do we always let the dangerous ones in?"

Julie smirks. "Because violence only affects the poor, not the rich who make the rules."

Mie nods. "Like in China. Poor not protected. Rich make stink if someone step on toe."

Julie nods back at Mie. "Right. And we're the ones paying all the taxes while the rich get to hide their money."

I keep flipping through the paperwork while the two of them talk politics. Julie appears to be trying to mend bridges, but I keep seeing the clock. Ten minutes are gone. The drive to the address is not far, but with the weather being the way it is...

"...and we really need your help, right Bruce?"

My name snaps me out of the fog. I glance over, and Mie is holding Julie's hand. There's a small trickle of wet on my wife's face, and her eyes are a little puffy. Has she told her everything?

"I'm sorry." I stand up. "I have to go."

Mie stands before I can take two steps. She places a hand on my chest.

"Partner mean partner. You have problem. I help."

Her deep eyes are almost black as they stare at me. There's a finality in her words that makes me not argue. I glance over to Julie, and she nods her head once.

"There's no reason for it. They want me alone."

Mie doesn't move her hand. "When this happen, we say to people it no matter. They have your child. It mean nothing. You see her? Talk with her?"

"Don't pull the cop card on me now, Mie. This is my daughter we're talking about. I know the stats and that there's a chance she's..." I can't say it.

Julie stares at me.

"I don't care what the stats say. She's my daughter, not yours. She's alive until I have proof. I'm going to capitalize on it." A quick glance at my phone. "Now, I only have forty-five minutes to get to the meeting."

She pushes hard against my chest. I take three steps back.

"You not think like cop. You think like father. If daughter alive, we work as team to get her free."

I shake my head. "And what can you do to help?"

A slight smile crosses her lips. "We have address. I have what be big message. Come see."

My puffy coat hides the small arsenal of weapons stashed about my body. The warmth in the elevator leaches out as we reach the first floor. The windows of the lobby are white with what looks like a blizzard raging outside. Mie walks into it without hesitation, her coat whipping in the wind. She reaches behind her head and gathers her long hair into a quick bunch, stuffing it under her collar.

There's a new model, white Tesla sedan, parked in the visitor's parking space nearest the front door to the building. The vehicle must be Canadian made, or its battery wouldn't work in sub-zero temperatures. Snow builds up on the vehicle. Mie wipes off the trunk and opens it. She pulls off her coat, replacing it with a white cover-all parka. The heavyweight of a flak jacket hits me. I strip off my coat, quickly putting it on. Still, I shake so much I can barely button up.

An old BMG .50 cal lies there. Painted white, cloth wraps the muzzle. A small cloaking diffusion shield is wedged into the back. Thermal goggles lay to the side along with an assortment of modern and traditional weapons. It's like she's ready for war.

Mie's finished strapping on the body armor. Dressed as she is, she's white against the snow and hard to see.

"That's a big gun," I say, pointing at the BMG 50.

"Range good. Suppressor take most noise. From far, no sound." She lifts a small friend or foe bracelet and slaps it on my wrist. The metal leaches out my warmth. "So me no shot you."

I've read about the bracelets but never saw one. I want to examine it, but time is running short. "Just be sure you don't hit Sarah if they bring her to the meeting. What's your plan?" I ask.

"We talk inside." She closes the trunk, nodding for me to get in the driver's side. "You drive." A fob is pressed into my hand.

"Okay," I say, not knowing what to expect.

She slips in the passenger side, and I get in the driver's. The seat is slid back for me as if she anticipated something.

The car comes to life as it senses the fob in my pocket. The thing's display is like a rocket ship's, but I don't have time to admire it. My hands shake as I slip the car out of park and pull out of the visitor's space.

I slow the car down to thirty, and Mie throws open her door. She rolls out onto the road and the door slams shut as I accelerate. In the storm, she's almost invisible. I keep driving, hoping the plan will work.

One klick. That's the distance she said she needed. I only hope they don't have a lot of cover.

The road is hazardous in the snow. Wheels spin as they try to bite in for traction, and the car adjusts power to keep a grip. It's frustrating watching the dash clock run down time while I roll forward.

I take the turn onto Cardico Drive and then a left into the parking lot. An RV trailer company has some of their vehicles on the lot but nothing too large. I stop at the building marked #4. The back lot is fenced in, but the gate is pulled aside. I head for that, catching a quick glimpse of a man holding a small assault rifle on the other side. This must be the right place.

A few meters in and I come to a stop. A lot of men are out there watching the perimeter. Each carries the same type of rifle as the one guarding the gate. They make no move to engage, just stand there in the blowing snow.

The car comes to a stop twenty meters from the men. I get out, hands raised, hoping they think I'm armed. They'll search me, but I've taken precautions to hide my weapons in the pockets and behind my back where most people will not look. That's when Bojing steps away from the crowd.

He walks agonizingly slow with a slight limp. I store that information away in case it's needed. The wind takes his hair as if the tiny strands don't want to be around him either. It would be comical in another world, but my daughter's life is at stake. The glow of a cigarette pierces through the snow as he takes a puff. One of his men stifles a cough.

A younger man follows him, holding nothing. His left hand is bandaged with blood stains where his little finger would be – only two paces between them.

Bojing stops as the young man steps toward me. He halts two paces away.

"Da kai wai tao," he says in a harsh tone.

I tilt my head. "I don't understand."

"Da kai ni de wai tao bai se mo gui," the man says, becoming angry.

I look to Bojing.

"You should understand him. Chinese becoming language of Toronto. He wants you open coat. He no trust white devil."

"It's a little cold for shit like this. Where's my daughter?" I demand.

Bojing laughs lightly. "You no position to demand, cop."

"Yes, I am." I take a deep breath. "Unless you can prove you have her, we're done."

The smile fades from his eyes. He looks back at the others and barks out a command in Chinese. Half of them nod and run to the building. A door is pushed open, and Sarah is pulled out into the cold. Thank God she's alive. But something's wrong. She's wearing a sweater too loose to be warm, not a coat. Her hair is tangled and falls forward across her brow. She looks up. The word "Daddy" touches her lips. With a twist of her body, she almost breaks free of her captures. They hold fast. Fingers clutch her arms tighter. Fire erupts in my stomach. My little girl . I have to get her home safely.

"Let her go."

Bojing smiles. "Open coat."

I open my coat. The butt of the Glock digs in a little. The young guy with the bloody hand comes forward and feels my chest, legs. A half-hearted search with only one hand touching my body.

He steps back and nods to Bojing.

They pull Sarah back into the building.

"We talk now," Bojing says.

"I don't have anything to say to you. Release my daughter or die."

Bojing lets out a little chuckle. "You not see what we ask." He reaches into his coat. "This for you and family. Take it. All you people take and look away." He tosses an envelope to my feet. "You get more. After few week we give daughter to you."

"She's coming home with me today." I don't even glance at the envelope.

"No, few week. No more talk. Take money. Buy small house somewhere. Live good life. We take care of you. Daughter free in few week."

I'm tired of his talking. "She's coming with me today. If you want to live, you'll not get in my way." I take a step forward.

The young man puts his left hand against my chest, eyes almost wincing. His right comes up with a blade. A good half meter of steel presses to my throat.

"He kill you if asked," Bojing says.

"And I kill him now." I raise my hand, point a finger, and drop my thumb as if firing.

The bullet hits the young man in the temple. At first, it does not appear as much, but his body jerks to the left and away just as the other side of his head explodes—bone and brain fly. Everyone scatters. I run to the car, pulling a Glock out as I do. One shot takes out the guard behind me. I dive against the back of the car, making sure my body is covered by the wheels.

Now it is all up to Mie.

January 12th, 2033 — Firefight

Bojing swears as blood, bone, and brain spray the snow beside the warehouse.

Move, you old fool! He rushes to the side, looking for anything to cover himself from the sniper. The cop double-crossed us. With quick revenge flowing through his mind, he scrambles toward the door. Inside he will be hidden. Inside he will live.

A 49er also heads for the same door. I'll need to deal with him. But before the man can reach the handle, his head explodes. Chunks of grey matter decorate the wall next to the door. Bojing swears again.

Shots ring out from the car. Roberts must be dug in there. It'll take a lot to get him out. The sniper has his men in a crossfire. There's little he can do to make sure they survive.

"Machines! Get on the snow machines!" Bojing yells out.

Some of his men run in the right direction, but the majority of them just cover-up, waiting in safety.

"There's only one sniper. Find him!" Bojing shouts.

"Sir. How do you know?" Ping calls back.

"They didn't have time to mobilize for a full-scale assault. He must have a friend out there, no more than one. Not enough shots for more. Find that one, and we'll survive."

Ping nods back and scampers off. Bojing wonders if he did it out of reflex or because of his command. He doesn't care.

The whine of engines breaks through the wind, and four machines take off into the south woods. Good. My men know what cover to use. It takes a few seconds before the shots from the car cease. Bojing spots a barrel and dashes to it. A round kicks up snow and asphalt as he dives behind it. Fire erupts from his knee as it smacks the ground.

I am going to kill this cop!

The last of the gang is behind barrels. I can only get a few shots off from my position before becoming a target as well. Mie keeps hitting heads with her shots. I drop the clip out of the Glock and slide another home.

With a fast roll, lying prone behind a tire, I aim at a leg sticking out too far. The round smacks the barrel. Correcting for wind, I take another shot. Hit! There's a howl of pain. I roll back into cover, bullets spray the car.

A man tries to come around the fence. His timing is wrong. I bring the Glock up and point at his center mass—a squeeze. The bullet hits the chest and punctures through the other side. Another one crumbles to the ground. One less target for Mia.

The thwap of a high-powered round strikes something soft to my right. I roll away.

A corpse hits the ground a few meters away; half its head is gone. Mie does a good job.

"You're pinned in a crossfire!" I yell out to Bojing. "Tell your men to throw down their arms, and they won't be killed."

Bullets hit the car. The answer is clear. Mie is taking her time when she should be firing at the barrels. Her rounds will go right through them, cause greater panic.

A round hits one of the barrels. The plastic keg slides back a good half meter, exposing the man behind it. I fire three rounds. One hits but it must be a flesh wound because the guy's still moving.

I spin. The whine of an engine erupts from behind the building. The sound fades. Fuck. They're making a run for it.

The wind dies. Heavy snowflakes fall in a steady downpour. They'll cover Mie's tracks, maybe even hide her, but it makes for hell aiming a gun without an infra-red scope like Mie's BMG.

I watch two barrels start to move. One looks like it's being dragged while the other is pushed toward the building's door. It must be Bojing. That's where I last saw him when Mie took out one of his men. I aim at the spot, counting slow. Waiting for the barrels to come into my sight instead of tracking them. I squeeze off five rapid shots. The barrels stop moving. A man slumps to the ground. It isn't Bojing. Shit.

No more bullets come from Mie. I have two clips besides the rounds left. I need to make them count.

Cold metal touches my neck.

"Drop gun," a guttural voice says.

Fuck! I start to open the fingers holding the Glock, but the gun's ripped from my hand, almost taking my finger with it.

"Hands on head. Stay still."

Rough hands search me. They find the knife, clips, and back-up guns. My arms are bent behind me, and a slip binding tightens around my wrists. My shoulders cry in pain. I grunt as someone hauls me to my feet. A crowd of them surround me.

"You will die for attack," the man behind me says in broken English.

"At least a bunch of you died first. You think I don't have a plan if you capture me?"

The man pushes me hard against the car. I fold over, cheek slamming against the metal. A humph escapes my lips as I slip to the ground. A kid, no more than eighteen, pulls me back up to standing. Pimples decorate his young face, a sign he indulges in too much fast food. His smile is tobacco stained. Crooked teeth turn the expression into a ghoul's grimace. His breath is foul. Left hand bandaged like the first guy who frisked me.

The low rumble of snowmobiles returning comes from the direction of the front gate. The noise of their engines tells me they're taking their time, not rushing. I glance over as they stop, and a figure is pulled off the back of a machine and pushed forward at gunpoint. Mie.

Bojing comes to me, a smile on his face. A cigarette hangs from one side of his mouth. He puffs at it like a baby sucks a soother. I want to shove the thing up his ass.

"You trouble, cop. Partner here. You here. Money here. You die soon. Nothing show for it. Maybe put money in account and tip off investigation. You get no money. You wife get no pension. You get no funeral. Die in disgrace." He lets out a chuckle. "Maybe I do daughter. How you like, cop?"

I struggle against the bonds. They won't budge. Instead, they dig into my wrists. My back is on fire from the position and from struggling, but I don't let them see it. I whisper some nonsensical words.

"What you say?" Bojing takes a step forward.

Not close enough. I whisper the same nonsensical words again.

Bojing takes another step forward. "You speak loud, you hear?"

He's a step away. I take it. Drive my forehead toward him—nothing. A hand slams my forehead and drives more fire to my back and shoulders.

"Enough," Bojing says. "I deal you later."

He turns to the others and shouts something in Chinese. The group gives out a shout and clap.

Mie is shoved against the car beside me. She has a black eye forming and a split lip. The three snowmobiles take off to the back of the building.

"We're doing well," I say to her.

"Stay near," she says.

Bojing glances at Mie. "Nice. I have you before. Good to have again. Maybe take time. Show you fun time, yes?"

Mie spits at him. Some lands on his face. He wipes it away, but the smile doesn't leave his face. "Good for you." He turns and yells something at the men behind us.

Mie stares into my eyes. "Good fight."

Pain erupts from my skull, and darkness engulfs me.

———

The veil of darkness lifts. Images clarify. Instead of a big, fuzzy blur, I can make out colors. They appear to be my legs.

The cold nibbles at my skin. My clothes are gone. That's for certain. My arms are still fastened in that weird position of one reaching up and over my back, and one twisted behind. A rope tied around my chest keeps me from falling off the chair. Something is clipped to my dick and balls. I can feel the rough bite. Not painful, but not comfortable. My head throbs as I lift it. The room comes into focus. Paneled walls without pictures, two low filing cabinets with two drawers are against one wall, and a desk sits in front of me. No windows adorn the walls— just a bright, white light coming from the ceiling. What surprises me the most is the silence.

A small keyboard illuminates the desk, as well as the screen saver program. I test the bonds that hold me. The one on my arms is tight. The chest rope has fallen now that I no longer slump against it. I swing my head around and instantly regret it. Pain erupts. This is the second strike to the head I've taken in so many days. Probably have a concussion again.

A door opens behind me. I try to look but can't move enough to see what is there. Voices explode into the room from outside, along with a cold draft. Goosebumps pimple my skin. The door closes, and the noise disappears. The room must be soundproof. A line from an old movie enters my mind. No one can hear you scream. I'm alone in the room.

The door opens again; this time, the noise from the outside is less. Hobbling footsteps enter. Rancid fumes assault my nose. The harshness of Asian cigarettes makes me want to gag. Only one person I know smokes them.

"Bojing?" I ask with a sore throat.

"You surprise, cop." Bojing hobbles to lean against the desk. "Most people not good at waking after hard hit. You... Well, you not like most people me think."

His lopsided smile is still there as I struggle against the bindings.

"You no get out. They tight. Bad position." Bojing pushes away from the desk and sits on the chair. He lets out a soft sigh. "You two cause many problem today. Men, time, machine. It be easy. Take money. Go vacation. Not investigate. But no. You poke nose where not belong. Make boss angry. He tell me fix. So here I fix. Have money, but not for you. For thing attach to you." He lets out a good chuckle. "Some like what happen, but most not. You like and not happen. No like and keep happen. Tell me what I need know."

To demonstrate, he runs a finger up his desk just a little bit. Electricity tickles my nuts and dick. He's rigged me for electrocution. Great.

The door opens again, and someone enters. Chains drag against the ground, and there's a muffled whimper. The voice is familiar. Bojing looks up, and his smile becomes wider.

"I have something for you," he says and comes over to stand in front of me. "You need see this."

He motions behind me, and Sarah is brought to my side. A gag is keeping her from speaking. She lets out a scream and reaches out for me, hands bound. Tears spill down my cheeks. Sarah's hands are tied but in front of her, not around the back like mine. Her clothes are tattered. Rips in the sweater show her bra is still on.

She breaks away from the man holding her and rushes to me. Her hands go up and around me. Hugs me close. She cries.

"You okay?" I ask between her sobs. She nods her head.

"You love child. Good." He snaps his fingers, and the guard pulls Sarah off me. She's kicking, and I get a mental picture of her giving Bojing the limp. Hopefully, she's the one who did it to the monster.

"You need know daughter here to watch. If answer wrong, this happen."

He runs his finger up the desk screen, making bars light up—electricity arcs through my body from my balls and dick. Pain rips through me as my bladder screams and anus puckers. My teeth clamp down. Sarah screams for Bojing to stop. I taste metal. Everything stops, except the pain. That takes a while to recede before I can open my eyes.

Bojing nods. "That only half."

There's pleasure in his eyes. Maybe even excitement. The asshole is getting off on this. Fuck. This is not how this rescue was supposed to end. No one but Julie knows where we are. At least she's smart. She'll get us help.

"I need know. Tell me what cops know of us."

My mind whirls. Stomach clenches. Bile burns my throat. But where do I start? The simple? The complicated? I look between my daughter and Bojing.

"Go to hell," I say.

Bojing sighs. "Hell promised to me." He pushes his finger up the desk.

The soft touch of a wet cloth brings me around. I lift my head, open my eyes, and see Sarah beside me. She's touching my face with a dirty rag. There's blood on it. Not a lot, just enough to be noticed. Her eyes are puffy, and tendrils run from her eyes down her face. With a trembling hand, she brings the cloth back to my face and wipes away at something.

"You bit your tongue. Then blacked out. Bojing walked out in a furry for that." She takes a trembling breath. "I'm sorry. It's all... all my fault."

"Ho... how long?" I ask.

"I don't know—a few minutes. I went out last night. Should've stayed home. Can you... If they come back, you should pretend to still be out." Sarah starts to tear up. "I got us into this."

My shoulders ache, but at least my arms are lashed to the chair with plastic ties instead of behind me now. I pull at them, but nothing budges.

"We'll talk about that later. For now, you're alive. Can you get to the desk?"

"I think so." Sarah gets up and takes a few steps toward the desk. Chains drag against the floor. "Yeah."

I look at her foot. A chain is shackled there and fastened to the wall.

"Did they hurt you?" I hold my breath.

"They tried to... they wanted to rape me. I remember what you said once, long ago." She looks down at her feet. "I pissed myself when they tried to take my pants off. It made most of them turn away, but a few..."

"You did good."

"A few looked turned on, but they noticed how the others acted and pretended to be revolted as well." She turns back to the desk. "What am I looking for?"

"Anything. Everything. We need to find a way to escape."

She walks around the desk, and the chain stretches taut. "I can reach a drawer." It opens, and she looks through it. "Nothing much here. I don't know what to…"

Sarah stares at something in the drawer. Color drains from her face. "What did you find?"

"Fingers. He has fingers in his drawer."

"What?"

She pulls out a napkin covered in blood and shows me. A finger cut just above the first knuckle joint. Christ. This guy is sick.

Sarah puts the finger back. She rummages around in the drawer a little more. "I see something but I'm having a hard time getting at it. The thing is slippery."

It takes a few seconds, but she pulls out a small knife. I breathe a sigh of relief—time to get out of here.

"Bring it over. You can cut through my bonds."

Sarah comes over with the blade in her hand. She tests the edge against the first bond, and it cuts into the plastic with ease. One hand is free, but it's numb with rope marks still screaming angrily. I can move it, but the feeling's not there.

"The other one," I say. She brings the blade to it.

The doorknob jiggles a little behind me. I look up into Sarah's eyes, and tears rush down her face.

"No, don't panic. That will give this all away." I look over my shoulder. "Hide the knife and disguise the broken bond. We can do this again once they're gone. I'll pretend to be out still."

She puts the knife under the desk by its back leg. Easy to reach for her, but out of sight. Then she works with the broken binding, twisting the cut ends together to make it appear still functional. Still, the door is being jostled as if someone is fumbling for keys.

"Grab the cloth and make it look like you're still cleaning me up."

Sarah uses the cloth. I lean back like I was before, and the cloth moves across my face. The door jostles one more time, and then it's quiet. I start to believe nothing will happen, but then it explodes inward on us, and a body drops to the ground striking Sarah's leg.

My daughter screams.

January 12th, 2033 – Rescued

Bojing walks out of his office and lights another cigarette. He frowns at the semi-sweet smoke twirling around his tongue. There's no bite, not bitter, not the acrid taste he expects. Just unwanted and horrible sweetness. He takes two puffs and snuffs the disgusting thing under his foot, throwing away the pack.

"Ping!" he yells. "You have any Chinese cigarettes?"

Ping looks over from the group he is with. "I have two."

"I have a shipment coming tomorrow. Can I get one of yours?"

Ping excuses himself from the group and walks toward Bojing. He fishes out his pack and offers it. A smile crosses the older man's face as he extracts one cigarette.

"Thank you, Ping." He hands it back. "I owe you one."

"Sir," Ping says. "We have news."

Bojing lights the cigarette and lets the bitter stinging smoke curl around his tongue. "Yes, what is it?"

"Cops are coming." Ping points back to his group. "We can take them out before they get here, or we can leave now. It is your choice."

"How many?"

"Three SWAT, ten cars."

Bojing takes another drag. He thinks about the forces at his disposal. Getting more men will take time. The newcomers will need visas and passports. Then he'll need to train them about the way to behave among Canadians, how to blend in with the other emigrants from China, the new way of snatching girls for initiation, and how to prop up the teens in the school to spread their legs for the new star they pick.

All of it a lot more time and work.

"How far out are they?"

Ping glances back at his group. One of them holds up seven fingers.

"Seven minutes, sir."

"Seven minutes." Bojing takes another drag. "Okay, we leave this place. Now. Tell men to gather only what they need. Wipe down everything, so those who are undiscovered stay that way, and have those who are known to cops report here to me in three minutes."

"Sir," Ping says.

"Do we have ways to delay them set up and ready?"

"Yes, several." Ping turns to the group. "Hong, come here."

A man in his mid-twenties breaks away from the group and trots over. His belly is large and face round. He huffs as he stops, putting both hands on his knees and bending over as if the ten-meter run almost killed him.

"Hong set up the delays last week." Ping turns to Hong. "Tell us what you done."

Hong straightens up. "I have three non-lethal works ready to go. They are two kilometers out from the base and on the road they are using. There are two lethal IEDs in the road as well, and we can trigger them remotely. Two cameras are set up at each to watch. How much time do you need?"

Bojing glances down at the half-gone cigarette. A few seconds pass, and he studies the two men.

"We need twenty minutes to evacuate. Are we sure the cops don't have air support?"

"We have seen none," Ping says. "Maybe they have drone. Our informant in the department said the cops didn't have time to get much put together. I think taking out the SWAT will be the best idea. They would have the drones."

"I agree." Bojing smiles at Ping. "You are thinking well for one so young. Keep it up. I'll let the base know."

"About the prisoners," Ping says. "Should we kill them?"

Bojing smiles. "No. Let them be found. They only saw Ping and me. The cop knows we can touch him now, and he'll be more eager to keep his family safe. As for Interpol... I have plans for her."

Shan rushes into the room, glances at me, and immediately goes to Sarah. His dark hands take hold of her shaking shoulders as he pulls her close, whispering soothing words into teenage ears.

Gunfire sounds outside the room. The odd, "Clear!" is shouted out to whoever is listening. I almost cry. The cavalry is here to save us, but how did they know? Really, I don't care.

"Shan," I say.

He turns those dark brown eyes at me. "Bruce."

"Yeah. Can you help a brother out?"

He stands, letting go of my daughter. "Sure thing."

Shan pulls out a small knife and cuts the last of my bindings, doing his best to avoid looking at my dick and balls. He does a good job until I reach under the chair and remove the wires. I go to push myself up but fall back down into the chair, legs tingling.

"We need a medic here!" Shan shouts to the door. "Don't move yet. Let them come in and take care of you."

"Yeah, good idea." I relax my arms. "Some clothes would be nice. God, I could do with a drink right now."

Shan pulls his coat off and drapes it over my lap. I look up as he looks away.

"God, Bruce. The LT is pissed at you."

"Yeah, figured he would be."

"Really? Why the hell did you go off like that?"

I nod toward Sarah. "I have my reasons." My legs are starting to do the pins and needles thing. Little pinpricks run up and down them. Even my balls ache. Hell, this is not going to be fun once the circulation is fully restored, and all the nerves start to complain. "Do you think he'll want my badge?"

Shan lets out a deep breath. "No, but maybe your balls." He mouths a sorry as Sarah lifts her head.

"I'm okay now," Sarah says and comes over to my side. She places a hand against my cheek. "I'm sorry."

"Nothing to be sorry about. Just glad you're safe."

"It's my fault." A tear runs down her cheek. "If it wasn't for me, this wouldn't have happened."

"Don't say that." I reach out and pull her close, bring my arms around and hug her. "This gang would've found you no matter what. At least they didn't catch your mother. Hell, they would have shot her for all the bitching she would've done."

Sarah lets out a short, soft laugh. "I got that one guy good, though. Hit his knee like you showed me. He started to really limp after that."

"I saw the results of your kick. Good job." I pat the back of her head and kiss her. My daughter is safe. That's all I care about right now. "Maybe the raid got him as well."

Shan shakes his head. "We were a few K's out when some fireworks went off. We had to slow in order to clear them. Then two IEDs took out two SWAT vans."

"How many dead?" I ask.

"Not sure, but a few men were injured." Shan puts a hand on my shoulder.

"I'm going to owe a lot of people after this is done," I say. Too many of us seem to owe each other. It's too much to remember.

"No, you don't." Shan squeezes my shoulder.

He shuffles back as two medics come into the room. They step to either side of the chair. One reaches out and takes Sarah aside to make sure she's all right while the other one pulls back the jacket.

"Nasty," he says. "Leads were attached?"

His question almost makes me cross my legs. "I'd rather not think about that."

"Are you feeling any pain?"

The words, what do you think, rattle through my skull. "Yeah. Legs are still a little numb, but pins and needles are coming full force."

The medic nods and pulls open his side pouch. He throws a blood pressure cuff around my arm and pokes a probe into my ear. A soft click, and he pulls out the device with a nod. "Your temp is good. Blood pressure is slightly elevated, but that's to be expected. Saturation reading is good as well. Stretcher or walk?"

"I'd like to walk but need some clothes."

Shan stops rummaging through the desk and comes around. Pants, shirt, and shoes held proudly.

"What, no socks?"

He drops them on the floor. "I'm not a personal shopper, you know."

I smile, remembering back when a homeowner complained we took all their good clothes after a break-in. He smiles back, probably playing the same scene in his mind. We are a fine example of the brotherhood.

It takes a few minutes for the feeling in my legs to return. Getting out of the chair offers another logistical issue. My parts are swollen, and the hole is too small. The medics help get me out. Shan left the room with Sarah for that procedure.

The pants scratch as I put them on, but that can be ignored. Walking shoots a reminder of the pain through my body, but I make it to the door just in time to see Mie on a stretcher, her eyes closed as if unconscious. The sheet is pulled up at her neck, but there are no bumps for arms and legs. The bastards took her limbs off. I hobble over before they can get the gurney into the bus.

"I'm going with her."

"No way," the redheaded woman responds.

"She's my partner. I'm going with her."

The woman looks at the other medic, and he nods.

"Okay, but stay out of my way."

"Sure." I wait until they load her into the bus and step up to sit on the end of the bench. "Did you get her arms and legs?"

"The prosthetics are being collected by the cops." She closes the doors. "One of the arms and both legs are junked. They must have beat her with them before trashing the things. Poor girl."

The lights flick on, and the driver gets us moving quickly. We take off out of the warehouse into the afternoon sun. The ambulance turns south.

"Which hospital?" I ask.

"Mackenzie," the medic says. She's examining Mie's left stump of an arm. Bruises cover the surface and the connection point for her prosthetic. The medic takes a few seconds to examine the metal end of the stump. Contact points in her arm stand out in gold while others give off light.

She's just a torso with a head. I bite my lower lip. I've only seen her remove one of her arms, and even then, I never took a good look. The complexities of the connections baffle me. They shine and blink. She said the fingers and toes felt real to her. Nerve transmission points are all embedded around them. Even the tiny hairs moved according to the rest of her body. Foolproof technology.

The medic stares at the stump, trying to find a place to insert the saline drip. She flashes a light, peels back a piece of rubber with a small icon on it. The needle goes in—fluid races down the tube. Everything fits perfectly.

A heart monitor starts to bleep a little fast, and the medic stares at it for a second, brow furrowing. She reaches over to the drawer and pulls out a package, ripping it open. The syringe is full of a clear liquid, and she empties into the IV line attached to my partner.

The ambulance tilts a little to the left as the driver turns onto Major Mackenzie Drive and then stops in a traffic jam. He hits the siren and transitions from one lane to another. "God damn fucking old people driving. Move your ass! Hold on!" the driver calls back.

The bus makes a quick swerve, and the driver hits the gas. We're moving but not as fast as I want us to. We slow again, the horn adding to the cacophony of sound as the driver swears some more. The monitor shows Mie's heart skipping a beat.

"Is that normal?" I ask.

"You wanted to ride with us, so shut up while I work," the red-headed medic says. She reaches over to the supplies again and pulls out another wrapped syringe. The contents flow through the IV and into Mie's body. Her heart rate speeds up.

"Fuck," the medic says.

"What?" I ask.

"She's getting tacky. You know CPR?"

"Yes."

"Good. I may use you, after all."

We make it through the intersection of Major Mackenzie and Leslie. The driver knows what he's doing. We're jostled from the erratic swerves. I swear he must be using the oncoming lane to get us to the hospital.

"She's arrhythmic, John," the medic calls to the front.

"Got it!" He picks up his radio mic and begins relaying the information to the hospital.

"What's that?" I ask.

"Hearts not beating right." She reaches into her supply and takes out another syringe. "We've got to stabilize her."

She puts the syringe contents into the IV, then pulls back the sheet and rips open Mie's shirt. There's a bra in the way, so she cuts it in the middle. The two cups slip away as her breasts are taken by gravity.

Two pads are slapped on her chest. One on the right just above the breast and one on the left just under it and to the side. The sheet is pulled back up.

The metallic voice makes me jump when it sings out.

"Analyzing. Stop compressions."

Ten seconds go by like they're hours.

"Shock recommended. Please stay clear and press the shock button."

I move away from the gurney, as does the medic. She hits a button, and a thunk sounds.

"Analyzing. Please stand by."

Time passes at an agonizing snail's pace. I count to ten-twenty times.

"Shock recommended. Please stay clear and press the shock button."

Again, the thunk sounds.

"Analyzing. Please stand by."

My beard grows waiting for the report.

"No shock recommended. Ensure the patient is breathing."

The medic leans over Mie and nods after a second.

"She's good?" I ask.

"Yeah, for now. Stable, at least."

Out goes the breath I hold. I reach out a hand to take Mie's but realize she doesn't have one.

"Here," the medic says. "Just put your hand on her shoulder. She'll know it's yours."

I put my hand on Mie's shoulder. Her eyes flicker open, bruising keeps them from opening fully. She looks around without focusing on anything until she hits my eyes.

"You're going to be okay," I say.

Mie moves her lips, but nothing comes out. Her shoulders roll under the blanket. She lifts her head. The medic puts hands against Mie's head and lowers it down.

"Don't move," she says.

"Bu, bu, bu," Mie whimpers, then she passes out.

We hit emerge just as the traffic starts to lighten up. The medics help me out and pull the gurney with Mie on it through the hospital's emergency doors. I follow them, not knowing what to do next.

The medics wheel Mie past the triage station and into an area surrounded by curtains. The medics leave as a doctor who looks to be Sarah's age comes in with a nurse in tow. I stand at the foot of the bed while the doctor examines her.

Mie's eyes flutter open, and she tries to move. The doctor gently urges her back down, but she struggles as soon as he lifts his hands. I come around and put my hands on Mie's shoulders.

"Mie, you're in a hospital. They're looking after you."

Her head turns, eyes focus on me. A small oxygen mask is placed over her face. Her breath causes it to fog up a little.

"What... What happen," she gets out.

"The cops stormed the place and got us out." I take one hand away from her shoulder but leave the other one there as a comfort. "They saved us, Mie."

A small smile touches her lips, then trembles away. Her eyelids flutter. Eyes rolling back.

"She's tachycardic." The doctor looks at me. "Is she on any meds? A pacemaker?"

"I don't think so." I try to remember the conversations we had. "Never told me anything."

The doctor pulls the blanket down and grabs the leads of the heart monitor. He doesn't pull the blanket up. His gaze lingers on the prosthetic connection. "The connections are metal with leads in them. Where's this arm?"

My gaze lingers on Mie's face. "Ruined at the scene."

"Nurse, lidocaine hydrochloride, stat." The doctor turns to me. "Call someone. Get it here."

I glance at the wall – an old-style phone. I grab it and dial Shan's cell. Tell him to get the left arm and bring it to the hospital fast.

"Clear!" the doctor calls out.

A familiar thud echoes in my ears. I try to remember how many times the body can stand being shocked without repercussions.

"Arm is on its way," I tell the doctor.

"Good." He stares at the heart monitor. "We're back to normal sinus rhythm."

"Doc, is she going to be okay?"

"I think so. But she's not out of the woods yet." He checks the monitor again. "The monitors indicate she has a heart condition. It looks like it was managed, but I don't know how. I'm ordering an echocardiogram to see if that gives us any answers."

I stare down at Mie's face. She looks peaceful. Very different than the first day I met her. No more worry lines or tough exterior. I would even say she's beautiful, though her nose is a little too flat for my taste.

"Hang in there, Mie."

"Bruce," she breathes out in a whisper. "My arm. Where is it?"

"They destroyed it. Your legs as well."

"Bruce," she says. "You do something?"

"Anything. Name it."

"Spare arm and leg at room. Box combination 66, 35, 99, 12, 55, 83. Bring here. Need them."

January 12th, 2033 – Warrant

The snowmobile jostles as it goes over a ridge. Bojing holds on tight, keeping his thoughts of slapping the driver to a minimum. His knee throbs from all the bumps as they escape from the warehouse. All that work finding, securing, and setting up operations flushed. But he's not worried. The backup location is not far away, and they can be ready to start the initiations and find a new crop of girls for their clients. Recording the sequences will allow the men to relax and gain trust once more. And the revenue from the China Girl sales will explode once again.

Ping is on a machine next to him, yelling into the wind. Bojing wants the man to shut up. He cannot understand his second with the sound of the machines and the wind so loud in his ears. Another storm must be coming in from the North. The wind makes the snow squalls on the trail difficult. Bojing waves Ping away and watches for vehicles as they approach the safe house. At least the storm will make it hard for the police to track them. It even keeps the helicopter out of the air. He smiles, wondering when he started liking the weather in this accursed country.

The next few days will be hard – lining up his alibi and engineering proof of his innocence. But their inside man will take care of most of the issues. It is good to have someone in his pocket to take care of what comes up. He'll need to approve a little extra for the spy getting the warning to them in time. It saved much.

A snowmobile towing a small sled holding weapons and equipment passes them on the left.

The money is still hidden in another safe house, along with the codes for all his overseas bank accounts and safe deposit boxes: so much planning and so little time to enact it. The rich people of the area will want another snuff film soon. Too bad he could not make one with that cop's daughter. She was nice looking. That was until she kicked his knee. How much damage had she inflicted? She knew exactly where to kick and on what angle to make him hurt for so long.

He will deal with the cop and his hateful child soon. Now, they need to get another girl. Maybe younger this time. Fifteen? Fourteen? Yes, fourteen. One of the men has a taste for the young. They'll need to find one that looks the part. Maybe braces and glasses with freckles. Yes, that will put the men in a good mood and surprise the rich who have subscribed to the feed.

Mie lies on the bed, monitors hooked up to her bleep. Every few minutes, I have to move my hand off her shoulder while the system takes a reading and sends a micro shock to her heart to get it back to the proper rhythm. The doc says she had a lot of trauma early in her life and that strained her heart, though she is in good shape regardless. I'll take his word for it.

She is peaceful and calm in light of what has happened to her. The private room is courtesy of Interpol and the guards outside, from the department. This way, we can keep her safe until things are back to normal for her.

"Bruce?" Julie says from the doorway.

I turn. Tears flood her face. Sarah rushes in and hugs me. Her grip is like iron, and she doesn't let go. I encircle her with both arms. Julie hugs both of us. It's a heart-warming moment. Not something we've had as a family over the last couple of years, and I'm hopeful we'll have a lot more of them.

The machine beeps, and the quiet sound of a discharge reminds me of what's going on.

"She's tacky?" Julie asks.

"That's what the docs say." I stroke Sarah's hair. "She has a condition due to past trauma."

Julie's brow rises. She lifts the side of the blanket and sees the arm, or what's left of it. Her gaze goes to the missing legs as well.

"Did this happen today?" She stares a little longer. "My God, Bruce, what happened to her?"

"Not really my story to tell." I place my hand back on Mie's shoulder.

Julie smooth's down the blanket and brushes the hair from Mie's eyes.

"I'm sorry I gave you such a hard time when we met," she says.

"Shan is getting her replacements from the hotel."

Sarah is crying, making my shoulder wet.

"The doc says the artificial limbs she has must regulate her heart in some way."

"Interesting. There is a lot about her I didn't know." Julie stands up and goes to the foot of the bed where she pulls the chart screen up.

"Yeah. Her father's rich. When it happened, he advanced limb replacement theory and developed an early model of what she has. Mie said she wears the newest version of the system or something like that."

Mie's eyes flutter open. She turns her head and looks at me. A little smile comes across her face and reaches the sad eyes.

"You get replacements?" she asks.

"No, not yet. They're coming."

Sarah lets go of me and turns to Mie. She reaches out and hugs my partner.

"Thank you," Sarah says.

Mie's brows go together, but she does not lose the softness in her tone. "For what?"

"Saving me," Sarah says.

Julie looks up. "Mie saved you?"

"Yes. I had kicked the man in the knee. He wanted to punish me for it, but Dad showed up. When we…" She turns away, then steps toward Mie and puts a hand on her head. "If it wasn't for Mie distracting the guards and getting beat up for it, they would have started in on me for hurting the man."

Julie's eyes go wide as she looks at Mie's face. "That's a sacrifice I won't easily forget."

"It job," Mie says. "Would do for anyone."

"But you did it for my daughter. That means something to me." Julie puts the chart down. "Thank you."

"You welcome."

The machine lets out a beep.

"Sarah, you'll need to let go of Mie for a moment," I say.

Mie's eyes curl up, and eyelashes flutter. A small chunk sounds as voltage races through her body to reset her heart's proper beat.

"She's going to be out for a little while," Julie says. I just nod. "Sarah, let's see if we can find something for Dad to wear."

"I kinda like the little gown," I say.

Julie chuckles. "Yes, but not everyone behind you will want to see that hairy ass of yours."

Shan found Mie's replacement parts and brought them to the hospital. The doc puts them in place and monitors her heart. After two hours, he removes the leads. Mie's color starts to return, and soon she's sitting up in bed, arguing about getting out. I tell her that we're here overnight and not to complain. It seems to sink in, and Mie settles down.

I make my way back to the room I'm assigned. It's a long walk, all of ten steps. They put me right next to her on the orders of the department. You only need two guards this way, not four. Julie brought some clothes from home, and I'm grateful. The air in the hospital is cold.

Shan drops by and slips me a piece for protection. I nod at the consideration. He's always looking out for our people in that way. I don't feel safe unless I have at least one gun on me, especially now.

The night goes by without a hitch. Morning rounds happen at

seven, and then breakfast is served. Nothing fancy. I clean the plate of the toast, egg, cheese, and fruit, not realizing how hungry I am. The tea is a nice touch. I sip it wondering if a second breakfast is in the works for me or not.

"Bruce." Cap stands at the door to my room.

"Hey, Cap." I put the tea down.

He flinches at the name like always, but instead of correcting me, he lets this one slide. Must be something to do with what's put me here.

"How you feeling?" Cap steps a few paces into the room.

"Good as new. Little swollen in the balls, but nothing time won't cure."

He winces again, must have heard what they did to me. "Look, if you need time. Take it. I'm going to see Mie next and tell her the same thing. Interpol will send a replacement if you're not ready to go back."

"I don't need time off."

"Look, I know it's none of my business, but if you're having a hard time with the wife... If you need, take a little while and help mend that."

I shake my head. "Nope. Already fixed that."

"You going to be signed out today? Not against doctor's recommendations?"

"He said I'll be discharged this afternoon." I pick up my tea and take a sip. "Mie is the same. They can't find anything wrong with her since the prosthetics were put in place."

He flinches a little. Not many knew about Mie's condition. Not even Cap. But everyone will know now. I just hope the jokes will be kept to a minimum.

"Yes, but are you ready to come back?"

I stare at the man for a second. "Are you looking at getting rid of me? Not going to happen. We have a job to do, and nothing's going to stop us from nabbing Wang. Remember, we are witnesses to the crime."

"That's the problem. You can't really be both enforcer and victim. The defense will pick that apart."

I shake my head. "No deal. And if we need someone else, we'll use Sarah."

"Your daughter?" He snorts a little. "Not going to happen. That's like putting chum in the water. She'll be torn apart and painted as trying to advance her father's case."

"Then what?"

"Not sure. We need to get a good angle on this in order for the D. A. to sign off on it." He takes a deep breath and releases it over a few seconds. "Let me see what I can come up with. If you don't hear anything before you're discharged, then come down to the precinct, and we'll discuss it."

He turns, walks to the door, and stops. "You're a good detective, Roberts. I'd hate to lose you over something that others can handle without the exposure."

Both Mie and I are discharged at the same time. Julie picks us up at eleven. They wheel us to the front door. As soon as we're outside in the biting cold, I shiver and duck into the car. At least the storm has passed, and the plows have moved everything off the roads.

We drive back to the apartment, and I change into my work clothes. Julie and Mie talk while I get ready. They quiet down when I come out of the bedroom, and Julie gives Mie a hug before we leave. Looks like another relationship is mended.

The drive to Mie's hotel is uneventful. We park and take the elevator to the business class suites near the top, the floor where the hotel does not book children. It's quiet, secure, and very nice.

Mie has a bedroom, bathroom, and lounge area. Little separates them from each other, so I plop myself down and turn on the TV while Mie heads to the bedroom to change and get ready. She's like me, doesn't take long and ready in less than half an hour. We walk out, and I take note of how everything is in perfect order: bed made, clothes folded and put aside for the maid to clean, bathroom with things everything in it's place. Not something you expect out of a single person. She's no slob, that's for sure.

At the precinct, as the elevator doors open, the whole room hushes up. They're up to something. We walk to our desks and sit down. I tap on my desk to bring up the report I'll need to fill out and see the object of their joke. A cock and ball warmer ad displays on my desk. Sound and everything is turned up.

"...and the warmer is made from real alpaca wool. Guaranteed to keep your member warm and balls swinging easy."

I mute it and close the screen. Laughter erupts in the room. I look up.

Mie is holding a doll with no arms or legs. Its black hair is longer than Mie's, but the doll has Asian features. A note hanging from it says, "The Mie Ling body part replacement factory." She frowns and holds it out for me to see.

Jokes are good. I actually got a good crack out of the one they did on me. But this one is not so funny. The laughter erupts again as the crowd sees Mie's face. I can't let this one go.

"Who's responsible for this?" I ask, holding the doll up. "Tell me now before I get it checked for prints."

Everyone in the squad room looks away. I'm able to narrow down the culprits to three. One of them is Phil. I pick him, knowing my hunch is probably right for the doll is naked.

"Phil, did you do this?" I call out.

"Come on, Bruce. What's wrong with having a little fun?"

"Funny is what you did to me. This thing"–I hold up the doll–"is an insult to a good cop who had a debilitating injury and fought back to overcome it. A moron would have seen how inappropriate this is."

I toss the doll at him. He fumbles to catch it but misses. The doll hits him in the chest and drops into his coffee cup, spilling the liquid all over his shirt. He gives a howl and runs to the bathroom. The coffee must've been hot. I don't care.

"Roberts!" Cap yells from his office door.

I turn to him, too angry to care about being caught in retaliatory action.

"Keep it down, next time. I'm working here." Cap closes his door.

I'm off the hook.

Mie's scowl softens, and she nods to me as we sit back down and fill out our sheets. Paperwork makes the world go 'round. At least it's all electronic. No actual paper wasted, and I get to type instead of write.

"Thank you," Mie says after a few minutes.

"Don't mention it. He's an asshole and shouldn't have been promoted to detective."

"Still, thank you." She doesn't lift her head. "We ask for warrant on Bojing?"

"Filling that out now. Getting ready to send."

"I see it?" she asks.

"If you want." I push away from the desk to let her get a look at the arrest warrant request. Once I send it, we'll get a response from the D.A. who will push it to a judge for signing. Probably take about an hour. From there, we can arrest Bojing. Probably will have to find him first.

"You misspell name," Mie says.

"What? Where?"

"Here." She points. "You have Wong. It Wang."

"Good catch." I type out the correction. "Something like that, unchecked, could lead to a release."

I do a double-check and then send it off. It shouldn't take more than an hour. We have too much evidence against the man to have it take longer.

Two hours go by, and still, nothing shows up. I glance at the request trail and see that three judges have turned down signing, which is strange considering the evidence we have in place. The Fourth judge is the last hope. He's more liberal with his decisions but could cause an issue at trial due to his viewpoint.

"I'm going to call the D.A. and find out what's going on."

"Yes. Getting food. Want something?" Mie asks.

"Sure, whatever you're getting. But take a uniform with you."

I pull up the number for the D.A. and call him on my cell. I hate using the desk interface. People tend to be more abrupt when you call them without face to face. It makes things more efficient. My cell rings through to voice mail, and I leave a message to get back to me. I hang up, and my phone vibrates with a text message.

I know why you're calling. Taking this as far as possible. The judges appear to be compromised in some way. Don't talk about it to anyone. There are ears in your department that are not friendly. I'll contact you once it is signed. D.

It takes two readings to ensure I understand the full meaning of the message. Mie drops a paper bag on my desk and sits down at hers. She pulls out a container and chopsticks. The aroma of ginger and garlic fill the air, and my stomach grumbles. I dig into my bag.

The container holds something I've not seen. Something like noodles but thick. The ginger and garlic mix well, and Mie is digging into hers like no tomorrow, so what the hell. I use the sticks to grab a piece of noodle, but it slips. A hard grasp is needed to put it into my mouth. Spices flood my pallet. I close my eyes and let the food fill my mouth as I chew. The noodle is meat. Probably pork or something, but I can't tell. I open my eyes to see a few of the cops gawking at me.

One of the Asian uniforms stares at me. "You know what you're eating?"

"Don't care, it's good."

My phone vibrates as the warrant comes through the desk.

"We got it, now we have to find him," I say to Mie.

"Find who, detective?" a voice says behind me.

I turn and see a man in a three-piece suit staring at me. What pulls my attention though, is Bojing standing beside him.

January 13th, 2033
— Interrogation

Bojing smiles as drawn weapons pointed toward him. Voices scream for him to put his hands up. He raises his hands in exaggerated slowness. His one hand pulls the zipper down, and the other opens the heavy coat to show he is unarmed.

At least they keep the place warm .

The desire for a cigarette almost makes him fish one. His lawyer holds out shaking hands to the police as if to hold back any possible violence.

Bojing pulls off his gloves and stuffs them into a pocket. Roberts stands, face flushed and angry as he approaches, gun in hand. The lawyer steps between them with an interjecting hand.

"Detective Roberts, please stand down," the lawyer says. "Mr. Wang is here to clear up some misunderstanding. His name is being dragged through the mud because of what is being said about him."

Roberts keeps his gun leveled and steps a little closer. "I suggest you step aside. We have a warrant for Wang's arrest, and he'll be spending a considerable amount of time in a cell."

"No, he won't. He's here to clear his name, and I'm going to make sure that happens. Put your weapon down. You can see he is unarmed."

Bojing steps forward, his hands out at his sides. "I no have weapon. Search if need."

Roberts holsters his gun and steps forward. Bojing opens his coat to show there are no weapons under it, but Roberts pulls him to the desk and pushes him forward. Hands hit the desk, and a foot goes between, forcing them apart.

"You'll spread them and not move while we search."

Rough hands pat Bojing down as rights are read. His possessions are dumped into a container – lighter, cigarettes, gum, wallet, watch, and phone.

"You'll need to voucher those items for my client as he will want them back," the lawyer says.

"If he gets out," Robert shoots back.

"He'll be out in an hour." The lawyer steps forward, card in hand. "Jacobs Smith, defense attorney. I suggest you treat Mr. Wang with respect."

Mie steps forward. "He do much wrong."

"In Canada?" The lawyer looks at Mie's long hair and pretty face with bruises. "We don't have an extradition treaty with China. Besides, he's here of his own free will."

"With a lawyer ready to get him out on bail just like he did the kid," Roberts says. "We're not taking chances. He's going into interrogation room three."

Handcuffs encircle Bojing's wrists, and he straightens up.

"On what charge?" the lawyer asks.

"Kidnapping, attempted murder, assault, and just about anything else I can throw in there," Roberts says.

"Then, you will show me the arrest warrant with that laid out and all pertinent information." The lawyer crosses his arms. "And I expect the cuffs to come off in the interrogation room."

Our interrogation rooms are small, three by four-meter boxes. A table sits in the center, a pair of chairs on either side. Overhead lights shine with intensity. Cameras point from each corner of the ceiling, lights blinking to notify the occupants they're being recorded.

I shove Bojing into the room. He's not resisting, just not moving fast enough for my liking. It could be the busted knee. Sarah really got him good.

Mie follows me in as well as the lawyer and Shan. He's on duty, and it's good to have another set of eyes on what is happening.

Bojing turns his back slightly and lifts the cuffs up to me for them to be undone. I just stare at him.

"Really? After what you did to Mie and me, you really believe I'll un-cuff you?"

"I do nothing. You have wrong man." Bojing smiles.

"We'll see about that." I turn to sit on the opposite side of the table.

"Detective, I want you to un-cuff my client now. He is cooperating fully." The lawyer puts his briefcase on the table and pulls out the two chairs. "Unless you want another civil suit filed against the department."

I hesitate. The threat holds some weight. We usually only keep the hardened criminals in cuffs at this point. Once a lawyer is present, we remove them. I look at Mie, who shakes her head, then at Shan, who gives a frown, but nods. He's right. I fish out my keys and unlock the cuffs.

Bojing rubs his wrists as he sits beside the lawyer and nods a thank you to me. He's smug, all right. But we have him—two witnesses to the crime and records of our cells in the area. The rest is just putting the pieces together, and he's behind bars.

"To start with, I'd like to give you this sworn statement of Mr. Wang's whereabouts on the day in question." The lawyer produces two binders from his case. One he keeps, and the other he pushes to me. "You'll see the signatories are highly respected."

I flip through the paperwork. There's a lot of stuff for someone who just came in to clear his name. I stop at the end page and see the signatures. The first name is Favolopolus. The second name is Judge Williams. The third, our mayor. What the hell? Our mayor? I glance up at the lawyer keeping my face passive to not give anything away. Then I turn back to the first page and start reading. It covers the evening I was in the hospital, and the day he tried to pay me off. All tied into a nice ball of lies. The statements of two public officials will outweigh that of my daughter and me without any collaborating witnesses or evidence of him at the scene.

Through the papers, it seems he's covered for the entire time we were in his hands. Even the raid time is perfect and gives him an alibi. I close the folder.

"This means nothing. He could have had a look-alike stand-in for him," I say.

"We have it on tape. One of the things we ask our clients for is any recordings of their whereabouts. And Mr. Wang has such a recording, time-stamped and authenticated."

I glare at Bojing, who only smiles back at me. "So, you're saying you were not at 4 Cardico Drive on January 12th from 09:00 hours to this morning?"

"He was not," the lawyer says.

"I want to hear the lie from him."

"Mr. Wang is not very good with English, as you may already know." The lawyer glances over at Bojing, and the man nods. "He is also not comfortable with the police, coming from a communist country like he has." The lawyer faces me again. "Because of that, he is having a hard time speaking to you."

"Then he can answer me," Mie says, stepping away from the wall, arms dropping to her side.

The lawyer turns his head sharply to Mie.

"Ne renwai nin de huongyan hui rang nin touli jianyu doujiu," Mie says to Bojing.

That god damned smile just sits on the man's face. Nothing is happening. He nods at Mie and just laughs a little. "Wo bu sahuang, wo he wo de pengyou zai yiqi."

"There, you have it. He was with friends." The lawyer takes the one folder containing the statement and puts it into his briefcase. "Unless you have evidence to show otherwise, I suggest you release my client and drop the charges."

"He's part of the Triad, you know," I say to the lawyer. "If you think they'll not take you down with them, think again. They're killers, cold-blooded and calculating."

The lawyer just smiles back at me.

"All I have to do is link one of these higher-ups somewhere other than with him, and he's away for a long time, then back to China for them to take care of."

"Then until you do that"–the lawyer snaps shut his briefcase–"I suggest you study the law and the rule of evidence. Mr. Wang and I are walking out of here, and unless you want an incident raised and a pending civil suit started, you will release both of us right now."

"We have witnesses," I say.

"Who? You, a cop. And you"–he looks at Mie–"an Interpol agent intent on framing an innocent man?" He shakes his head. "Against a well-respected businessman, a Federal Court Judge, and the Mayor of Toronto? Who would you believe?"

My phone vibrates. I know it's Cap wanting me to bounce the man. We haven't had enough time to comb the crime scene, let alone level any real charges against him. They will appear drummed up and fake against the witnesses they have. We'll need to investigate them as well. But which judge would sign off on an investigation against the bench?

The lawyer points at my phone. "You may want to get that."

I pick up my phone. It's not Cap. It's the judge who signed the warrant.

"Don't make him wait too much longer," the lawyer warns.

I stand, turn my back to the two of them, and answer the phone.

"Detective Roberts," I say.

" Roberts? Do you have Bojing Wang in custody? "

I glance at the caller ID. Judge Micheal Felps.

"Yes, sir. He's here with his lawyer, and we're–"

" Listen to me, Detective. That man is feeding millions of dollars into cancer research. Cancer fucking research. He's funded a wing of the Shriner's Hospital in Quebec for god's sake. " A rattling deep breath full of phlegm is inhaled at the other end. " I was with him last night. There is no way he was involved with anything. I want you to release him with our sincerest apologies. Is that understood? "

"Sir, I was–"

"I don't care. Did you hear what I said, or do I have to call the Chief and have him relieve you of duty?"

My phone vibrates in my pocket. I ignore it. The desk screen is blank, and there are still forms to fill out on what happened with Bojing and the lawyer. I really don't want anything to do with police work right now.

Having the wind taken out of your sails really makes for a lousy afternoon. I think Mie feels it as well. We have our sworn statements but also statements from three officials who will trump what we have to say. The whole thing stinks. Bojing is getting away with it, and there's nothing we can do. And to try to get it done today will kill the evening plans Julie and I have for being together.

A message lights up my desk. William Louis III has sent an active message for me. I open it, and all I can see are the words "Pick Up!"

My phone vibrates again.

I want to ignore it, but it could be important. I answer.

"Roberts speaking."

"Roberts. Louis here. What the hell happened?"

Crap. I recount the fifteen minutes we had Bojing and his lawyer in the interview room to him. There's nothing more to be said. Just wait for the downfall.

"Roberts, I want you to get out of the precinct now. We have to talk, and they're monitoring. Do you live nearby?"

"No, up in Markham... Who's monitoring?"

"Damn. No time to explain. We need to meet. Text me your address."

I type in my address. "What are we doing?"

"We'll talk soon. I'll send you a time. Probably tomorrow."

Sunday. I'll need to get Mie involved. "How about Mie?"

"Yes, if she can be there, that would be best."

The text came in later that day to meet at my place around one. Gives me just enough time to get Sarah out of the home and to a girlfriend's. Julie is working, so don't have to worry about her being around and asking questions.

I'm just sitting watching TV—nothing much on Sunday. I have the streaming service pushing an old movie to me, and coffee is warming. A commercial comes on advertising cheap vacations to Cuba and how wonderful it is down there. The last time I went was on my honeymoon. Food was okay, but I didn't like being asked about buying cigars from everyone on the beach. Never did trust those locals.

A knock on the door brings me around. Must have dozed off or something. The time shows 12:50 pm. The guy is early. Mie's not even here. But how did he get into the building without being buzzed in? Maybe someone went out—

The knock repeats.

I cross over to the door and hit the viewer. Mie stands there, arm lifted to rap again. I open the door.

"Asleep?" she asks.

"Can you tell?"

She points to my hair. Must be standing up or something. "At least I'm dressed."

A little smile crosses her lips. Must be growing on her. She never smiles at anything, not really. Familiarity breeds contempt, they say. She walks in carrying a few bags in one hand, and drops them to the floor to take off her coat.

"What's in the bags?"

"Food." She picks them up and goes to the kitchen. I follow out of habit. A dog looking for crumbs.

"I have food here, you know. Teenagers and all. Kinda need to keep the fridge stocked."

"This for me." She opens the bags and takes out a bunch of stuff I don't recognize. All have Chinese writing on them.

"Where'd you get this stuff?"

"Chinese market down street. Good, most. You need watch. They have out of date food there. Chicken smell bad. I get duck."

She pulls out a duck, still in the package. I recognize it. King Cole.

"Did you go to their outlet?"

"Yes. Long drive. Almost lost. GPS help. No drive off cliff." She smiles and puts the duck into the sink. "You got sharp knife?"

I point to the knife block. "They should be sharp."

"Need bowl. Big one. Big pot. Chopping board."

I fish out what she needs and stand aside. She's good in the kitchen. I just let her do what she does.

The phone rings. I walk into the living room, and the lobby camera is on William. He's bundled up but still wearing a suit. A briefcase is in one hand, and he looks around everywhere but at the camera. I hit the talk.

"Louis, I'll ring you in. Come up to the twelfth floor. Door twenty to the left."

"Be right up," he says and puts a hand on the door.

I buzz it open and wait until the door closes. The screen returns to normal. Some fishing show resumes.

Chopping comes from the kitchen, and I return. Mie is finishing dressing the duck. It's all in pieces and going into the pot with water. The stove is set to boil. She's putting other things in the pot as well.

"Louis is coming up." I motion to the pot. "How long will this take?"

"Not long. Few minute to boil. Once ready, make taste good." She throws more vegetables into the pot. "Mother taught me soup good on cold day. Today cold."

I nod like a bobblehead. Soup is always good.

The pot boils. She has it at the max to make it come up fast. A quick twist, and it's back to simmer. More ingredients go into the pot, and I take in the aroma of fresh food.

A knock on the door brings me back to the moment. I cross to the living room and check the door camera. Louis is there. I open the door, and he hurries in like a man worried he's being followed.

"You okay?" I ask him.

"No." He shucks off his coat, and I take it. "Damn near driven off the road by kids driving daddy's car. How do you drive so far every day?"

"It's not so bad. You get used to it." I hang up his coat. "The hard part is in the summer when all the bikers are out."

Louis looks shocked. "You have bike gangs up here?"

I shake my head. "Not bike gangs. Bicyclists. They never share the road, especially up north, where you may want to drive because of no transit."

Louis nods. "Any place to sit?"

I point to the dining area just off the living room. He walks to the table and puts his briefcase on it.

"Smells good, whatever it is," he says.

"Duck noodle soup," Mie says.

Louis opens his briefcase and pulls out a little square plastic box; it's like a cell phone only thicker. He puts a finger to his lips as he flips it on. The box lights up. "My Mom used to make soup all the time." He's talking louder than needed as he waves the device in a circle. "It helps on a cold day." The lights on the device go red, and he walks toward the clock we have on the wall. "Is that a family recipe?"

"Yes. Mother taught. I make when day like today."

Louis puts the device in his pocket and takes the clock off the wall. "My mother said the same thing." He checks the back of it and pulls out a small tab-like piece of plastic before putting the clock back. The device is out of his pocket, and he's moving about the room. "did your mother teach you to make dumplings as well?"

"Yes. But Bruce not have steamer, so I no make."

The device goes nuts again with the lights—this time near the TV. Louis motions me to help him move it a little.

"You don't really need a steamer, you know. Just a pot with water and a strainer to hold the dumplings in."

We pull the TV out quietly, and he comes up with another plastic tab thing. I start to say something, but he just shakes his head.

"I try later if you like. Lot of food."

He keeps circling the rooms: kitchen, living room, dining room, and bedrooms. After half an hour of small talk with Mie, who doesn't bat an eye at what he's doing or what he finds, we have twenty of the tab things on the table. He pulls out a small box from his briefcase and opens it.

The lid sits on the table, and he puts the tabs into it. He motions to me to turn off the TV.

"Well, that soup is good, but I have something to show you in my car. Come with me." He stands up, goes to the door, opens it for a few seconds, and then closes it. Walking lightly, he goes to the table, puts the tabs in the box, closes the lid, and sits down, shoulders slumping.

"Okay, now we can talk."

January 13th, 2033 – Private

Crisp air bites at Bojing as he walks from the lawyer's office to the waiting car. A smile touches his lips as the driver opens the door. The simple pleasures of life far outweigh the responsibilities. He slides inside, and the door is closed.

"Where to, sir," the young man asks.

"Home," Bojing says.

Home, the top floor of a high-end apartment building overlooking the busy streets of Highway 7 and Birchmount Road. The Triad paid for the building and gave Bojing the penthouse, providing him with a semi-private elevator so he could come and go without being noticed.

"Call Ping and tell him to have something special waiting for me. Two... no, three girls. Make them young with blonde hair."

"Yes, sir."

He hits the privacy button, and the window between him and the driver rolls up. The small cabin of the vehicle falls silent. He is encased in armor. Nothing can penetrate the walls around him. Plating thicker than his finger now separates the outside and inside. He reaches over and increases the heat. Stupid country. Cold most months and freezing the others.

Time to listen in.

Bojing takes out his phone and plugs it into the vehicle's system. He engages the app and waits. Last report, the cop, and Interpol agent were meeting today. About one, they said.

Chopping sounds. Small talk. Three are in the apartment. Louis? Who is that? He turns up the sound. Someone is cooking. Another is moving about. Roberts is not talking. The door opens and then closes. Nothing but silence follows.

He waits, straining his ears to pick up anything from the bugs planted in the apartment. Nothing. Not even the sound of the wind he usually hears. He pulls up the menu and checks reception. No signal. The bugs are not transmitting any more.

Bojing slams his fist against the window.

I stare at the box on the table.

"Okay, Louis. What the hell is that?" I ask.

Mie walks into the room and glances at the box. "Faraday cage." She walks back to the kitchen, and dishes clang together.

"She's right," Louis says. "A Farris cage. It blocks the sending and receiving of electronic signals. Your home was bugged."

My head spins. How and when was my place bugged? By who? Why? There's no reason for it. What are they going to get? Sarah watching TV? Then it hits me.

"Bojing," I say.

"Probably. Or his gang." Louis puts the box into his briefcase. "You're going to need better security."

"You think someone's bugged the precinct as well?"

"I don't doubt it. And my office." He takes the little electronic box out of his pocket. "I found more than this in my building just last week. Seems someone is very snoopy for information. Happened when we started getting reports of run-a-ways. More than we usually get."

I put my chin in a palm. The situation makes more sense now. Bojing has always been one step ahead of us. If he's bugged my house, he's bugged the department, and maybe... I think back to the China Girl that played into my mind. God. If that is what's happening here, we should see more bodies...

"Can we trace the signal?" I ask.

"No. These bugs are using a small electromagnetic field to transmit. They have a range of about fifty meters, and a booster does the rest of the work. No telling where that is. It only amplifies the signal, and that signal can be picked up for about thirty kilometers."

Mie comes into the room and puts a bowl of soup in front of us. The aroma is strong, almost sweet. It calls up memories of warm summer days by the lake before the contamination got too bad. Two spoons are dropped on the table.

"Thinking always better on full stomach."

I grab a spoon and dig into the bowl. Never been one to like waterfowl, but the duck is perfect. Leafy vegetables along with a slightly salty taste of soy mix well with whatever else is in the thing. I look up at Mie, who has joined us with her own bowl. "This is fantastic. Julie would love this."

"Lot in pot." She slurps up vegetables.

"I'm impressed," Louis says. "Best I've tasted in a long time."

"Thank you."

We eat in silence, each enjoying the meal. It warms my stomach and gives me a better focus on the problem at hand. How to get the Triad. How to stop the kidnappings. How to lock away Bojing.

"I think you guys put a dent in Bojing's operations this week." Louis sets his spoon in the bowl. "He'll need to regroup and get a new base."

"So, you believe in what we've done so far?" I ask.

"Yes." He pushes the bowl away. "Can you imagine how much scrambling the Triad needed to do in order to get that alibi letter made up? The favors they called in? What they now owe to those people? Yes, the kid's father signed without thinking, but the Judge and Mayor. Hell, I'm going to start digging into those two on Monday."

I finish the last of my bowl. "The Judge will be the problem. He's well connected."

"But if I do it right, people will start distancing themselves from him. Let the office hear a few snippets of what I'm looking into. I'll start with bank accounts, then relationships, and pull a warrant for investment information. People build their own little conspiracy theories when they hear a person's investments and friends are being tracked."

"We don't want to tip our hand," I say. "We have so much information right now, and the names listed on the affidavit have given us a lot to go on."

"I get China office apply pressure," Mie says.

I think about it. The investigation from the D.A.'s office will back the gang into a corner while pressure in China will pull resources back from them. But if they have a lot of resources...

"Can you get a dump of their internet traffic?" I ask.

"What you think?" Mie asks.

I feel the itching of a plan coming up. "You remember when we found the device on Sarah?"

Mie nods.

"That one night, Sarah's system got a download. A huge download. Like maybe a whole movie. Never thought much of it." I get up and go into my bedroom. The China Girl rig is locked away in my gun safe. I open it and pull out the device. The download is complete. I walk back into the dining area. "Here. It was downloaded on the 12th. The IP address the file came from is recorded in the phone's log."

"What the hell is that?" Louis asks.

I look at him and grimace. "A parent's worst nightmare."

Louis lies on my couch. The China Girl rig fits on his head. The interface in the band hits just the correct spots, according to Mie. I watch the man. He appears to be asleep, but I know better. The immersive playback has his mind locked down with whatever is being played for him. His body offers a few twitches and responds to the stimuli.

The phone's battery discharges at an alarming rate without a charger attached, but that's better than tearing the unit off. It could take him a few hours to recover if that happened. But I watch, making sure nothing interrupts the playback unexpectedly.

Thirty minutes in, the battery dies, and Louis blinks his eyes open.

He's dazed, but we help him up and to a chair. He shakes, eyes wide and face ashen. Tears stream, and he buries his head in his hands. After a minute, he glances from Mie to me without blinking.

"What the hell was that?" he asks.

"I don't know. Didn't watch it," I say.

"I was laying there"—he points to the couch—"and then I'm in this large room. It was cold. No clothes on, and a bunch of people standing around a bed. They kept chanting 'fuck her' to me." He takes a deep breath, and Mie hands him a glass of water.

"It was intense. Then they parted and the girl. Oh god. She was tied up spread eagle, and as I approached her, men patted me on the back. It was like I was there doing it, but I couldn't control what was happening." He stops for a few seconds trying to gather his thoughts. "I fucked her. My hands went to her neck, and she screamed. God did she scream."

"What happened after that?" I asked.

"I... I could feel the life leaving her body as I squeezed her throat. Then it stopped, and I saw both of you watching me."

"Battery run out," Mie says. "Record go to killing girl when cum."

Louis swallows. "Fuck."

"It's the China Girl technology out of China. From what you explained, it was a ritual the Triad perform to initiate a new member into the 49ers." I pick up the device. "From what Mie has told me, the device links into the brain using magnetic and electronic stimulation and overrides the user's basic connections from the body. This allows you to relive the experience of the person who wore it."

Louis reaches out for the device then pulls his hand back. "God. Something that could be used for so much good. Used now for porn. No, for snuff films."

"They actually sell the footage," I say.

"I'm going to be sick." Louis holds his stomach and leans forward.

"I'll get a bucket unless you can make it to the bathroom," I say.

"No, I'll be okay." He looks up at Mie. "How did you get involved in this?"

Mie returns his gaze. "They took me when young."

I've seen people pale before, but Louis loses all the blood from his face. He swallows. "But you're alive?"

"They only start killing year ago."

Her face is deadpan. The same expression she had on when she met me. I don't think she likes talking about her own experience, but most people would be better off knowing there is real evil out there. I desperately want her to talk to Sarah about what they put her through. It will add just that much more of a reason for her to be safe.

"I'm sorry." He motions to Mie's arms and legs. "That's why you have them?"

Mie stands. "I have them from Father. I have this from them." She disconnects an arm and pulls back her sleeve to show Louis the stump with the connecting socket. A few lights blink. "The limbs help heart. They injure me and heart bad."

"They act as a pacemaker?" I ask, making sure I understand their full function.

"Yes. Monitor heart and blood and body. Make small adjustment to beating. Check to ensure blood clean."

"They really did a number on you," Louis says.

Mie nods. "Yes."

"Cyber Crime Unit didn't know how to turn on one of these units until Mie came along. She advanced their knowledge of China Girl. They owe her a lot. We just haven't gotten the word out that we know what these are. Keeping our cards close to our chest."

Louis shakes the cell phone and playback headset in front of him. "This is going to change everything." He stands up, wavers a little, but becomes steady. "We can really put them away if we can link them to this. Crap, I didn't see any faces. Those around me all wore masks, except the girl."

"Like I said, if we can link them to the IP used to distribute the stuff, then we can link them to the murders and kidnappings. It would help if we could find a body as well."

"How are they getting rid of the bodies?" Louis wonders.

"Burn. Acid for bone." Mie sits down on the couch.

"If they burn the body, it would still leave a trace. Maybe acid period. If they can reduce it to sludge then neutralize the acid, they can use an industrial dump site to get rid of it. No DNA would survive the acid bath."

Louis brings out his phone.

"What are you doing?" I ask.

"I'm VPNing to the office. Going to email the medical examiner to find out what type of acid is needed to liquefy a body, and if there are restrictions on it."

"Stop," I say. "It'll be seen."

"I'm using our VPN. They can't trace that."

"Right, but they have been bugging. They may have something to intercept your emails and route copies of them. It wouldn't be an issue for someone to do that if they've been able to get bugs into your office."

He stops typing. "You're right. I'll actually go over and talk to him."

"We need to keep our communications on this low tech. They have the ability to bug us. We'll need to set up a schedule to meet, so they don't intercept phone calls." I look at my watch. "Crime doesn't sleep. We should work on this as much as possible. Louis, can you get that list from the M.E. quick?"

"Call me Bill." He smiles. "I can sit on his lap until he runs the information. But I don't think it will come to that.

"Okay, Lou... I mean, Bill. You have that on your plate. Mie and I will go through the missing children's file and see if any of them match what the bastards like to have. They seem to prey on young women of a certain type. Just have to run it from what we know they've been after. At least we have a few models to go on."

"Most like skinny girls, long hair." Mie picks up Bill's glass and walks it to the kitchen.

"We have a lot of research to do." I stand. "Can I get one of those gizmos from you?"

"The bug sniffer? Yeah, take this one. I can pick up another one on the way to the office."

He hands over the device and gives me a quick demo. The thing is easy to work, even charges with a USB port.

"How far do you think the Triad's corruption goes?" I ask Bill.

"Far." He takes a deep breath. "Don't trust anyone. Not even someone you've worked with for a long time." He picks up his briefcase and heads to the door. "Since this has been underground and deeply buried for so long, the cockroaches will scatter as we shine a light. People could have been bought and paid for a long time ago only to keep them in their back pocket. I suggest scanning the apartment every day if you go out for any length of time, just to make sure. Maybe install a camera."

"You better do it too. Do you have a gun?" I ask.

"No, just a protection detail if needed... Shit, you don't think..."

I nod. "As you say, they could have paid off anyone at any time. Better to be your own protector than trust someone who could be paid off. Know how to use a gun?"

"Not really." He rubs the back of his neck. "Never had any reason to do so."

I reach into the closet and open the gun safe. A Beretta is there. Nothing too elaborate.

"Here." I hand him the weapon. "Semi-automatic. Low recoil. Safety is there. Make sure you use it. The trigger is a two position. One unlocks the other part releases the firing pin. Meet me at the range tomorrow, and I'll go over how to use it without shooting your foot off."

Bill takes the weapon and examines it. He flips the safety on and off to ensure a knowledge that most don't have. I show him the clip release and hand him a few loads.

"Something you should know," I say. "Most people freeze when they have a gun in their hand. The gun is only an extension. Don't always count on it. Remember to keep your distance from the person. If they get too close to you, the gun will be useless."

"Keep at a distance. Don't freeze." He put the safety on.

"People always pull the trigger. This takes the gun's aim point off. Pulling it hard or with a jerky movement will cause the round to go off in the direction of your tug. If you're right-handed, the round will go to the right. If you're left, it goes left. Be aware and breathe."

"Breathe, right."

"And for the most part, if you aim at something, you should be ready to squeeze the trigger. Having the gun out means you're in danger of being killed. Don't hesitate to use it."

"I won't. Anything else?"

I put a hand on his shoulder. "If you're not licensed to carry, you're breaking the law. Keep it hidden. Don't put it in your belt, or you'll shoot off your dick."

He laughs.

"I'm serious. It's happened to a lot of gang members over the years, and they handle guns all the time. Don't be the one who shoots his dick off."

"Okay, I hear you on that one."

I take a deep breath. "The gun has no serial number. It's highly illegal. If you're caught with it, you'll be put in jail. We all know what that means to your career as a D.A., right?"

He nods. "I'm screwed."

"So, if someone makes you, use it, wipe it down, and toss it away. The bottom of a garbage bin that's full is the best place. Beat cops do most of the searching for evidence. They hate jumping into the bins to search if they don't know there's something in it. After that, look for a sewage grate and toss it in there if you need to. Don't worry about it being traced to you or me. If your prints aren't on it, you'll be safe." I look him in the eye. "Do you have any questions?"

He stares into my eyes. "No, but I think you do."

I shake my head. "Not at this time. Just be safe, will you, Bill?"

January 14th, 2033 – Frustration

I t takes two delivery men an hour to bring in the new desk and remove the old one. Bojing does not smile. His hand trembles slightly while he works. The hook-ups slide into place, and the men exit carrying the old desktop, careful not to slice their hands on the shattered remains of the supposed shatterproof glass top.

"I need you to sign that the desk is hooked up and working to your satisfaction," the large delivery man says, holding out a datapad.

Bojing ignores the pad presented to him and walks around to the desk. He starts up the embedded computer system, and he goes through the initialization steps. In three minutes, he's typing in his code name and connecting to the VPN servers the Triad keeps backup information on. Data streams into the desk as the base operating system with all the spyware and advertising is overwritten by a base Centos Twelve operating system and rebooted.

"You know that voids the warranty," the delivery man says.

He does not look up but keeps typing information and passwords as the system reboots and comes back online.

Satisfied, Bojing takes the pad and scribbles his signature on it. He hands it back to the delivery man, who puts it into a pocket.

"Yes?" Bojing asks.

"Sir, it may be none of my business, but the tops of these desks are pretty strong." The man rubs the back of his neck. "It takes a good amount of weight to break one, or a really strong blow with a hammer."

"Your Point?" Bojing asks.

"Well, I've only had to replace one of these desks in the six years I've worked for the company. That time, it was destroyed in a fire. I'm just curious. What happened?"

Bojing turns back to the desk. "That all?"

The man holds his spot for a few seconds before turning and grasping the other end of the ruined desk.

"Thank you for shopping at Microsoft," he says over his shoulder. He grunts, lifting his side of the desk and hauls it out of the room.

Ping clears his throat from the doorway.

"Come in." Bojing checks the download of his personal files. He should just keep them on-site instead, but something about the security of the VPN connection makes him more relaxed.

"We haven't been able to secure the home of the cop. From what we can tell, the bugs have all been swept."

Bojing drops into his seat, steeples his hands, and leans back. "He knows."

"Yes, sir. That's what we believe as well."

I need a cigarette.

Bojing looks at Ping, but the man is out of cigarettes as well. The shipment expected on Friday with a fresh supply of his habit is still tied up with customs and won't be released until Monday at the earliest. All the cigarettes from home are smoked. He owes a number of packs to his men. And as a matter of honor, he will pay them back—every one of them.

"You remember the tracking numbers?" Bojing asks.

"Yes, I have them here." Ping steps forward and pulls out his phone. After a swipe, he lays it on the desk in front of Bojing.

"Can you send someone out to get more cigarettes for me?" Bojing asks.

Ping nods, reaches back a hand, and snaps his fingers. A young man, maybe twenty, with a short buzz cut rushes in.

"Go to the island reserve, Port Perry. Island Road, you'll find a store called Smoke Shack. Get five... no, ten cartons of deadheads."

The young man smiles, showing crooked and tobacco-stained teeth.

"Hide them from view and don't smoke on the way out. It's illegal to take the cigarettes off the reserve, and the cops may be out and watching."

The smile fades from the man's face, and he gives a slight bow before turning and running out of the office.

Ping turns back. Bojing looks at him with a raised eyebrow.

"Some of the men say the place is as close to the cigarettes from home." Ping opens his hands in front of him. "Cheap too."

"You forget something."

Ping looks to the ground both left and right as if searching for something. "What?"

"He will drive right past the Casino."

The gun jumps a little in my hands as I fire off five rounds.

"Clear," I say while opening the breach and placing the weapon on the small table in front of me, muzzle still pointing away from us. The target starts its way up range, and I take off my ear protectors.

"Nice shooting," Bill says.

The grouping is okay, but nothing spectacular: three rounds center mass and two just off to the left.

"Could be better." I take down the target and put up a new one. "Your turn." I point to the weapon on the table next to mine. Same small handgun I gave him the day before. Light but still lethal. Enough to put someone down but not if they're wearing a vest. "Remember what I told you."

"Act as if the weapon is loaded and ready to fire at all times." He picks up the gun and checks the breach, then the clip. "So, when do I get real bullets?"

"After you fire about a hundred rubber ones," I tell him.

The target goes down range ten meters. I hand him a clip.

"Here's your first five."

He takes it and pulls the empty clip from the gun, slamming the practice one into the butt.

"You're right," I say.

"About what?"

"You've never really done this before."

He frowns at me. "How can you tell?"

"People don't slam clips into their weapons. It's a good way to get a jam or misfire. Just slide the clip in till you hear a click. That tells you it's in place."

"But what if I'm in a hurry?"

"Don't rush it. The last thing you need is having a misfire or jam while in a firefight. Take your time and remove the possible problem before it happens. Aim at the chest."

"Oh," he says and releases the breach, pushing a round into the firing chamber.

I put my headset back on and tap him on the shoulder. He squeezes off a round and winces. He puts his ear protectors on.

"You could have said something about that," he yells at me.

"What? How can you hear me after firing without ear protectors on?" I grin at him. "Better to learn like this than to have me try and drill it into you. Besides, now you know how loud they can be."

He squeezes off four more rounds and puts the gun down beside mine. I wait. Bill looks at me.

"Well?" he asks.

I just stare at him. It takes a few seconds, then he calls out, "Clear!"

We remove our ear protectors.

"Range safety is no joke. If you don't do it, someone will get hurt."

The target stops in front of us. Nothing hit it.

"Well, you don't have to be a good shot if you can talk your way out," I say.

"Funny," Bill replies. "So, what did I do wrong?"

"You pulled when you should have squeezed."

He stares at me for a few seconds, then shakes his head. "No, honestly. What did I do wrong?"

I hit the return switch, and the target travels down range. Before he knows it, I've got my Glock in hand and ear protectors on. He scrambles to catch up to me. The clip slides into the receiver, and I release the breach, loading a round. I pull the trigger back, look at him, then squeeze it. The light goes on behind his eyes.

"So, you just squeeze then?"

"Right. When you pull, the gun will jerk depending on which hand you have it in. Squeezing will keep the gun lined up on your target."

I put down my gun, and he picks his up. Five rounds are fired at the target, which I then bring back up to the table. One shot is center mass while the others are a little scattered, but four of the bullets actually hit this time.

"How many more?" he asks.

"Until I'm satisfied you won't shoot your foot off. About a hundred more rounds."

Mie walks into the small range and puts on ear protectors. She comes up to us and examines the target with a critical eye.

"You shoot?" she asks Bill.

"Not until today," he replies. "First time on a range as well."

She puts a new target on the clips and sends it down range. Before either of us says anything, she pulls out a large pistol that looks like a cross between a desert eagle and magnum .45. I've not seen her carry that gun before. She fires off six rounds from the hand cannon without her hands moving. The concussion from the shots echoes in the range for a second and hurts my ears. She must be hunting tanks with that thing.

Bill just glares at her as she brings the target back. I let out a short whistle at what I see. Two holes center mass, two holes in the forehead, and two holes in the crotch.

Bill fires the last round in the clip down range and hits the target. He's getting a little smug, now that he has over fifty rounds fired. The air is thick with burnt gun powder, and my head pounds from the uneven firing pattern of a rookie.

The target comes up range, and I look at the grouping. He's doing better. Most of the shots are within twenty centimeters of each other.

"Keep that up, and you'll be at Mie's level in no time," I say.

Mie smirks and sends her last target down range. The cannon goes off eight times - a full clip. As the target comes back, I smile. Looks like only three hit, but that can't be right. I call up the target's camera footage on the monitor. There's always a high speed one at the end of the range to capture shots in case someone contests the shooting during a competition. After watching, I let my jaw drop. All eight shots went into the center mass hole she put in the target.

"Fuck," Bill says. "If we need to be in a firefight, I want her on my side."

Mie holds out her cannon, but first to Bill. "You try?"

Bill takes the thing with tentative fingers. As she lets go, the gun dips.

"A lot heavier than I expected," he says.

"Yes, much." She sends another target down range and hands over a clip. "Do not blow foot off."

When the target stops, Bill lifts the weapon up and points down range. He squeezes. His hands jerk back, almost bringing the post on the muzzle to his head. He puts the gun down and massages his wrist.

"I'm not going to fire that again. Damn near tore my hand off my wrist."

Mie looks at me and nods to her weapon. "You try?"

I put my hands up. "Not me. I know when not to play in a sandbox."

Her left brow furrows, and the right one arcs up. "I think you joke."

"Yeah, but not a good one," Bill says, jabbing at me. "Not man enough to shoot your partner's gun?"

I glance at the weapon. It's a gorgeous pistol, but I know when something is bigger than me. "Nope. Not man enough." I give Mie a wink.

"So, I man?" Mie stands, hands on her hips.

Crap! Sounds like she's been talking to Julie too much. A topic change is needed.

"We need to talk," I say.

Mie nods, and Bill looks around nervously. "I'll need to sweep."

"Don't worry. The room is clear of surveillance." I motion to the walls. "The range is soundproof, and the walls will stop even Mie's hand cannon. Check your cell to see if you have a signal."

He pulls out his phone and swipes it a little. "No signal, but this is not the be-all and end-all of checking. The device I gave you yesterday will pick anything up."

"Yes, it would. That's why I swept the area before you got here. And even if they could bug this place, we fired off enough rounds that anyone listening would be deaf by now."

Bill stops messaging his wrists. "I've started digging into the financial records of the Judge and Mayor. It isn't easy without a warrant, and keeping it quiet is another thing."

I understand how difficult it is to keep an investigation under wraps. We'll have to pressure James Favolopolus and his father somehow without doing much investigating. The one thing Bill has at his disposal is the records from the public offices. A routine check to uncover any anomalies.

Bill glances up between Mie and me. "Do you have anything new?"

I look at Mie, who nods. She pulls out her cell and puts it on the table.

"Here is Favolopolus home." A holograph jumps out from the screen and hovers there ten centimeters high. "Layout normal but for one wall." She points to what appears to be a study. "False wall from measurement. Something behind. Maybe a meter deep."

"Records?" I ask.

"Maybe. Not sure. Need get in to look."

"We need a warrant," Bill says.

"Yeah, but when?" I lean forward. Mie brings up another menu.

"Guard on ground and in house. Big house, but not for area. Two-acre lot and right in middle." She pushes out the view until we see the whole map. "Guard walk around even in winter. They armed rifle. Twenty minute sometimes, other time more or less. Stagger. You not know. Professional."

I nod. We try to teach cops on guard duty to keep their time staggered. Do stuff on the strange hours like 1:43 or something. Never make a pattern. It can be predictable.

"Alarm inside," Mie says. "Keypad and blue tooth activate. We clone phone and we in."

Great, clone a phone. How the hell are we going to do that? I look to the other two. "We need some tech."

They both nod.

Nygen's Technology is on the corner of Sheppard and Yonge. It's across the street from the McDonald's and diagonal from the Yonge Sheppard Center. Nothing really to write home about, but the guy is known on the streets to have the best tech there is for any job – and not the legal ones. Metal bars decorate the front of his shop, and the door is a steel alloy composite with internal locks. I hit the buzzer to see if anyone's in, but nothing happens. Snow coats my shoulders and feet. The big fluffy flakes that are terrible for snowballs unless a little melted.

I bang on the door and ring the bell again. The shop has to be open.

"Hello?" a voice says over a tinny speaker.

"Nygen. Open up. We need something," I say.

A screen lights up, and an old Asian face looks back at me. "What you want? I no deal with pigs." He reaches up to shut off the camera.

"No, we're not really pigs. I'm a detective, and we're looking for something special," I say.

"Special? Like illegal? I no deal illegal."

The screen goes off. I lean against the door and mumble a little. Mie places a hand on my arm.

"We get Bojing other way."

The monitor flickers on. "You say Bojing?"

"Yes," Mie says. "Bojing. We need tech to get him."

An angry woman's voice yells at Nygen, and he responds in kind. It carries on for several exchanges until the man gives the finger to someone off-screen.

"Wife not want you in. I want Bojing Wang gone. Come in."

With a buzz I push the door open.

I don't know what to expect, but the level of technology in the shop stifles me. There are drones of all sizes, even ones with a section to hold a revolver. Cameras point all over the store, and TV screens show us from different angles. Even angles I'm not able to see a camera pointing at. Pens with stickers explaining how long a recording they can store and little sticky cameras lay in a display case. I wonder if I'll see any of the bugs that were in my apartment.

Nygen motions me forward and leans in. "Bojing run racket. All shops pay up but me. Wife want to just pay but we not go out but to shop food. No one get me. Lot of camera to record what happen. Safe for now."

I nod. "I need a specific piece of technology."

Nygen smiles and holds out his arms. "Sure, you got it! What you need. I have."

"Cell cloner."

Nygen's hands drop. "No. Illegal. Me legit businessman. No illegal."

I bark a laugh. "Half the stuff I see here is illegal."

"Yes, but not for sale," he says.

"I don't have time for this." I take out my gun and slap it on the display case. "Look, I need to clone a cell phone, and I know you have the device here somewhere. I'll buy it, but in order to do that, you'll need to show it to me."

"No clone." He holds up his arms. "No need. All on cloud."

He wriggles away from me over to a computer. "Here, Google server. I run backup farm for them. Just need name and find record. Image of phone there. Download and install overlay from current phone. No clone needed."

I should have thought of the cloud. Of course, we could get everything we need from them if they're using specific phones.

"Peter Favolopolus. 21 Country Estates Dr."

Nygen takes his hands off the keyboard.

"Well?"

"Feng kuang de bai ren nan ren cao ni," he says, gaze darting from me to Mie.

"Zun zhong ta ren," Mie says.

I glance at Nygen. "You'll have to excuse my partner. Maybe you didn't know that she speaks Chinese, and you thought she was born here. But no, she's on loan from Interpol and has a very short temper."

Nygen swears, but his fingers start typing. It only takes a second.

"Here he is." He points to the screen. "Phone Google Fi Foe. I have one. Expensive. Big value on data. Take while to load."

"I thought you said it would be no problem?"

"No problem to make copy. Data encrypted in storage. Need break encryption before load phone. You have time?"

January 14th, 2033
- Crossing a Line

The car rolls onto the street as Bojing lights a cigarette. Smoke curls as tobacco catches fire, and the familiar sting of nicotine rolls in his mouth. Finally, a good cigarette.

Another evening of the white stuff. I cannot live in this weather. Snow rushes across the road as the wind picks up. It is a headache to travel in.

Bojing hits the button to lower the privacy glass. The driver glances into the rearview mirror with a raised eyebrow.

"Home, sir?"

Bojing just stares out the window, wishing for summer to come soon. "No. Take me to dancers."

"Club Pro or Whiskey, sir?"

"Whiskey."

The vehicle turns left, and Bojing raises the privacy glass.

Bojing wants breasts in his face. A skinny young thing naked on his lap. Someone he can talk into coming home with him. The three Ping brought him did nothing to satisfy his desires. There were too many girls to strangle. They left, and his blood lust went unsatisfied. If he can just get one woman to come back with him... The lure of money works on most girls, but not all. He will have to spend a lot to get the woman interested. It always takes a lot.

The vehicle glides over the road as Bojing reaches into the hidden compartment and takes out a China Girl viewer. He thinks back to the girl they captured a week ago. She was nice, but giving her to a 49er for initiation was a mistake. She could have been a better draw with someone who lasted longer.

He puts the device on, plugs it into an outlet, and slips the memory card into place–a little something to occupy his mind during the drive.

The cigarette burns between his fingers, totally forgotten as he immerses himself in the playback, and the joy of taking Mie Ling for the second time, ultimately leaving her defenseless, plays in his mind from the device.

The limo slides on the snow. The pumping sound of antilock brakes fills the cab. Swearing comes through the sound deadening privacy glass as the limo fishtails until it jerks to a stop with a crunch of metal against metal.

Bojing swears as he turns off the feed. His arm is sore from being twisted in the seatbelt. Fire races up the limb, telling him nothing is broken, but an injury sears through the muscles. He looks out the window at the tailgate of an F150, all white with chrome bumpers. The yell of a man from outside makes its way into the cabin. The door to the truck opens, and a man standing over two meters gets out and approaches the limo. The man turns his face to the back of the truck, then back to the limo. He comes up to the passenger side and knocks on the window.

"Fuckin' slant eyed asshole!" the man screams. "Someone take your test for you? That why you hit me?"

Bojing lowers his outside window. "We okay. No help need."

The man's face reddens. He approaches the back and leans down to eye Bojing with cigarette recovered and in his mouth. The truck driver hesitates a second, then continues to the back of the limo, meaty hands clenched into fists.

"Who's going to fix my truck?"

Bojing sits up, examines the truck through the front window, and then looks to the man dismissively. "No damage your car. Mine have dent."

"I don't care what you think you see. My truck is brand new! Still got the new car smell. Yours, on the other hand"–the man presses against the frame–"needs paint and shit. I'm not leaving until you come out and look it over with me. I need your insurance and the driver's information."

"Car still drive-able?" Bojing asks the driver in a hushed voice.

"Yes, sir."

Bojing takes papers from the folder beside him and holds them out to the window. The man comes over and reaches out for them. A shot shatters through the air. The man tumbles back and to the ground—a small line of blood pools behind the head with eyes staring up to the heavens.

"Drive," Bojing says.

We get the cell phone just as dusk falls. No better time than the present to cross the line. It's not the first and won't be the last. Maybe we'll have a little more authority in the future, but criminals seem to have more rights than their victims.

Snow falls but not like the last few days. Plows roll out to clean up, and that'll make for slow driving. Best to get things over with. I turn to Mie, and she walks toward her car. I don't mind her driving. Julie usually makes me drive everywhere we go. That means a lot of staying sober, even if the party is for one of my friends or me. The silly thing is she rarely drinks.

Getting out of the parking lot is difficult. The steady flow of traffic heading north makes taking a left turn near impossible. It's the way Mie decided to go. I would have suggested Sheppard then left on Yonge, but it's usually better to keep one's mouth shut unless you are the person driving. After five minutes, we make it out.

Using the on-board terminal, I check the social media sites for a Favolopolus in Markham. His personal page shows the family attending a fundraiser tonight, regardless of the weather. People should be more

careful about what they put on social media. It leaves them open for
problems, like the one we're going to give them. It also gives us three
hours to search. That is if all goes well.

"We have about thirty minutes before they leave the house," I
tell Mie.

"Good. They out for long time?"

"About three hours." I pull up the information for the fundraiser.
No electronics allowed blinks under the event address. "They won't
have their cells on them."

"Nice of event."

Traffic lightens up as we pass Steeles Avenue, but closer to
Highway 407 it gets thicker. 16th is not traveled a lot, so I hold my
breath. The flashing red and blue lights at the corner make my stomach
tighten.

"Trouble ahead."

"We need stop," Mie says.

"Yeah, see what's up."

The whole intersection is cordoned off. The holo tape blocks the
intersection just after the lights, instructing us to find an alternate.
Those smart enough turn at the intersection. We continue on.

The snow comes down good and hard now—wind whips from the
north-west, right across one of the lakes, dumping fun for everyone. The
officer watching the blockade has two vehicles before us – it's an excel-
lent time to get our story straight.

By the time we're at the cop, we have it down pat. Two off duty
detectives just trying to help.

The officer holds his hand up, and Mie slows us to a stop.

The cop is a little shorter than Mie, but that's because he's hunched
over a little to try and stay warm. Battling the wind and snow is not easy,
but he's making a good go of it. He pulls down his scarf and smiles one
of those "I'd rather be in front of my fireplace curled up with my dog,"
smiles. I don't blame him.

"The intersection is closed. You'll need to go back and take Baycliffe
or Carlton," she says to Mie and I bring out my badge. "Oh, you got
called in?"

"No," Mie says. "We heard the intersection issue. Came to help."

The officer shakes her head. "Why would you come out on a Sunday night in this weather?"

Mie jerks a thumb at me. "He need overtime. I just like work."

"Okay, just take it easy on the street up there. They've called off the plows in order to try and find evidence."

"What happened?" I ask.

"Some poor guy got hit. Seems like a bump, shoot, and run job." He points up to the intersection. "Just about a meter when you turn right at the lights."

"We can do coffee run," Mie offers.

"Thanks, got a thermos of it in the car." He backs away from the window. "Like I said, take the road carefully. Lots of ice build-up."

Mie nods, and I wave. The window goes up, stopping the bitter cold from trying to kill us anymore, and Mie takes us to the intersection, nice and slow.

There's a bus or ambulance at the corner. They're a good five meters from the intersection. Kept back by the cops. That way, they don't contaminate the crime scene too much. Five cars with flashers going are at the intersection and a few at the roadways. I can see one further up the road by a walking path. They must be keeping back the gawkers. Flashes of light go off as someone takes images of the scene. A white truck sits where someone would be if they were waiting for a light to change— white Ford F150 during winter. Smart move.

We stop at the first vehicle and get out. It's an instant regret. The wind picks up and sneaks its way through my pants and up into my body. Fucking cold.

One of the detectives at the scene breaks away from the rest and jogs over to us. At first, all we see is a bulky coat covering up a body just a little beyond fat. But when he stops, it's obvious the coat struggles to hold him in. Three chins waggle as he talks to Mie. I take a few steps toward the crime scene.

A body lays in the snow right behind the truck. The back bumper has some paint on it. A very different shade of blue. Very dark, almost a navy. The tire tracks are all but covered with the drifting snow, but someone did seem to have the forethought of covering part of the prints. The man is definitely dead. Even with the covering tarp, the blood-soaked snow tells me he bled out, or the shot was sufficient to let all the blood in him leave the body before winter froze it. Either way, no evidence of robbery or any other such crime. Could be the guy who hit him just wanted to get rid of the headache of insurance.

"Who's the vic?" I ask.

"Some wanna-be rich guy." The officer I speak to shivers under his parka. They're never are warm enough.

"Wanna-be?"

"Yeah, he lives further north. In one of the cheaper homes. Up on Royal West. Could be here as a contractor or something."

I glance at the back of the truck. "No stickers or advertising. Don't think he's a contractor. They usually splash their name on every vehicle they own."

"Makes sense." The cop pulls out his cell and exchanges some words. "Just got it. Works for a bank. Low level IT person it seems."

"Everything okay here?" I ask.

"Yeah. We have all we're going to get. Damn snow covered a lot of evidence." He walks to the body. "We think he was killed about two hours ago. But why no one saw him, I don't know. Not even the blinkers on."

"Could be anything. Maybe the truck ran out of gas."

The cop walks to the truck and opens the door. Nothing lights up. He presses a button on the dash, and there's a dim glow that goes dark fast–dead battery.

"Good call on that," he says, walking back. "Tank is drained. Must have had all the electronics going when he stopped. The battery is dead as well."

Why was someone killed in plain sight and left to freeze? It's puzzling.

"I've got to get back to my partner."

"You better. Jules will talk her ear off. He likes the sound of his own voice."

"Thanks." I turn and walk back to the car and Mie.

True enough, Jules is rambling on about a lot of stuff. From the look Mie gives me, I can tell she needs to be rescued. I hold out my hand to Jules. He grasps mine and we shake.

I drop his hand. "I gotta get Mie home."

"Really? We were just having a great talk about the usage of rubber bullets." He looks at me, the same look Sarah gives me when she has a lot to say but doesn't know where to start.

"Yeah, really. We have a lot of paperwork to do, and VPNing into the network from home lets us leave early. Our cap will be watching to make sure we're not playing hooky or something."

He holds out a card. "I'm the union rep for the area. If you ever need anything like a captain off your back, let me know. I can keep him so tied up he'll have no time to give you crap." He takes a breath. It appears talking has the same effect on him that running to the car did. "And if you need anything, like advice or something, just let me know. I'm a rep not only for this area, but will help anyone of our fellow officers. It's just something I do. My home number is on the card as well. If you need union representation and your rep isn't available, just give me a call, and I'll be there."

"Thanks, I'll keep that in mind." I walk around the car to the passenger door.

"Yes, keep that in mind. James for the Rules. I had that slogan made for me. The other reps don't care as much as I do, but we have rules with the union, and I make sure they're used to protect you. Remember to call if you need me or something. I just like helping out good cops doing a shitty job." He takes another deep breath. "Remember, we need better working conditions and equipment. Do you use your own vehicle for the job? You know there's a thing now that allows you to not only claim car payments but also the insurance costs. Make sure you list your car as being used for police business."

"I will. See you." I step into the car and slam the door before he can say anything else. "God, I think he can breathe through his ears."

"All cops like him in union?" Mie asks.

"Only the ones we haven't shot yet," I say.

She gives another smile at that and turns onto 16th. We pass the other tape and cop before turning on Country Estates Drive.

The homes are outlandish. Each has three-car garages and interlocking brick driveways devoid of snow. Some of the houses are built like castles. This is the way the very wealthy live—a whole new world.

Mie gawks at the homes. They're huge, expensive, and just a little too gaudy for my taste. We follow the road looking for the house in question.

The building we want comes up quickly. It has a large stone fence that comes almost out to the curb. The barrier looks new, for the bricks have not faded while the driveway has. Keeping a property like this could cost a small fortune in itself. I wonder why the son is in public school. Maybe being kicked out of the other schools has led them to enroll him with the common people. Either that or it was done as a punishment.

At the gate, I pull out the cloned cell. A quick tap of the app unlocks and swings the barrier out of the way, and I'm not worried about the guards. They'll get a notification the owner is back unexpectedly, and they'll do nothing unless another alarm is raised. Mie takes us up to the home.

As we approach, the app on the phone asks if we want the garage door opened. I respond, yes. Better to have the car out of sight. It stands out against other vehicles in the area.

A garage door opens. Mie glides the car into the space. There's a Lexus SUV, two Ferrari's, and one Lamborghini. This family is loaded.

Mie and I exit the car, and I check the app for any cameras. There are only two at the front gate. I need to take care of the footage from those.

The garage door closes, and we make our way to the internal house door. This is easier than I thought it would be. No dogs, no issue with the guards. We'll be in and out fast.

We get to the door, and Mie points down. There's a good trail of water behind me. I shrug. The floor must have radiant heat. They won't even know we've been here if I just wipe the floor a little.

The internal door is unlocked, and we find ourselves just outside the kitchen in a hallway. I go to one end as Mie takes the other. The recording equipment for the cameras will be in a room away from the main house, and I want to take care of that first.

Security rooms inside a house are rarely alarmed. This one is no exception. Inside, a bank of monitors attached to a blade server. I pull one of the drives. The server goes down. The drive is a spinner, not an

SSD like most. The sticker calls it a SAS drive, so this kills the recordings by taking it out. I don't want to be obvious. The second and third drives come out with a soft pull. I swap their positions and walk out. That'll destroy all records when they reboot the system.

I walk into the kitchen and stop.

Mie stands there with a man in front of her. They're ten paces apart and staring at each other. Both have their weapons out. Neither of them blinks.

January 14th, 2033 - Night Night

The girl sits on Bojing's lap as the song ends. Her nude body glistens with a light sheen of sweat, but he does not mind. Once the music starts again, she'll resume dancing. Her breasts are firm and large, not hanging down like the other dancers in the club. A thin waist and hips are precisely what he looks for in a woman. Long blonde hair spills against her shoulders and makes her nipples play peek-a-boo in the most arousing way. He likes this one.

With a flourish, he takes the small towel off the table and hands it to her. She accepts it with a smile and wipes sweat off her breasts.

"I know you like them," she says.

He smiles, not letting her know just how much he is enjoying the show. Soon he'll ask her to come home with him. He wonders how much it will cost him tonight and if she understands what will be asked of her. But most don't. All they think is they'll get screwed and a few thousand dollars. Little do they know.

This is the first and last visit to this strip club. Not using the same source for women helps him keep a low profile.

"Good," he says with a grin and nods.

The music starts.

She pushes his legs apart and slips between them. The dance begins again. She swings her hips to the music and turns in place to the beat until her back is to him. With short shuffling steps, she backs up and bends forward, showing herself to him.

Bojing knows the rules. He cannot reach out and touch her there, but if she guides his hand, that's another story. She reaches between her legs, a soft hand taking his as she brings his fingers closer to her crotch. But she does not bring him into her. Instead, she glides his hand over the wetness of her womanhood. Slick dampness he wants to enjoy.

She leans back, taking his one finger into herself while he cups a breast. The dance of pleasure begins to take him to bliss.

"Do you want me tonight?" she breaths into his ear.

"Tonight. All night," he replies.

"You're not a cop, are you?"

"No, businessman."

She tightens upon his finger. "From China?"

"Yes, China."

"Five big."

"Cash," Bojing says.

"I have an hour left to dance. They have me on stage next. Three dances." She pants. Wetness flows from her. "I need to keep dancing for at least ten after that."

"Dance for me," he says.

She pushes forward, and his finger comes out of her. Looking over her shoulder, she smiles. "I'll be back in three songs."

I step back from the scene until my hand touches a doorknob. A quick turn opens it. I slam the door shut. Three thuds echo with the smack of flesh being hit hard. A snap breaks the air, and then a bag hits the ground. I step forward. Mie stands over the guard.

"He look away," she says.

"I thought you could use the distraction. Did he get a good look at you?"

"No, he watch gun. Hair also in face when I turn." She looks back at me, hair draped over her forehead and covering one side of her face. It hides enough that I would not recognize her if I only have a quick glance or a gun is pointing at me.

"What are we going to do with him?"

She looks down and then bends over. The man is flipped over on his side, and Mie removes his laces. She ties him up like a hog. I check a few of the drawers until I find dish towels and toss one to her. She shoves it into his mouth. The jaw looks awkward as if broken. I toss another towel, and she glances at me with a questioning look.

"Around his eyes." I make a motion of tying a blindfold. "That way, we have less chance of him seeing you again."

She nods and covers his eyes. A few steps back, and she admires her handy work. "We have no time."

I poke my head into the room attached to the kitchen. "Look for a den or office. Should be where he keeps most of his records."

Mie walks through an archway and into the main foyer. I follow her, hoping she knows what she's doing. She stops and looks from side to side. Quick steps take her to the right, and she opens a door, then shuts it quick.

"Guard outside." She nods at the front door. Tall panes of glass stand on either side of the entranceway, frosted with a slight bevel that distorts the view. A light sweeps back and forth as it moves from the left to the right and out of sight.

"He's clear," I say.

Mie opens the door again and slides in. I enter right behind. It's the den. Even the smell of it tells me what it's for.

Sweet tobacco permeates the air, cedar panels decorate the walls, and a huge wooden desk sits near one wall. A bookcase is built into the wall behind the desk and goes from the floor to the ceiling. Heavy tomes fill the shelves.

Mie goes to the desk. She sticks a USB into a port and boots the system using it. A few seconds pass, and she logs into it, directing the system to copy the contents of the desk's ME drives.

"Five minutes," she says.

I examine the walls, look behind pictures, and spin the wooden globe. It doesn't turn.

"I found something."

Mie comes up behind me and stares at me as I examine the globe. My fingers run under the lip of a wooden ring that runs around the globe. I find a latch. It moves with the slightest of pressure, and the top of the globe lifts a little. Bingo!

Multiple flash drives sit nestled in holders inside the globe. I pull one and read the name on it. Another one and another name. All woman. The small storage devices are each listed as 250 gigs. After each name are the initials CG.

"China Girl," Mie says.

"There's got to be over a hundred of them here." I hold another one up.

"We take?"

Taking and handing them in for investigation would be good for charges if they contain under-aged girls. But then we have to tell the forensic guys how we got them, and that wouldn't hold well. We're here illegally, and the evidence cannot be used against him. But knowing where they are, we can secure a search warrant and take them that way. A charge of pedophilia can get the owner put away for a long time.

"We need a warrant."

Mie closes the globe. "Need reason."

There it is, the biggest thing between the good guys and the bad. The proof is needed in order to search.

A bleep comes from the desk.

"Done," Mie says. She goes to the desk and pulls the USB. A quick double-tap and the O/S reboot back to Windows. It's like she was never there.

We take another route to my apartment. Mie goes to her hotel, and I head up in the elevator. The numbers click by as my floor approaches. We need to actually find out more information regarding the site that pushed the last China Girl download to Sarah's phone. The information on everyone who owns a headset could also be stored on the server. We just need to find the IP. But maybe we'll need a warrant for it as well. There was a big uprising concerning net neutrality several years ago. I pull out my phone as the elevator stops on my floor. Bill will know.

I type – What do we need to track an IP?

My phone vibrates as I reach my apartment.

Bill – Whois.

I type – Me, Bruce.

Bill – No, LOL. Whois. Google it.

I put the phone in my pocket and open the door. Cigarette smoke fills the air.

"Good to see you, detective," Bojing says. "Waiting for you."

I drop my phone and grab my Glock just as cold metal touches my temple.

"No gun," a man says.

"Best listen to Ping, Detective Roberts."

I let go of the Glock's grip and slide my hand out of my coat. Ping reaches in, takes my pistol, and shoves it into his pants. The nose of the weapon comes away from my temple, and it motions to the couch beside Bojing. The door alarm and three of my security cameras lay on the table before him.

"You have made some friends of mine nervous," Bojing says as I sit down. "They like privacy, and you and a friend seem to be digging where you not welcome."

Ping stands at the door, gun in hand, trying to stifle a yawn. A rattle comes from the kitchen, and another man enters the front room, a bowl in one hand, and the other using a spoon to shovel noodles into his mouth. Chinese words come from the bedroom down the hall to my right. I start to get up, but Ping straightens and lifts the gun, pointing it at me. I sit back down.

"No do anything wrong, Detective Roberts. Ping gets anxious when we visit new places." Bojing lowers the gun and pulls out a pack of cigarettes. He offers me one. I decline. It doesn't phase him as he puts a cancer stick in his mouth and lights it. The stink is more pungent than it was when I entered. Julie's going to be upset.

"What do you want, Bojing?"

He sucks on the cigarette and blows smoke out. "I want you back off."

It seems Mie and I have hit a nerve.

I sit back and cross my arms. "Back off what?"

Bojing smiles. "You know."

"No, I don't."

He blows more smoke. "Someone looking into judge. It stop. Now."

"And what do I get if we do?" I ask.

Bojing hesitates. It catches him off guard. Especially since I turned down all his prior bribes.

"What you need?" Bojing says.

I think for a second. Something that will make him believe I'm actually putting something together. But I already know what I want to say. I just want him to think there's a possibility of him getting me in his pocket.

"Well?" he asks.

"Yes, I have it." I lean forward. "There's a really sharp knife in the kitchen. Go in there, drop your pants, and cut your dick off. I'll take that for payment."

His smile drops to a frown, and eyes narrow. He takes a puff then puts out the cigarette on the arm of the couch.

"You play dangerous game," he says.

"Really?" I stand. Ping holds up his gun but doesn't point it at me.

"Yes." Bojing stands as well.

"How do you know I don't have cameras recording what you're doing?"

Ping's eyes go wide. A man walks out of the hallway from the bedrooms. He's holding one of Julie's bras.

"I could also have other recording devices on me, keeping track of everything being said. It's not a very smart thing to do, breaking into the home of a cop who's investigating you. Maybe you'll figure it out. Anyone can record a conversation. So maybe you should take your three little boys here and walk out the front door." I take a few steps to the door and put a hand on the knob. With my other hand, I reach out and pull my Glock from Ping's pants. It's a ballsy move, but I think once my hand is on the butt, he's not going to move any.

"Ni wan yi ge wei xain de you xi, jing cha," Bojing says.

The man with the bowl puts it on the dining room table. Bra guy puts the garment on the couch. They both walk toward me. I open the door, and Ping steps sideways to get around me. My right foot holds the door as I watch the three men exit before Bojing.

I wait. Bojing stares at me for a few more seconds before walking to the door, limping slightly on the leg my daughter kicked. It makes me smile. He's still not over the injury. Hopefully, it'll plague him for a few more days.

At the door, he stops, head slumping–smoke circles around his head from another cigarette.

"You should know there's no smoking in the hallway or elevator."

Bojing turns to face me, a smile edging the corner of his mouth.

"You lucky." He takes the cigarette out of his mouth. "Last time you told where daughter was. Next time, you not so fortunate." He takes another drag and blows the smoke into the apartment. "Or maybe wife get lucky with someone soon."

I grip my gun hard. It takes all I have to not bring it up and put a round through his forehead. The light threat against my wife and daughter is not lost on me. And that stupid grin of his doesn't help.

Bojing blows more smoke into the apartment. I recognize the type of cigarettes he's smoking. Reserve cigarettes. Now we have him on something. Minor though it is, it's something. Possession of Reservation cigarettes by a non-native is an offense. But there's no way for me to do something about it while he has the thugs with him.

"It'll be nice to put you in jail. There's no smoking where you'll be going." I start to close the door.

Bojing's smile grows even wider. "You so sure of self. A cop tried once to put me into jail."

I take the bait. "And?"

"He bury his wife. She fit in small bag."

I stand there, staring at the closed door for ten minutes, then go around and open the windows a crack before pulling out the summer fans. With any luck, the smell will be gone soon, but I don't hold my breath.

Picking up the cigarette butts takes a little bit of time as well. It makes me wonder what that man's lungs look like. He's a chain smoker. I'd heard of such but never really met anyone like that. Who could afford it?

The arm of the couch is ruined. Julie's going to be pissed. The only thing that keeps me from calling her about the visit is knowing she still has another three hours left in her shift. I text Sarah. She's still at her friend's apartment.

I check the kitchen for anything strange. They could have done anything while they were here. Being safe, I pull out any open food. This is going to hurt. I hate waste, but if something was put in the food, it would be in the open packages.

It's getting late. Sarah's only a few floors down. She needs to be the one warned against what happened and what can happen. She's the vulnerable one. Easier to get at than Julie.

I use the bug detector to scan the room and find them hidden behind the toilet and in the bedrooms. The toilet becomes their end as they circle the bowl and make their way down the drain. I pull out my phone, Sarah picks up on the first ring. Guess our relationship is healing.

The explanation of what went on takes a few seconds, but the questions she asks come out like a machine gun. She promises to bring something up to clear the air in the apartment and demands to know if her room was violated. When I tell her it was, she says she'll be up in a minute.

Her key hits the lock while I'm closing the windows, hoping the smell of cigarettes has dissipated.

"Shit!" She stands there, sleeve under her nose. "Dad, what the hell?"

I walk toward her, and she holds out her arms. Her gesture for a hug is something I've missed over the last eight years. Now it's like she really wants to make sure we love each other.

"Your mom's going to have a crap at the smell."

"You think?"

I take her hand and walk toward the bedroom.

The door is closed because I opened her window a lot to clear it out fast, just like my bedroom. The only thing is the room is freezing. We close the windows, and she starts picking up some clothes. It's interesting she's doing that now. Her room is like a bomb went off in it most of the time, but not anymore.

I help.

"At least they didn't smoke in here. It would make me sick." She throws her clothes into the laundry hamper.

"We may have something on him. It opens the door to a whole investigation." I put the clothes on her dresser. Better to let her put them into the drawers she wants.

"But how are you going to get him?"

"We're following his friends. Some of them perjured themselves on an affidavit that helped him walk."

"I still don't understand how he was able to get off without even being in jail." Sarah shoves her clothes into the drawers. "Three of us are witnesses."

"Two cops with a grudge and the daughter of one of them." I scratch the back of my head. "The courts would have fun with that one. He'd become the victim of a revenge scheme."

"But how are you going to get him now?"

"Pressure on the friends. We follow them and investigate until we find the money exchanging hands or being moved about without any proof of where it comes from. The great thing is, Mie and I have done some groundwork. You're not still seeing that boy, James, right?"

She stops and picks at her fingernails. "No. I called it off after I found out what he did."

"Good. That way, we can make sure you're not hurt."

"I'm not hurt, really. But if I see him in class, I'll cut his dick off."

January 15th, 2033 – Tracking

Blood spatters the sink as Bojing clears his nose. Good, it's not broken . He lights a cigarette and takes a deep drag. The smoke does not come out of his nose. Nothing comes out of his nose but blood and bubbles.

He leans forward once again and tries to clear it. Blood colors the water in the sink. He reaches out his hand and turns on the tap. Water splashes. His cigarette rips from the filter. He stares as it circles the drain and tries to go down. The paper disintegrates with agonizing slowness, and the tobacco strings down the hole. He's thankful there are more, but soon he'll need to send a runner back to the reserve for another few cartons.

Face cloth in hand, he walks out of the bathroom and into the foyer. It's good he has enough money to afford the penthouse. At least the room he sleeps in can be cleaned up, but the broken lamp will need to be replaced.

She struggled well. He didn't expect the punch or the force with which she delivered it. Not many women can overcome a man when he is on top of her. He walks to the bedroom, and the mess of the fight shows everywhere.

The dancer lays on the bed, body naked and nipples pointing to the ceiling. He sits beside her and strokes the hair away from her face. She was such a pretty thing. The bruises on the neck leave no doubt about what happened. Nor do the marks on her cheek from his slapping. The bruise on her left eye didn't have a chance to expand before she died. He places a hand on a breast. Still warm. His penis engorges. His body is still good for another go.

He takes off the robe and lets it tumble to the ground. Small pinprick marks of cigarette burns decorate his otherwise smooth arms. She had stroked and kissed them when they started—likewise, the scar on his left breast. A long knife wound inflicted when he was a 49er so many years ago.

She did convince him she enjoyed the sex. The night felt real, but it was just a dream, a hazy illusion by an actor playing her part. All she really cared about was the money. But her interest didn't matter. No amount of money will bring her back from the dead. He sits beside her again and rests a hand on her breast. The excitement builds, and he mounts the body.

My stomach rumbles as it digests. Mie brought breakfast for me, and the spicy food churns in my stomach, reminding me of how early it is. The food was good, but the mixture of peppers and coffee sits badly. I cover my mouth as another belch escapes.

We park, and I plug in the car. The elevator opens. Three uniforms walk out before we enter.

Mie and I don't have a lot to talk about. I told her about Bojing's visit last night. She agrees we need to step up the investigation and get my family's protection in place. I agree, but when you think about the situation, we need to take the Triad to task. They have violated my private life, something gangs in Canada don't do anymore. They either pay you off or move to someone less ethical. It's just the way. Beat cops are easy to get rid of if you wave enough money at them. Killing them usually makes for a messy deal with others as you try to cover it up. So why is Bojing doing exactly that?

"We report?" Mie asks.

I nod. "Cap will want to have a debriefing on what happened today."

"Trust Cap?"

"Just as much as I can trust anyone," I say.

We hit the main floor. The elevator doors open. A beat cop pushes in a man reeking of stale sweat and bodily fluids. He mouths an apology while pushing the perp to the corner. Mie and I stand as far away as possible. He gets off on the third floor, but the smell stays. Urine is puddled where the prisoner stood.

The doors open on our floor; we get out as Phil enters. He turns quick and plugs his nose. "Did you guys have to let one go?"

The doors close, and I smile. Serves him right.

We get to our desks and sit. It takes no time to compile a report on Bojing's activities; we've been filling it out from the beginning. An email blinks urgently for me from Bill. I open it.

"Bills coming down for our debrief with the Cap," I say.

Mie raises an eyebrow. "This usual?"

"No. It's damn strange. The DA usually keeps their distance when it comes to sharing information. Well, with the higher-ups, that is." I glance at her display. "You finished?"

Mie pushes the electronic form from her desk to mine. "Last part. You in hurry to see Cap?"

I smile. Another person now uses the name he hates.

The elevator door opens, and a man and woman get off. They head directly to Cap's office and enter it without even knocking. They pull the blinds.

"Cap's got someone horning in on him," I say.

"Horning?" Mie asks.

One of the guys in the squad room sends me an instant message via his desk. I raise an eyebrow.

"Internal Affairs. Not good for someone. Wonder what IAD is doing down here?" I type in the last part of the report.

The door to Cap's office opens, and he sticks his head out. "Roberts! Ling! On the double!"

I look at Mie, who shrugs.

What is IAD doing here? And why are we being called into Cap's office? Is someone playing us? We push away from our desks and stand.

"What about?" Mie asks.

I shake my head. "Not sure. But suspect Wang has something to do with it."

We cross the room and enter Cap's office. The two detectives I assume are from Internal Affairs are there, the guy sitting and the woman leaning against a credenza. The man is older, maybe in his late forties. A gut rolls over his belt; his shirt is wrinkled – not a clean person.

The woman looks right out of training. She leans. It shows off how trim and fit she is. Nothing comes over the belt on her. That is if she can find a belt small enough for her waist. Probably doesn't need it.

A folder sits on Cap's desk. Papers are spread out.

"What's up, Cap?" I ask as we enter.

"Close the door, Bruce." Cap sits down at his desk. He leans back in his chair and steeples his fingers. "Have you met Detective Lance and Jenkins from IAD?"

"Can't say I've had the privilege." I reach out a hand to the woman who takes it. The man stands, and I shake hands with him. Mie mirrors my actions but adds a slight bow.

"Detectives, I called both Detective Roberts and Ling in because they're partnered on a specific investigation that can shed light on your findings. Do you want to start?"

Lance leans forward and grabs some of the paperwork. He stands and steps to the side of the office opposite his partner. I get an instant dislike for the guy.

"After a few calls were received from the public, we started a fast track investigation. During the course, we discovered a number of discrepancies with finance and behavior." He takes a breath and looks at the papers. "Detective Roberts, do you know a Chinese Natural by the name of Bojing Wang?"

I glance between him and Mie, then Cap. "Yes, I've had dealings with him."

"Damn it, Bruce!" Cap says. "Full disclosure is your best defense."

"Do I need a lawyer?" I ask Cap.

"You can ask for one," the skinny woman says. I decide to just call her Bones . "It won't look good if you do, though. We'll have to make everything official, and that could lead to something a little–"

"Enough, Detective," Cap says.

I look over to the other IAD officer. "Yes, I know Bojing Wang. He tried to bribe me a few days ago and then kidnapped my kid. Last night he came to my home, broke in, and waited for me to return. He threatened my family."

Lance raises an eyebrow. "Why haven't you put the information into the system?"

"Bruce in hospital," Mie says. "You not read reports?"

Lance growls. "I read all his reports. Nothing says he was in the hospital."

"It in mine. He unconscious at time." Mie tilts her head a bit. "Maybe you go read all reports?"

"Ling, don't be a smart ass," Cap says. "Detective Lance, I told you not to worry about these two."

I remember something Bill said and take out the bug detector.

Lance opens his mouth to say something, but the bug detector lights up like a Christmas tree.

We find ten bugs in Cap's office. Exact duplicates of what we found in my home. Two of them are on the clothes of the IAD officers. I put them into a cup and place it outside the office. I find it easier to deal with IAD when you have something on them.

Everyone is standing. I pull another two chairs in from the squad room, and we all sit around a small table in Cap's office. We're all on a level playing field now, no one trying to catch the other in a lie or anything because of the bugs. Seems good to me.

I explain about the first kidnapping, the encounter at the school, China Girl, then the kidnapping of my kid, our encounter with Bojing Wang and his crew, and the eventual rescue of Sarah and me. Then I spilled about the visit last night. Both take notes, but I'm sure they have their cells recording everything for playback later. They start putting their proverbial cards on the table for us.

"It started four days ago, on the 13th," Jenkins says. "IAD got a call about suspected bribery happening. We started tagging your activities then." She pulls out a few pictures. Actual pictures! Not images on a cell. "Here's Bojing Wang handing you a package. Here's another time he hands you a package. And another."

I look at the pictures. Different angles, same place. "Those are the same pictures."

Jenkins stares at them. "You sure?"

"Noodle place downstairs," I explain. "See, same suit on both of us, they doctored the color of his tie, but that's it. You can catch the clock in the corner of one picture and the display from across the street in this one."

She circles them and nods. "Damn."

We also have these." Lance pulls records from his folder. "Shows debt being paid off. A lot of it."

"Not nice, is it?" I ask. "But that's what happens when you secure a loan to consolidate."

Lance flips another sheet at me. "How about this?"

I look down at it. A deposit report from Bank of Montreal shows 1.2 million.

"Well, if I had that money, you think I'd be living in the apartment I'm in?"

He taps the page. "It shows you've had the money for a few weeks."

"Record can be fake," Mie says. "You check bank and backtrack deposit?"

"Not yet," Jenkins says. "Something like this is reported first, and we do some interviews to see if there's merit to it. The primary reports supported approaching Captain Max with the findings. He argued we should approach you, and we agreed."

"Much better to confront someone who might be innocent and see if their story trips them up, right?" I ask.

Lance flushes, which is interesting. I guess he must be human, after all.

Cap sits back in his chair. "Everything we have here is circumstantial evidence. I'm sure Detective Roberts will be happy to open up his books to show you what has been happening in his life, as well as supply evidence that will dispute what you have here. I don't think we need to investigate any further, and I'm definitely not in a hurry to pull him off a case he's been making progress on over the last week. So, unless you have anything else..."

A knock at the door interrupts anyone from responding. Bill peeks through the small amount of window between the door and the blind.

I get up and open the door before anyone can protest.

Bill takes two steps and stops, looking at everyone in the room. He's probably never met anyone from IAD, so it's hard to figure out what he's thinking right now. I give him a little shove, and he goes with it.

"William Louis, District Attorney's office," he says, reaching out a hand first to Cap and then the other two he's not met.

"Bill, Captain Braden Max, the other two are from IAD, Detectives Lance, and Jenkins." I motion him to sit in my seat.

"IAD? Why are they here?"

"Our friend has been planting evidence against me." I point to the pictures and the bank statement. "Problem is, we've been able to disprove it all."

"Good." Bill reaches over and takes the bank statement. "Well, what are you going to do with this?" He puts a finger on the 1.2 million deposit.

I glance at Cap. "Maybe we should think of it as a donation to the department. Get a few extra squad cars or replace all the rounds shot at the raid."

Cap starts to laugh. "It would be a good deposit on the man-hours you're going to rack up figuring out how to nail this gang."

"No, wait a minute," Lance says. "The money is in an account with your name on it, Roberts. If you touch it, we'll have to come down on you."

"Why?" I say.

"I'd have to advise you not to," Bill says. "No one from my department will back you on that. And when it comes down to help, IAD needs all they can get when prosecuting cops."

"It is in my name." I wink at Bill.

"You could get a really good lawyer for that." He tosses the paper on the table. "Heck, I'll take leave to represent you."

"Awful nice of you, Bill. I just may take you up on that."

Mie leans forward. "What cops do with money taken from criminals?"

Cap smiles. "We actually use a lot of it. Some go to the victims of crime if they petition for it, and the rest gets dumped into our budget for the following year."

It's news to me. We confiscate a lot of cash each year, and it never dawned on me to find out where it goes. But it goes. Someone is making a shit load of cash.

"Anyway, we've already started to push buttons in order to get something going." I indicate Bill. "The judge who signed that affidavit saying Wang was with him when we know that wasn't true. Well, Bill is doing a quiet probe into his dealings. Mie and I have started investigating the Favolopolus family. I can tell you the father is sick."

"I didn't read anything in your reports about an investigation on the Favolopolus," Jenkins says.

"Because it is not in the formal reports." I cross my arms. "It's off the books."

She looks up. "Off the books?"

Lance nods. "I take it you covered your tracks?"

"Covered up what? You mean something illegal?" Jenkins asks.

"Not really illegal. We just didn't want to get a search warrant. If we had, the evidence would surely have been moved." I take a few steps toward Lance. "Favolopolus has a stash of China Girl recordings that date back about a year."

Jenkins nods. "Has anyone been able to view them without having to wear the device?"

I look over to Mie.

"No. Complicated. Hard to decipher signal from device. Too much data dumping at one time." She reaches into her pocket and pulls out a recording. "Terrabytes of information. Have you tried device?"

Lance leans forward. "Wasn't aware of it until today. Not sure if I should."

Jenkins leans forward. "I'll try it."

We empty the lunchroom to get privacy. Jenkins takes off her jacket and sits on the small couch as Mie takes the device out of the box. I still can't believe such a small thing can do what it does. Everything shrunk down to the smallest of parts.

"Does it hurt?" Jenkins asks.

"No, but it is uncomfortable when you start seeing and feeling the recording." I sit down beside her. "Whatever you do, don't pull the device off. If you do, you'll sever the connection and get a headache like you've never had before."

"Will I feel anything from the outside?"

"No, just a little numbness at first. Then as the system takes over, you'll not feel anything. Your limbs will only move if you really will them to. We can monitor you from here, but it is only you who will see what's going on."

Jenkins loosens her tie. "How do you know so much about this?"

"I tried it once as well. Mie's our resident expert on the device." I look over, Mie is getting everything laid out for use. She rummages in the box a little and looks around with brow furrowed. "What's wrong, Mie?"

"Missing recording. Should have five, but only four."

Cap comes into the room. "What's the problem?"

"Who said there was a problem?" I ask.

"The look on your face just now."

Mie held out the recordings. "One missing."

"I'll call down to evidence and see who checked out the kit."

He leaves us, and I glance at Jenkins. "You really want to go through with this? It's very intense."

"Yes. I need to justify the crossing of the line. With usual cases, there's evidence we'd check, read reports, eye witness accounts. This one is very different." She takes a deep breath. "This one seems more than personal to you. Like a violation happened."

I glance down, then back up into her eyes. "My daughter's ex-boyfriend. He's one of the people who used the technology to record them... you know. He had the gang spread it to the rich. This has got to stop for everyone's sake. Some things just have to be kept private. He violated her trust, and the gang made money off it. Probably still making money off it."

Jenkins gives me a little corner mouth smile. "Well, I'll let you know what I think when it's over."

I lower the headset on her. "Just remember. Don't take the rig off while it's playing. Just try to say the word stop. Yell it if you can."

"I'll yell," she says and leans back in her seat.

Mie glances over. "Never hooked a woman into a man recording before."

I look back at her. "Never? Well, what could go wrong?"

She taps the player, and it starts.

Jenkins jerks back on the couch. Her face goes ashen, and a tear makes its way down her cheek.

January 15th, 2033 – Live

Bojing watches the monitor on his desk. The display shows the break room of the precinct, the one room the police failed to scan. He watches in silence as the skinny cop sits on the couch with a China Girl in hand. The corner of his mouth lifts slightly. He anticipates what will happen when the sabotaged drives deliver a virus-laden recording to the wearer.

A soft knock on the door draws his attention away. He scowls, but his stomach grumbles. This better be lunch .

"Come," he calls out.

The door opens, and a young Asian girl enters. She's not Chinese, but a young, pretty Japanese girl. He wonders where his crew found her.

The girl moves forward without a sound. A skin-tight bodysuit snuggles all the small curves. Bojing sits back. Yes, a break from watching these fools would be nice. He turns away from the monitors. The thought of food and a pretty face is a welcome repast for him.

The door closes, but the girl remains. Her hair is pulled back and tied in place. She shakes. The soup bowl vibrates on the small plate in her hands. She walks around the desk at Bojing's beckoning and places the bowl in front of him. First, she hesitates, then turns to leave. The long hair swishes across her back. It reaches just past slender hips and settles down there. Bojing reaches out and lets a few strands of it slip through his fingers.

"Stay," Bojing says.

The girl stops. Her shoulders tremble.

"You afraid of me?" Bojing asks. Fear of him heightens his awareness of the girl's scent.

Her quivering increases. Bojing reaches out and places a hand on her shoulder. He turns her to face him. The proverbial mask he likes to wear around his victims comes up. Eyes soften and expand. Face relaxes and becomes the saddened father.

"There is nothing to fear," he reassures her.

Her lip trembles.

"What do you want?" Bojing asks.

The girl glances at the soup and then at Bojing. Her mouth opens slightly but closes fast.

"You can tell me," he says.

"Hungry," the girl says in broken Chinese with a Japanese accent.

"Then join me. There is more soup here than I can eat." Bojing indicates the bowl. It is large, and his hunger can be sated with a couple of spoons of the broth. The more substantial meal of a young girl stands before him.

The girl reaches for the spoon but stops just before touching it. She looks to Bojing, who nods.

As she picks up the spoon, Bojing strokes her back. The girl's trembling lessens under his touch. He points to the screen.

"You know where this is?"

The girl shakes her head.

"What is your name?"

"Sakura," she says in a soft voice.

Bojing smiles. Cherry Blossom. Her parents named her a traditional name. "Sakura, such a nice name for a pretty little girl. How old are you?"

The spoon stops halfway to her mouth. "Fifteen."

"Such a nice age for a pretty lady. Please, keep eating."

"You not hungry?" she asks.

"Yes, but you seem more hungry than I." His hand brushes against her cheek.

She brings the spoon to her lips and sips the liquid. Bojing watches her pucker and draw in the broth. Desire wells inside him.

Commotion on the screen draws his attention. The police have started the China Girl playback. The woman cop will be under in no time and in a coma if all goes to plan. He looks back at the little girl.

Bojing opens a drawer in his desk and pulls out a spoon. "I have a celebration to do."

Sakura takes another sip, not taking her eyes off the soup.

"This is a good day. Something to celebrate and rejoice in." Bojing puts his spoon in the bowl.

The girl glances at Bojing as he draws her closer to him, hands moving across her body.

Jenkins lays on the couch, tears streaming from her closed eyes. Lance steps forward and puts a hand on her shoulder. The woman's complexion becomes more ashen. I'm helping lower her so she can lie down.

She convulses. Foam fills her mouth and forms bubbles. I turn her to the side and try to keep her comfortable.

"What's happening to her?" Lance asks.

I look over to Mie, who shrugs.

"She's experiencing the recording. Should be over in a few minutes," I say.

"Did I do this when it was played?" I ask Mie.

"No, you just close eyes," she says.

"Then what the hell is happening to her?" Lance asks. He takes a tentative step forward.

"Don't know." Mie glances at the playback device, checking to see that everything is in order. "All look right."

Lance goes to remove the China Girl interface from Jenkins, but I stop him. "That could cause a lot of damage."

"And this isn't?" He looks to Mie. "Get this off her."

Mie hits the device, and Jenkins settles down. The foaming at the mouth slows to drool, and her body stops spasming.

"Is it off?" Lance asks.

"Yes, off," Mie replies.

Lance reaches out and takes the device off Jenkins. His hand trembles against her forehead. He has no wedding ring. He's gentle, more than most would be. I'm probably reading more into it, but it's almost like he's acting like she's more than a partner.

Mie studies the device and pulls the recording. She puts the sim card into her phone and taps out a few commands.

"We need to get her to a hospital," I say.

Lance turns to me, face flushed. "You did this."

"It wasn't my idea. She wanted to experience why we need to take this organization down. She wanted justification."

"Well, I'm pulling you from active duty." He turns back to his partner. "Some things are too important to lose."

"Not Bruce fault," Mie says. "Strange code on sim."

We both look at her. She has her phone out to show us. "Here. Usual CG recording look like this when analyze." A wavy pattern floats just over her wrist. Something like a waveform analysis. "This one we use." She swipes, and a new waveform displays. It's not smooth. A lot of jagged lines run up and down the waveform. The whole image is chaotic compared to the other one. Like someone decided to play a trick. "It cause issue, nothing else."

"You said this would be the same recording as the one you experienced," Lance says.

I glance over to Mie. "Was it?"

"Yes, same one." She pulls the nail drive out of her phone and examines it. "But it look different."

"Different? How?"

She hands the sim to me. "Serial number different."

There's a tag on the sim that identifies it as evidence on the case. It's numbered with a code twelve numbers and letters long. It looks the same. The sim itself has a serial number on it—something the manufacturer places there so people can keep track of it if they need to. The number is huge—about twenty characters.

"How the hell can you tell?" I ask.

"Numbers on sim not same as before." She holds up the sim. "See serial? It have different numbers."

"What proof do you have of that?" Lance says.

She hands over the inventory bag. "Sim serial recorded here." She points to the inventory listing. It has the tag numbers and any identifiable information. "The number not same as any other sim in box."

The EMTs are baffled over Jenkins's condition but take her away on a stretcher. Cap is back from the evidence locker. We sit with him in his office again. Time passes fast today, and he's behind in his paperwork due to helping get information for our investigation. His desk shows the listing of all those who had access to the device and recordings. There are a few. All men. Two from our department.

Lance uses Cap's desk to access his office computer.

"I'm cross-referencing the listing of those who signed out the evidence." He types information and executes the search. "We're going to have their full dossiers in a few minutes."

"What are we looking for?" I ask.

"Anything out of the ordinary." Lance points to the paperwork on me. "Stuff like we dug out on you. Bank records. Strange transactions. Registration of property. Something that indicates alternative income or strange behavior."

Cap points to a name on the list. "I want to call in Phil. He had the unit out a couple of times. Once overnight."

Lance nods. "Sounds suspicious to me." He turns to me. "I'll take the lead on the questions."

"No." Cap taps a few commands into his desk, and not thirty seconds later, Phil stands at the door.

"You want to see me, Captain?"

"Sit down, Phil. I have some questions to ask you." Cap indicates a chair on the other side of his desk.

Phil sits and fidgets. "Everything okay?"

"Phil, do you know the reasons behind not letting those not involved in a case sign out evidence?" Cap asks.

Phil looks at me, then Mie, then Lance. "To keep you out of the public eye?"

"Basically, right. Suppose you sign out evidence, and something happens to it. In that case, the DA could call you up on charges of interfering with an investigation. I don't want to see that."

Phil starts to sweat. Small beads of perspiration decorate his forehead. He taps the heal of his foot against the floor as if he has restless leg syndrome. "I didn't do anything wrong, right?"

"What do you mean?" Cap asks. Question with a question. Pulling the person into a loop of evidence to see if there's a break.

"I mean, others have done it."

"Done what?"

Phil sits forward a little. "Signed out that tech."

Cap sits forward with him. "What tech?"

Phil nods toward the box containing the China Girl evidence. "That gear."

Cap glances at the box. "Why would someone want to sign that out?"

The sweat on Phil's forehead starts to run. "To... you know, experience it."

"I'm not sure I understand your meaning.

Cap's calm. Calmer than I would be. He's sitting forward and not showing any emotion.

I'm roiling on the inside. Even though I've never been a friend of Phil's, there is a professional courtesy about police work. You cover each other in case something goes wrong. Phil is now basically saying he wanted to experience the raping and killing of another human being. I want to reach out and slap him on the back of the head. Tell him something like that is not what we do. Instead, I just listen to him rant.

"Well, the guys have been talking about the tech. You get to be someone in the game and do things that normally you wouldn't be able to do." He takes a breath. "I just took it home instead of doing it in the bathroom like the others." He glances at Mie. Her expression is a mask. "They kept saying there's a mix of girls recorded. You could try any of them." He reaches into his pocket and pulls out his phone. "They even gave me the site where you could get more recordings."

He shows his phone to Cap, who makes a note. Phil has the missing information we need. The URL of the download site.

"You just sign in and download. They gave me a code to use, and that's what got me curious about it."

He went to the well too many times, and now he's caught. "How many times did you sign out the device?" Cap asks.

"Three...no, four. I was able to get that guy on Yonge to duplicate it."

"Nygen's Technology?" I ask, taking a stab in the dark.

"Yeah, that's the one." Phil points to me and looks back at Cap. "See, even Bruce knows about him. The guy has a good racket. He makes copies of tech you bring in. He actually makes some of the home-made stuff like that thing"–he points to the evidence box–"and doesn't charge you a king's ransom for it."

"You mean you have one of these devices at home?" Cap asks.

Phil swallows. He's in the trap now. "Yeah...I didn't want to keep signing the thing out. It's addictive."

Cap sits back and looks at Lance, who nods.

"You know how many have those devices? This week that tech store made twenty headsets! Twenty! Heck, I even saw Roberts in there the other night. I don't know what the problem is. Really? What is going on?" Phil glances at Lance, who stands.

Cap leans forward. "Phil, you need to surrender the device and the recordings you have."

"But Captain, there's nothing wrong with the recordings. It's just porn." He looks between Mie and me. "Isn't it?"

I stand up and walk to the door where Bill is now.

"What's the DA doing here?" Phil asks.

"He's going to review the interview we just had and recommend what charges to lay," Lance says.

Phil pushes his chair back and stands. He leans forward and stares into Cap's eyes. "You tricked me!"

"I didn't trick you, Phil. You buried yourself," Cap says.

I open the door for Bill to come in.

"You didn't recommend I speak to a union rep or get a lawyer," Phil accuses. "I'm not going down for anything said here."

Bill stops. "Phil, you don't have to be advised of anything until we lay charges. Your interview here was not coerced in any way. You just answered questions."

"But if you're investigating me, then you have to let me know!" He turns to Lance. "You did this!" He then turns to me. "And you! If you fucked up and I'm in trouble for it, then I'll take you down!"

Bill takes a step forward. "We'll cut you a deal for tampering with evidence. That is if you come clean on what is happening with the group involved in circulating the recordings."

"A deal?" Phil says. "For what? Watching a little porn?"

"It's not porn," I say. The disgust in me mounts, along with anger. "They're child rape and snuff films."

"They're actors. Everyone knows it!" Phil yells.

I glance at Mie and walk over to stare Phil right in the eyes.

"There was one named Sarah. Did you watch that one?"

"Yeah. She was eighteen, at least."

I can't hold it back and punch him...My fist connects with him right on the jaw. He stumbles back. A hand goes to his face. He looks up at me in shock. "What the fuck, Bruce! It was great! They didn't even do the fake killing!"

I walk out of the room just as Mie says, "Sarah Bruce daughter."

Cap doesn't want Mie or me in his office during the interrogation. I don't want to be in the room, but then again, I want to tear Phil apart. His actions against the case and callous disregard for the rules have cost him. He'll get jail time for this, but if he helps with the case, he'll get a little less. Still, possession of child pornography is against the law. I hope Sarah doesn't have to be pulled into this as a witness. She may need to authenticate the recording and her age if that happens. It'll cause more issues for her, and I don't want that in her life.

Cap's door opens, and Lance escorts Phil out of the office in cuffs. He's not being handled any too kindly by the IAD agent. Pushed, shoved, and led out the door. It could have been worse. It could have been me guiding him out.

Mie sits at the desk, and Bill comes by. He has a smug smile on his face and pulls up a chair to sit beside us. From his earnest look, there's news, and he's just about ready to explode in order to give it to us.

I sit back, waiting. Mie doesn't say anything. My desk chimes. Cap sent me a message. All it says is to fill out a report on me striking Phil but not to submit it officially. Just send it to him in case the guy decides to push against something and uses me as the focal point.

But before I can start writing it, Bill slaps the desk.

"Man! That was intense." He sits back in the chair. "Is it always like that when you collar someone?"

Mie just looks up at me.

"Not always. This one is different. It's one of our own." I start typing the report.

"I didn't know how intense your jobs can be. It makes mine look boring as all hell." He leans forward. "Wow! You walked out at the wrong time."

"I had to. If I waited any longer, I would've put a bullet in his head."

Bill hesitates. The synapses in his brain must be firing, and he's thinking about what he is about to say before saying it. "I'm sorry your daughter is mixed up in this."

"This whole thing is fucked up. He better not get out or I'll..." I type some more, my fingers impacting the letters with force.

"Well, if we get him to roll over, we'll shave a little time off his sentence. Not that much. He's still being charged with pedophilia, possession of restricted images, promotion of violence, and tampering with evidence for personal gain."

"Think you can make all that stick?" I ask.

"After listening to the interview, yes." Bill smiles. "He's looking at about thirty years. I'll offer twenty-five with the possibility of parole after ten. His days as a cop are over. That is if he gives us something that can be used."

"I want Wang behind bars," I say.

"That could be sooner than you think." Bill leans forward. "From what Phil said, he's known of the guy for a while. Knows where they do a lot of the shooting of films. Met him once. They took him to one of the teen shoots, telling him they were actors."

I don't feel any better because of it, but that's not something I can decide to do anything about.

"Just give me the chance to get Wang in my sights so I can put a bullet between his eyes."

January 15th, 2033
- Out on a Limb

The cold soup sits on the corner of the desk. Bojing ignores it while he scans the recorded vid of the police station break room. Something didn't work the way he wanted it to.

The cop who donned the China Girl interface lived through the brain worm code. It should have hammered her psyche with the male embedded brain waves, causing horrible feedback and hormone imbalance beyond a recoverable point. That small opening in security, tailored to worm its way into the mind of any woman experiencing the planted feed, would lower the protective barriers, but it didn't work. Why?

He absently scratches his crotch, not even thinking of the little girl the men had brought him. She was no virgin. Didn't even smell right. And now his dick itches from the encounter. He needs to wash, but this is more important.

The video shows all the right things happening. Loading of the program. The sim into the machine. Lead attachments. Headgear in place. The program started. The initial virus was delivered, making the female cop blackout. But then she should have thrashed even when they turned off the device. A non-recoverable scenario. How did she survive?

Bojing uses his access to enter the police human resources computer. Nothing spectacular about the officer. Top shape. No injuries during training. The background check was completed without any major incident–a name change at eighteen. Something is wrong.

He scours the system once again. Goes back to the initial documents of birth from 2012. Toronto Hospital, but doesn't find her. The parents are there, checked in for pending birth—a healthy baby boy of four kilos. There needs to be... He stops and replays the information—a boy. The officer is a man! But all the records show a woman. How... it hits Bojing. A sex change.

Historical records from other hospitals. He needs to check them. A hit comes up in The Hospital for Sick Children. The doctor is listed as retired. A record of an operation at ten cites gender confusion as to the reason. Parents signed off on the reassignment—the patient's name listed as Mark Jenkins. The name change shows the same. New name Maria Jenkins. A school record indicates campus change with the new name.

It makes sense to him. This is why the virus didn't work. The brain didn't change, just the outside of the person. The tailor-made virus would not affect men, just women.

Bojing sits back in his chair. The bugs have all been removed but the one in the break room. Unfortunately, it does not show anything besides that room. He will need to pressure the cleaners to plant more.

It's fun watching Bill work his magic with the judges. He messages one who says they'll not sign off on the warrant for the police in question and another who hesitates but relents on the evidence. She even signs off on the warrant for the prior judge. Maybe she knows something about him that Bill doesn't. All I know is we are cleaning house. Cap's not too happy that about half of the department signed out the China Girl rig.

The first raid will be the tech store. If we can seize records there, it'll be a good jump on the game. Getting corroboration of the tech being created and distributed will mean a great deal to the case. And linking it back to the Triads here will also help.

Bill doesn't want to give anyone the heads up about the upcoming arrests, but is hitting a roadblock with one judge. Surprise is the key. We need to take this down without a hitch.

Cap made contact with another precinct an hour ago, and they sent three squads to the tech store and are waiting for the warrant or sign of anyone being tipped off. That's our only concern. It's hard for a judge to tip someone off about the warrant, but it's been known to happen. This one judge is just difficult, though. She's asking for clarification on the information – how do we know there's something at this place we'll need. Phil's statement isn't swaying her. Building something that can be used for a crime is not the same as building something meant for a crime. She doesn't believe there's a foundation, which means the evidence could be thrown out of court and jeopardize the case.

Bill disconnects and places his phone on the desk. The unit starts charging.

"Well?" I ask.

"We'll have a warrant in a few minutes." He stretches. "Once it's in, I'll transmit it to the squad leader, and they'll start the first raid."

I stand and glance at Bill. "You want to see a raid happen? It's not like what you see on TV."

Bill looks at his watch. "Hell, I've got time."

Nygen's Technology is open. The neon sign in the window screams for people to come inside and buy something. Good for him. But the store is empty. The owner is nowhere to be seen.

Bill is in the back seat of my car, the warrant scanned into his phone and ready to display. The squads keep back, even knowing about the warrant. Something is happening, and they wanted to get some more recordings of the store.

An ugly utility truck, one of those really high-roofed ones, sits in the parking lot. Among the antennas and equipment placed on the outside is a directional mic to pick up any sound we point the thing at. All disguised as a wind meter. Who says cops don't have a sense of humor?

Three clicks come over the radio. A sign they've stopped the recording.

I check my vest cam. Cap threw it at me and ordered it used today. He doesn't want any loose ends. This way, he can see exactly what happens for his report. It also protects me if something goes sideways.

Mie and I exit the car but keep ourselves out of sight of the shop. A bus pulls up and stops in front of the parking area. When the doors open, ten police file out, all in black. They carry assault rifles. One of them holds a battering ram.

A smile tugs at the side of my mouth.

I walk into the shop. A chime rings out, but there's no one inside. The counter has a multitude of hardware strewn about it. Work not yet complete.

The door at the back of the shop opens, and an Asian man steps into the open area. He wears normal street clothes under an undone bulky coat. His hands are in the pockets, keeping the thing from swinging open. There's a nervous half-smile on his face as he walks to the counter and glances up at me.

"You here for pick up or drop off," he says with a heavy accent.

Okay, I'll play with him. "Pick up."

"Name?"

"It's not under my name." I indicate the back. "Is the owner here?"

"He unloading truck."

A lie. There's no truck delivery out back. A few men with automatic weapons and a search warrant, yes. But no truck. I decide to play it coy.

"I can come back..."

"No, if you have something to pick up, I get it. Need name."

"Phil Dwight," I say.

"Oh, he say something. You want new unit?" The guy starts typing on a keyboard.

"Yeah, something like that." I glance at the back. "You sure he's not available? We have an arrangement."

"No, he working hard. Lots of stuff."

"He said he had something special for me..."

"You cop?" The guy steps back from the counter.

"It's better that I speak to him." I turn a little. Make it look like I'll leave.

"No, I help. You order here somewhere." He types on the keyboard with one hand. "I see nothing."

"Like I said, special order." I put my hand in the pocket of my coat. Take a good grip on my Glock.

"No order on system."

"Did you spell my name right?" I lean forward to see the screen. It's blank.

"You shouldn't do that," he says, the other hand coming out of the coat with a gun. "Now, you problem."

"I'm not the problem. How about I ask you a question?" I pull my Glock out. His weapon is smaller and not pointed at me. Mine comes up and points at his head. "Get the door. Now!"

A bang sounds from the back. Metal hitting metal. Men yell in Chinese. The guy swings his gun up. I squeeze off a round, hitting him in his shoulder. He drops the gun and grabs at the wound. His legs fold as he hits the ground, screaming. Mayhem erupts. Another man runs out from the back into the store. He carries a small handgun.

"Freeze!"

He starts to raise the weapon, and I put a bullet into his leg. His weapon falls to the ground, followed by his body. Blood bursts from the hole in his leg. He grabs it.

I'm over the counter and throw cuffs on the fake clerk, kicking his gun away from him. He's secure. I glance at the other. The guy inches his way to his fallen gun. I run over and kick the weapon away and straddle him. A quick grab and I have cinch ties in hand. I force the plastic cuffs around his wrists. He's tied up quick. Hard to fight with a bullet in your leg.

Two shots come from the back and the sound of heavy boots hitting the ground. The back door opens again. Mie is there. She looks around, her weapon pointed at the ground.

"I got him. How's the back?"

"Secure. Two shot. They had weapons."

I stand up. "Two bullet holes here. This guy and the other." I walk to the door. "Coming in!"

The backroom is loaded with boxes and electronics. The shop

owner is in a chair out cold. Two bodies are on the floor, a man covering each.

"We have a medic here?" I ask.

"Coming," one of the men says, and he steps out from the pack. "You hit?"

"No." I motion to the front of the store. "Two down. Bullet wounds. We need to keep them alive for interrogation."

"On it," he says and rushes to the front of the store.

Bill walks in. He's shaking. Probably adrenaline. "Man, that's intense."

"Just a day's work." I holster my Glock. "You good?"

He looks up at me. "Yeah, just pumped from that."

The owner is alive. A little beat up but still breathing. We'll need a bus to take him to the hospital to get checked out. The other two can go on separate buses with escorts—time for us to secure evidence.

Bill opens one of the small boxes and whistles. "Nice."

I walk over and see a shining China Girl rig still in bubble wrap. There's about twenty more from the size of the packages. We stopped a problem.

Bill smiles and holds one out jokingly. "Want one?"

"No, thanks." I check out another smaller box. Black cases fill the insides. All have Chinese writing on them. "Wonder what these are?"

Bill comes over just as I open one of the cases. It holds sims. CG sims. They were using the store to distribute the things. My stomach roils. It was right here under our noses, and we didn't know. How many girls have they taped? How many of them were raped? How many did they kill? There's going to be a lot of work identifying all this, especially since there are no names on the sims.

Two of the men go to the front. Three buses are called, and we search the back storage while they make their way to the store. Mie hunts, recording everything. Depending on how much they sold the units for, we really put a dent in the operations.

All told, we have twenty-two China Girl sets and almost fifty groups of sim boxes. Each has sixty sims. A dent indeed.

Ron Lance drops a file folder on my desk. It's thick, but then again, arrest reports usually are when they involve cops–fourteen in all with child porn possession and bribery charges. The squad room is so empty now.

Scraping fills the air as Ron drags a chair over to my desk. He's got a strange look on his face, but I'm not one to be able to tell much, only knowing a little about him. He seems to be comfortable around me.

I take the folder and open it. Pages contain the names to investigate and why a warrant is needed. Other pages show the execution time of each warrant. They all have the same time. A well-coordinated strike. All within an hour of the raid on the tech store. No one was injured. Seventeen China Girl units seized. Hundreds of China Girl sims taken. Ten wives will probably file for divorce. I don't know how many children will be affected.

The only thing I do know is we've taken down the Triad's link to the police. Will it make a difference? Only time will tell.

"We're still going through the bank records from what we found with the warrants." He leans back. "Could mean a lot of pizza lunches for a few years."

"Wonder what he did with the money." I keep turning pages. It appears Phil and a number of others kept track of the names of the girls they watched. "Think we cleared out all the bad ones?"

"Doubt it," Ron says. "There could be a lot more, or others could fill their places."

Mie types out something on her desk. I can't tell because the letters appear to be Chinese.

Ron glances over to Mie then back to me. "Have you filled out the twelve-twenty-fours yet?"

I look up. "What?"

"The twelve-twenty-fours." He reaches over and taps a few commands on my desk. Forms appear. "When IAD is involved in a bust based on what is found out from another officer who is not IAD, the officer involved fills it out."

I leaf through the forms. There are a lots of pages. It has one name of the investigating officer, the IAD agent, and the officer being investigated.

"I don't have to fill one of these out for each arrest, do I?" The answer is already at the top of my mind.

"Sort of," Ron says. "I fill out most of it, but you need to send in a twenty-twenty form for each one asking me to fill in the forms." He reaches over and brings up another form. The thing is twice as long as the prior one.

"No way," I say. "This is crap!"

"Yeah, it is crap." He's smiling. "Sorry, it's something we pull on those we're interested in coming on board with us."

I glance around the squad room. "You want me to transfer to IAD?"

Ron pulls the chair closer and leans in. "Yes. You're a good detective and honest. Something we really need in our department."

"But, I've had discipline marks in my file."

"Yeah, so what? Do you know how many I had before transferring over?"

He leans back and takes me in, looking me up and down with a long stare. It's uncomfortable. Strange.

"Think about it. I have some pull with our Captain, and Maria is going to be out for a while." He takes a deep breath. "She's out of the coma, but her coordination is off. And she's having a hard time with what the machine tried to do to her."

It's good news. I feel like a shit not going to see her, but Ron seemed to find the time. "I got to get over there to see her."

"No worries. You really don't know her."

"So, why would I go to IAD?"

I push away the empty plate. Julie is at work, and Sarah cooked mac and cheese. Not bad, but a little dry. At least she's trying to help out. Life is different today. It's a good thing. I have my daughter back.

The wind keeps hitting the windows, but at least the snow is no longer falling. The temperature is dropping fast, though.

We talk. Not about much, but telling her about the raid and arrests seems to lighten her spirit a little.

I still don't know how to connect with my daughter. She's sixteen going on twenty-three. A bit wild, though the kidnapping seems to have taken a little out of her sails. What do you talk about with a young lady? It baffles me. The whole boyfriend thing is a mystery to me. She never let us know, and we didn't even meet him until I had to arrest him.

The silence at the table while we eat drives me a little mad. Maybe if I talk about my day or asking her about what she did will work.

"So, what did you do today?" I ask.

"Not much," she says, shoveling another spoon of the dried noodles and cheese into her mouth.

"What about school. Anything happening there?"

"Nope."

"Finished your homework?"

"Nope."

"You going to finish it tonight?"

"Nope."

"I just thought... What do you mean, nope?"

I catch the smile on her face through the carpet of hair she has let fall forward.

"Just thought I'd see if you were listening."

She has me. "When did you become such a detective?"

"It runs in the family."

I pick up my plate and stand. "Well, if you want, you can put in for cadet training in a couple of years."

"What?"

With my plate in hand, I walk into the kitchen and run water over it. "You heard me."

Sarah lets out a laugh. "With my luck, we'd end up in the same precinct."

I walk back into the dining room. "Could be worse."

My cell rings. "We're going to talk about this in a few minutes."

"But I want to talk about it now," Sarah says.

"Okay, we will, but not right now, in a few minutes." I look at the cell. Cap is calling. "Look, I have to take this."

"But what about me joining the police?"

"Bruce speaking." I press mute. "It's my captain. Give me a minute."

"Roberts. We have activity on the server."

"What?"

"We've traced the Triad to their new hideout."

January 17th, 2033
- Master Blaster

The bed is too soft.

Bojing rolls onto his side. The new bedroom and office is more a Western-style, not one for a man, but a pampered child. And sleeping alone is not something he enjoys. But sometimes he needs to just sleep. And now is the time.

The feng shui of the new building is not good. A door on the wrong wall, toilet incorrectly placed. He even hates the color of the paint. But he's had no time to change things. It should have been done months ago, but the contractor folded. Bankrupt without notice. The man didn't have enough business to keep his company busy and too little profit to pay his employees. That's why it took so long to get little done. Why the workers used poor colors. It was too bad, Bojing actually liked the man. But the contractor lost all the money paid to him and needed to be punished. And punish him they did. He will not be able to do construction again. Not rip off others with poor workmanship and continual extensions of deadlines. Not without his hands, that is.

A breeze enters the bedroom. Goosebumps form on his skin. The one thing about the building he really hates is the lack of insulation. Warmth hardly stays in the building, and the furnace continuously runs. The thing cannot keep up against the bitter cold outside.

Hell, he'll have to make sure motion sensors are up and running tomorrow. With the cops on their tail, they need to be ready for anything, and this move was so untimely. Little done and lots to do.

He will have to crack the whip on the men. Maybe wake them at four in the morning as punishment for not having the place ready. Harden them up. That is, if he can sleep any time soon.

The clock next to the bed shows one. It is late. Rest is needed.

He rolls over and closes his eyes, willing himself into a restless slumber.

I stare at the Portlands projected on the wall, a small man-made peninsula of lower Toronto. We've called in another precinct to help, and their headquarters are busting with activity, even with the darkness around us.

Cap explains the operation with the other precinct's captain. It's a raid. Over a hundred cops being coordinated on this. No small feat to organize. But it needs to be done. We're not sure how many Triad are holed up, but the size of the place we're hitting demands more feet on the ground.

Bill is with us. As the DA assigned to the case, he wants to make sure everything goes off without a hitch. He has search warrants tucked away, ready to produce when needed. It didn't take long for him to get a judge to sign them. Everyone heard about the China Girl arrests on the news, and there's a lot of interest in removing any more of the Triad from the area. With two judges arrested and charged with possession of child pornography related to China Girl, the others have to be on their best behavior, and now everyone in the court system wants to distance themselves from the Triad.

The building plans are laid out on the table. The place is huge. Larger than the last center of operations they had. But not as usable. Known as The Hearn, it was a coal-fired generating plant opened in the 1950s. In 1983 they decommissioned it. The building changed hands a number of times, but the last one turned out to be a year ago when a shell company picked it up for pennies on the dollar. Easy enough to do when the soil is contaminated, the building run down, and no way of reclaiming the site. Until the Triad came in.

Tax rolls show the shell company is owned by an Ontario numbered company, which is, in turn, owned by another. That one is owned by a Canada numbered company which has three subsidiaries. After the holdings change hands seven more times, we can see an offshore corporation in China controls the end of the string. Mie confirmed the firm in China, designated a holding company, is Triad based.

The captains run over the dangers of the building from its rundown state to the many rooms and offices. Several coal chutes are still open, and an urban explorer lost his life back in 2008 while trespassing. The place has earned a reputation for being dangerous.

"Satellite images of the outside show activity." Cap indicates the screen. Lights move in the yard of the building. Vehicles are running; the heat plums of their engines show up red in the infra-red scan. "We've been able to identify over fifty people going in and out of the location, so keep that in mind during the raid." The screen changes. "We've uploaded a copy of the floor plan to your phones. This is the last know layout, but it is based on data from 2018 when a production crew used the building for filming."

"Live long and prosper!" someone shouts from the back. The room laughs.

"Yes, we all watched that Star Trek movie." He changes the view to the outside of the actual building. It's a mess. Garbage is strewn everywhere, and old pipes cover the ground. "Last images we have are from the 2022 Luminato festival. This is where the building was condemned. Part of one wall fell, killing five and wounding over a dozen people."

The room is quiet. I wonder if we're all thinking the same question — why would they buy such a building?

"We're inserting here, here, and here." The other captain indicates the points on the overhead shot. "We'll have troops across the canal to pick up anyone attempting to flee from that side. Snowmobiles will be employed, and we'll have spotters here, here, and here." Again, he points to the map. "We'll coordinate the raid from this location just outside the property."

"All right, you all know your assignments," Cap says. My cap, not the other one. "If you have any questions, see your squad leaders. Let's be safe tonight. No one goes out without body armor and a helmet. I'm not going to attend a funeral on this one. Don't put your life at risk. No heroes."

Ron Lance steps forward from the side of the room. "What you have heard is an official statement from your captains. Being IAD, I will tell you this, you have a green light to shoot as needed. Each member of the raid will wear a transponder like this." He holds up a small, square device. "Everyone on our team attaches this to their shoulder. If you look through your faceplate and see a red light on the person you're looking at, they're a member of our team." He takes a deep breath. "If anyone shoots a member of our team, I'll personally ramrod them to the wall. Understood?"

The room grows silent, and every officer in the room nods. It's what they need to hear in order to have the instructions sink home. They're good to shoot the bad guys but be careful not to shoot a good guy.

Ron steps back.

Cap clears his throat. "Your body cams will activate at the start of the raid. We're watching everything that happens, so make sure you follow the rules and come out of this alive. Dismissed."

Mie and I hold back as the rest of the cops shuffle out of the room. It's not that we want to talk to the captains, just that we need to.

Ron and Bill are with the caps, talking about the operation.

We hang back, letting the two caps discuss what's needed. Bill breaks their chat short, and Mie takes the first step forward. She's more sure of herself, being from Interpol and all. They can't bust her down, but she can make their lives a nightmare with the right wording on a report. I think they already know that, for they are more polite to her.

"What can I do for you, Mie?" Cap One says. I decide our captain is Cap One, and the other is Cap Two. Just like Thing One and Thing Two in the children's story.

"Information on Triad. Office say leaders no pleased of Bojing being found out. They cut off support. He alone now. No backup," she says.

"What does that mean?" Bill asks.

"It means he's not going to have a lot of money to pay for a fancy lawyer," I say. "They've emptied his accounts."

Bill smiles. Cap One lets out a deep breath.

Ron takes a step back, stares at the image of Bojing on the screen. "He's trapped."

I nod. "Yeah, trapped. Nowhere to go and no one to turn to."

"He big problem now," Mie says.

Bill turns to us. "But he's run out of resources and support. He's going to be easy to take down now, right?"

Mie shakes her head. "He like caged tiger. Nothing to lose. All gone. Will eat hand with food."

Three SWAT teams meet us in the command unit. They're dressed for the weather just like us, white combats and weapons with white tape where it needs it. Each will be invisible to people looking for something to shoot, but only while we're outside. In each group is a sniper and spotter. That gives us three god-like powers. They can touch without being touched. BMG's weigh heavy on the shoulders of the three short shooters. They'll take out the ones trying to escape by snowmobile or foot.

The teams integrate well. Each member takes their group to the designated area. We're waiting for the right time and a pre-determined set of events to happen before giving the go-ahead. It all depends on the scouts we've deployed.

Most people think we just show up and raid places. In fact, it's a highly organized plan of attack. We minimize casualties that way.

The command trailer is a twenty-foot long camper type vehicle. It's specially made for us with thick walls, and no windows – save small slots of darkened glass. The glass can be slid aside for a weapon to be fired out of it. The ballistic glass can stop any normal slug from penetrating it. I hope no one tries to test that theory.

Along one side are monitors, each displaying information about the raid. One section has the readings of eight cops on each. Another bank is hooked up to the drones we have ready to deploy. Another set monitors the weather, airspeed, temp, you name it. Highly organized.

Mie and I stand amidst the techs, watching as the main groups reach position. When they do, a soft click is sent through their radios to tell us they're ready and waiting for instructions. It takes a heart—stopping twenty minutes for everyone to be in place. It's now 2:30 am.

"All teams reporting in. They've reached their designated areas and are holding for orders," one of the techs calls out.

"Have them stand by," Cap One says.

"Surveillance, what'd you got?" Cap Two asks.

"Nothing out of the ordinary on the heat signals, sir. Launching drones now." Another tech flips five switches and grabs a joystick. Four others follow his lead. The monitors in front of them go from dark to light as night vision imaging takes over. Things appear black and green on the screens as they send the drones up and away; their silent motors turn micro blades without disturbing the night.

Three of the drones circle the outside of the building, while two make their way through broken windows or walls. The interior of the place comes to life on our monitors, but it's empty. No one walks the wide-open space in the building. There's nothing to say anyone is there. They flying around looking for anything that will tell them people are here. But nothing shows up.

"The information we traced was sound," Bill says. "Our intelligence reports all of Bojing's group is assembled there."

"Not seeing anything in the building, sir," a tech reports.

"So far, you've only looked at the main open area." Cap Two steps to the tech's side. "Over there. High and to the South. You've got offices there."

The tech directs the drone to the spot. Light comes from one window. Movement. People.

"I want IDs on them now," Cap Two says.

"Running recognition. Will let you know," a tech says, her hands flying over a keyboard.

The image jumps and goes out of focus. It's like riding a roller coaster for a few seconds, and the drone goes offline. The tech removes his hand from the joystick and looks over.

"What happened?" Cap One asks.

"Not sure," the tech replies. "I'm running a diagnostic on the last received data."

"Come on," Cap two says. "We need to make sure. Drone three, you have anything?"

"Nothing from outside, sir."

"Drone five, you inside?"

"Yes, sir. Nothing to report."

"Anything out of the ordinary? Anything? Fly farts. I don't care what it was," Cap two says.

"My gyroscope wobbled for a second, but it stabilized quick," the tech says.

"Time frame?"

"02:47:38, sir."

"What time did your drone start to come down?" Cap One asks the tech, still staring at a log file.

"02:47:39, sir."

"Gyroscope readings?"

It takes a second. "02:47:38, sir."

"They have something. Go to stealth," Cap Two says.

The techs still flying hit controls. The drones slow. All lights are extinguished. The drones become shadows in the night.

Each tech verifies their drone are in stealth mode and what power level they're at. Most don't hit under 75%. Still have time to look around and return. Drone five moves to the same spot where the other drone was downed but approaches at a different angle. The night vision goes off, and a telephoto lens takes over. A man walks a gangway watching the empty space. He carries a large weapon in his hands, but it doesn't look like any rifle I've seen.

"Magnatron," the tech says. "He's scanning two dimensional. Coming up from under."

The drone tilts and dips. The pilot is good, but these things aren't meant to fly tilted. He captures a good picture of the face and turns back to night vision and under the gangplank.

An image shows up on the screen above the tech. It sharpens out, and the database is searched. We hit in seconds. Ping Leung. The guy has a rap sheet, but all from China: tech specialist, computer hacker, tendency to violence – it's off the scale, smokes but doesn't drink. I recognize him as one of the bastards in the room when Bojing tortured me.

"I want him," I say.

The image from drone five changes to an upshot. The drone flies silently, so it is under the man. The grating on the walkway is small but not that small. A crosshair shows up.

"What are you doing?" Cap One asks.

"Someone says they wanted this one. I'm getting ready," the operator says.

"Belay that." Cap One turns to me. "Careful what you say, Roberts. They would have taken this guy out, but it would also alert the others."

"He's taken out one of our drones. Don't you think he knows we're here?" I ask.

Cap One stares at me. "He could think it's just some kid's toy he just downed. Heck, the thing wasn't running silent."

I think about that for a second. He's right.

"I want to know how many people are in there," Cap Two says. "Find a way."

———

We have a count. Seventy confirmed heat signatures.

The wait is for a go on the raid. Everyone is ready. Frozen, but ready. Mie and I don our armor and check weapons when Ron comes up to us. The command trailer is long, but nothing is sectioned off.

"I want you to do something for me," he says.

"Sure, anything." I struggle with the laces on my boots. Been too long since I wore this crap.

"I'll bet that Bojing guy had something to do with Maria's incident."

"Yes, he would," Mie says. "It him who direct the actions of gang here."

Ron takes a deep breath. "They won't let me take part in the raid. I want to somehow be able to tell Maria I got the son-of-a-bitch who did this thing to her, but without being there, I'd be lying."

I finish the lace and stand up, looking Ron in the eyes. "I understand. But something you need to know as well." I put a hand on his shoulder. "You've green-lighted this project. That means you're involved deeply. If not, you wouldn't be here. When we get the bastard, he'll know you had something to do with it. It's cops like you that give us a good name. Honest and always digging for the truth."

Ron almost smiles at that. "Thanks. But I want you to do one thing for me."

"Anything," I say.

He hands me a pistol. It's huge—a Desert Eagle. I pull the clip. Seven rounds. 50 AE. Heavy load. It'll go through any flak jacket up to level III, but even then, it will break ribs on a center mass shot. I pull out my Glock. Less power, more rounds. There's something to say about having firepower, though. And the site of it will make just about anyone piss their pants.

It takes a few more seconds, but I hand him my Glock. "Keep that safe." I put the eagle into the holster. It fits, but just barely.

Ron takes my weapon and hands over seven clips for the eagle. "In case you need them."

"Thanks." I swap out the Glock mags with the ones for the eagle. "I'll be using the assault rifle for now, but if I see Wang, I'll definitely put a cap in his ass from your gun."

"I'd appreciate that."

I finish strapping up and look over at Mie. She's ready and waiting for me and holds a very small and oddly shaped weapon – like a handgun, but thinner. I give her a questing look.

"Needle gun." She holds it out but doesn't let it go. "Air propelled fine plastic needle. No shell. Will penetrate any armor." Her voice lowers to a whisper. "He die tonight."

January 17th, 2033 — Quagmire

The clock on the table flashes 12:00, but Bojing knows it's not that time. He reaches out and taps his cell. Numbers appear. 3:27. Still early, but sleep continues to elude him.

Windowless, the only lights are the clock's flashing numbers and the dimming display of his cell phone. The too soft bed cradles him but is not the reason for the lack of sleep. Something is wrong. He can feel it deep inside. He sits up. The cold room wraps around him.

A kilometer away, the city is waking up. Still, no noise reaches him, and the strangeness of the location broods in his mind. The building is too big for their needs, and many repairs are still incomplete.

He shuffles off the bed, turns on the light next to his cell, and dresses. The economy of movement happens by instinct. Clothes are donned quick and without fuss. Shoes are tied. A jacket put on. And cigarette lit.

Smoke trails up into the air while he walks to the door and opens it. Movement catches his eye. He turns sharply to the right. A small object hovers less than a meter from his head. The slow movement of it allows him to focus in the low light. A small drone pivots in a clockwise direction. For some reason, it doesn't focus on him, but then again, he is quiet. A habit forced upon him at a young age.

He grabs the drone. Electricity stings his hand, but he ignores it. Using his momentum, he slams the intruding device against the door frame, smashing the outside casing and ceasing the electric shock defense. A small camera mounted on the top front turns toward him. He places a finger over it, blocking prying eyes, and rips it away.

They have found us.

Our squad follows the railroad tracks from the Portlands Energy Centre to the small tree line opposite a snow-covered parking lot. Over fifty cars litter the area. Two people sit in each, maybe more. With our raiding party's size, if things go the wrong way, it could get messy.

A group of five officers wait at a tree just fifty meters in front of us. Mie and I see them from the red dots showing on our faceplates. No other people are around. A light flashes on the ground between us, a small pinprick hid from the building. Another group signals for us to join them.

In a crouch, Mie dashes across the distance, avoiding the small shrubs that lay between us. I count to ten and follow.

"Switch to channel three on your faceplate," whispers a man. He indicates a small switch on the inside of the helmet.

I reach in and hit the tiny button. An overlay appears in the upper right corner of my vision; it's footage from a drone. It's another fifty meters to the west of us doing a circuit and examining the Triad building's openings for any signs of weapons.

"Corner of the building in twos," the squad leader whispers. "First two go."

The squad splits. Two figures dash across the open field to the corner of the building. They get there safely.

"Second two, go."

Two more dash over to the corner.

"Third two, go."

Mie and I dash, following the same path as the other two partners. I get to the corner, heart pumping. Sweat threatens to run down my face, but the cold is enough to hold it back.

The squad leader runs in a crouch to the corner and puts his back against it.

"Catch your breath. Long measured intakes," he says, his words barely audible. "There's an opening in the wall about fifty meters. We'll single file to it and wait for the go signal."

The minute he allows us gets our heart rates back down, but the raid's anxiety still makes the adrenaline run. When he signals, we all move in a crouched line, weapons pointed at the ground but ready. We're low enough that the busted windows in the building are higher than our heads. It's uncomfortable, slow, but necessary to approach on the raid. The drone image shows the wall, but we're just specks against it with little red dots on our shoulders.

It's a big hole in the wall. Two can enter at once.

"Ear protection down," the squad leader says.

We all reach up and pull straps under our helmets. The ear protectors come down and muffle out the world around us.

"Squads, report," Cap One says over the radio.

"Squad one, in position," a voice replies.

We're squad eight, a pivotal entrance group. We believe the gang lives in the old office section on the fifth floor, directly above where we're entering. We'll be taking the stairs.

All squads report in position. It's happening—a little over a week. We're taking them down.

"Flashbangs, ready," Cap One says.

The squad leader dashes to the other side of the hole, a small canister in one hand.

"Pins out. On three," Cap One says, his voice strangely muffled over the radio. "Three, two, one, throw."

I throw my can into the building. The muffs keep me from hearing the obvious metallic clink of it bouncing on the floor. Four seconds. A muffled bang and blinding light. Shouts come from inside.

"By two – in!" the squad leader yells.

We enter, Mie and I last. Shots fire. I scan the area. Red dots appear far away and to the left and right–our people. Don't shoot our people. Sparks fly in front of us.

"Twelve high," our squad leader calls out.

Three of us aim up, searching. The others keep an eye out, protecting. Movement catches my eye. I squeeze off two rounds. The assault rifle belches out rounds. The other two zero in on what I saw and add two rounds each. A second later, a body falls from high up.

"Cover," the squad leader directs.

We split up in our pairs. Mie and I go forward and left.

"Advance odds." Our leader. We're evens. The odds move forward.

We advance in a staggered formation. The structure inside is comprised of girders and floor. There're railings, some of them purposeful around holes in the floor, others just scattered about. Once used coal shuts are now blocked off with natural gas pipes leading up to where the old generators used to be. There's cover everywhere.

More shots, but not from our team. Cap One keeps asking for status reports from each group, but we're not on the command channel and thus don't hear what the squad leaders report back to him. Our course is taking us to the stairs, not ten meters in front of us. We'll be sitting ducks for anyone firing from above when we finally make for it.

"Dash!"

The command comes over our squad channel. We all stand and run to the stairs. Presumably, the other squads are covering us. Nothing happens. We make it, not a shot fired. This is too easy.

"I don't like this, Cap," I say over the radio. "We need intel."

"Stand by," he replies.

We start climbing the stairs. The first flight is twenty meters high—a double run. Legs burn. Knees complain. I ignore them.

The first landing is gained, and we're back into formation, two by two. Our squad leader brings up the back, scanning behind. The formation we all know and trust takes us across to the first group of offices. An open door leads in–our first two peel off and into the area.

"Intel shows the main floor empty," Cap One says.

"Tell us something we don't know," I mutter.

Cap Two comes online. "Keep chatter to a minimum. Squad leaders only on the main channel."

I let up the pressure on my muffs and tap Mie to do the same. "I don't like this."

She glances around. "I understand. Me too."

"The offices are clear," the two scouts report.

We continue across the walkway to the next door and two more split off to verify. They report the same. Clear.

Another squad is up to the next floor, checking as well.

"Signs of life, but nothing else here," the scout reports.

"Secure the building," Cap Two says. "We're coming in."

Snow hits my faceplate as the command center turns off Unwin Avenue. Mie and I wait by the tracks as it lumbers forward, crushing the fluffy white stuff under heavy tread tires. The vehicle slows as it reaches the tracks, and we climb aboard through the opened door.

Techs are turned in their seats but occasionally glace back at their monitors to ensure the drones are hovering on standby.

The staff is just starting to get out of their seats and perform the mundane cleaning task. A map of the building sits on a table positioned in the middle of the compartment. Brandon Max, Cap One, stands by it, marking off rooms as Cap Two reads out the information. This is the second time they have people looking into each area to ensure nothing was missed.

"We should recall the drones," Cap Two says.

Cap puts both hands palm down on the table. I decide to just call him Cap now. "How the hell did we miss them?"

Cap Two glances at the techs. "Somehow, our intel was wrong. Didn't one of you spot someone?"

"Yeah, it was me." One of the techs spins around. "When drone two went down, I spotted the person who took it out. They were..." He turns to his monitor, and it blanks out. "What the hell?"

"You get a malfunction?" Cap Two asks.

The tech's fingers dance on the keyboard. The last few seconds play out as the drone wrenches in the air and goes dark. He rewinds the footage. The lens is covered by something.

"Is that a finger?" I ask.

Heat blooms appear on the satellite imaging. Another drone hits the ground, still transmitting.

"Sir, reports are coming in from some of the units," someone calls out.

"Let's hear it," Cap says.

A jumble of voices splits the air. Too many people talking at once. A few screams. Weapons fire.

"Fuck!" I yell, grabbing my helmet and slamming it on my head.

Mie and I are at the door when thunking sounds against both walls. Instinct kicks in. I hit the floor.

People cower. They whimper and cower. Probably the techs. I charge my rifle, lift my head, slide back a protective cover from the slit window. I just about shit.

Ten men on the Westside walk to our vehicle. The weapons they carry spit out fire and slugs. The truck jerks and tilts to the side, tires blown. The other side gives way as well. We're flat on rims.

Rounds ping off the walls. The armored sides deflect bullet after bullet, but even it has a limited life span. Nothing can keep up against sustained abuse.

"Don't we have weapons on this thing?" Cap calls out.

"Yes, but–" The vehicle rocks, and Cap Two stumbles forward, head striking one of the control panels.

"Shit! Can anyone man our weapons and fire back?" Cap calls out as he rushes to one of the panels.

The tech for drone five gets to his feet and takes a seat next to a panel. "I have them."

"Shoot their fucking asses," Cap commands.

A small part of the roof bumps up, and a ladder drops from the ceiling. It's not all the way to the floor but will do.

"Someone will have to man the turret," the tech yells.

I rush over and start to climb the ladder. There's little room in the turret to fit. I need to pull myself into the small seat and almost lay down. There's not even a meter in height. My feet hit peddles, and pressing one turns the turret in that direction. Sticks come up; each has a trigger. I spin to the right, a small shield slides away from the front, and ballistic glass allows me to see the enemy advancing. I tilt the gun and squeeze both triggers.

Two mini-guns spin to life. Death runs a trail from left to right, cutting into bodies, taking legs off, removing heads. In seconds the one wave at the east is destroyed.

"Yeah! We need one of these, Cap!" I call out.

Rounds ping off the back of the turret, and I spin it around. My fingers squeeze the triggers. I cut into a group of advancing forms on the other side. They scatter, knowing death is now against them. The guns stop firing but are still whining. I'm out of ammo already.

"Reload," I call down.

"Move the guns to face forward. We can only reload it in that position," someone yells from below.

I spin the turret until it's looking forward.

"Reload!"

Chunking and clicks fills my ears. A red light flashes on the board in front of me, and two counters, both at zero, start to blink. The clicking stops, the light turns green and flashes off. The counters are now at five hundred each.

Stray bullets strike against the side of the turret. I spin it but only get halfway to the side. A grinding noise sounds out.

"Something is wedged. Stop trying to force it," someone calls out from below.

The ladder shakes a bit as a head pops up beside me. "A round is caught in the gearing. We'll need to clear it." Her dark face is illuminated by the soft glow of the numbers.

Black eyes reflect in the center of the whites of her eyes, and she reaches out a shaking hand. I grab it and haul her up, but she slaps it away and reaches over her head. A small panel slides away, and she fishes with her fingers.

Her eyes go wide in a second. "Got it!" Her elation is cut short by a scream. She pulls her hand back. It comes out bloody and missing two fingers. She falls back.

"Get someone here to help her," I yell, turning my attention back to protecting us.

The gears are free. I swing the turret over, point to the approaching group.

"Time to die!"

I squeeze the triggers.

A figure runs out from the shadows. It streaks across my field of view, and I move the mini-guns into position. A light red dot appears on the back of it, and I stop. Silhouette with a red dot. A friendly.

The figure moves fast. Faster than anyone I know, except one person.

Mie.

I swing the guns back and cut down two more advancing combatants. At least we're safe here.

My feet hit the floor, and I let go of the ladder. The tech who freed up the gun sits on the floor, hand wrapped in gauze. Cap moves around, making sure everyone is okay, but his face is ashen, and his left arm is in a sling.

I come up to him, take a roll of gauze off him, start tending to the wounded. My ears ring from the sustained firing of the mini-guns. I look over. Cap is talking to me, but nothing is getting through. He points to something behind me, and I turn. A tech is at his seat but doing nothing. I go over to him, wondering what could be wrong.

The buzzing in my ears lessens. I can almost make out words. There's a lot of chatter out there. Not all of it is good. People have died today.

We still have a working drone. Must have been one of the high fliers. It's on its way down to the Hearn building, gliding in from above. An open window confirms a way in, and the tech flies it deftly, ignoring any interference from obstacles. Once at the top level, he spins it around and gets a good view of what's happening in the building.

I point at movement on the screen. "Zoom in there."

The tech zooms in, and the lens goes to night vision. I can make out Mie as she runs into the building.

I catch something from the tech but can't make it out. "Follow her," I say.

He brings the drone down and behind Mie. Collateral damage is spilled out before us. Bodies lay on the ground with red blooms on them. I glance at the other line of monitors showing the life readouts of our people. The drone's screen grabs my attention again. Mie has that needle gun thing out and firing.

"That thing is silent," the tech says from a few hundred meters away.

"What?"

"That gun of hers, it's not making any noise whatsoever!"

I hear that statement, but still, I need to check in order to be sure he's still not talking.

Cap puts a hand on my shoulder.

"Your hearing will come back soon. Give it a few minutes."

Mie's taken out twenty of the 49ers, sprinting from one body to the next. Some she removes the shoulder marker, and others she grabs their med-pack and does something. The ones she tends to get to keep their shoulder badges. The odd one gets cuffed with the zip ties. She's marking the living for pickup but using methodical, quick movements with little wasted time.

At the staircase, she climbs two steps at a time. On the first landing, she lets out two more shots from her weapon and then advances up more stairs. On the second landing, she repeats the process. Two more 49ers fall. She's a killing machine. Her speed is hard to believe, knowing how much running she's performed today.

The drone circles in and jerks. The tech smiles. "I got one!"

The tech moves the drone from the staircase and brings it up to the next landing ahead of Mie. He's making sure the coast is clear for her, playing the part of helpful overseer.

At the top of the stairs, he fires, killing another one. But a stray bullet hits the unit. One of the blades is damaged.

"I can hold it here, but only here," he says.

"The thing has done enough." I pick up my assault rifle. "Time to get back into the fight."

January 17th, 2033
- Helping Hand

Chaos ensues. Bojing's men run around without thought of where they are going. He shakes his head and kicks at the small device in front of him. The drone careens at the edge of the walkway for a second, then tumbles over the edge. Only the cops would have such a thing deployed. But how did they find him so fast?

He closes the sound-deadening door behind him. It seamlessly disappears against the dark texture of the wall. One of many such hiding places he insisted be built into the building. Most are below, in the small walkways under the building, where most of the men sleep, eat, and entertain themselves with the women they brought.

An acrid scent floats in the air. Gun power, smoke, death. And his pistol is inside the room he just left.

With long strides, he walks across the gangway but changes to a run to get into their control center at the opposite side of the building, and down into the tunnels. Safe. Protected. Hidden.

He takes the stairs two at a time. After three flights, his lungs start to protest. His legs burn, and one knee complains while the injured one screams for him to stop. He keeps pushing downward.

The stairs end at ground level, but he needs to be down farther. Two more stories to go. A quick turn to the left where a firefight rages.

Flashes of light and lines of tracer rounds fill the air. His men remembered the emergency plan.

He steps over the body of a policeman in riot gear. His men have killed a lot of uniforms tonight. They've taken the whole group by surprise. Good. He'll need to praise them for choosing the right course of action. But the whine of a powered machine gun splits the air. Men die. The opening in the wall is close, and he makes his way to it. He needs to know what's happening.

A large vehicle in the distance spits fire from a turret on the top. His men are cut down. Fire rains from the vehicle. It is done. The vehicle is disabled, but the charge to the outside to repel the invaders ended many of his men's lives. All those men lost. If they weren't 49ers he would feel the loss. But that is what they are for. They are foot soldiers. Throw them against the attacking force. More will line up to join without hesitation. He can rebuild his troops. A quick call is all he needs to make.

The gun stops firing. He glances out. Men retreat, run away, but still, there are those who fight on. But when the gun starts up again, death touches its cold finger on those remaining.

Bojing takes his gaze away from the sight. He needs a weapon. Any weapon. The bodies.

Little light spills into the building, but he finds a body with an assault rifle still slung over the shoulder along with a Glock, knife, and clip. He will make it out alive.

———

I walk through a hundred and fifty metres of death. Those I didn't take down with the mini-guns lay on the ground dead or dying from Mie's relentless run into the building. She's a machine. One well-oiled angel of death being visited on the Triad.

I hit the wall, my back against the cold bricks. My heart pounds. Breath comes in gasps. The glass of the faceplate attached to the helmet fogs. I lift it just enough to let the plumes escaping my mouth rush under it. Concentrate. Lower your heart rate with deeper breaths and you'll calm down. Calm means life, and no rash thoughts or actions.

Dropping to a knee, I glance around the broken bricks and into the building. The sight makes my stomach revolt. I hold back the rising bile —so many dead. I wonder if it's worth it.

Mie is one red dot up four levels and moving swiftly. She must be searching for Wang.

My head is flung backward, twisting my neck. The ballistic glass of the faceplate shatters. I drop to my stomach. A sharp retort sounds as someone continues to fire.

Someone is alive. And either they don't have a helmet or don't care who is shot. Must be the gang. Cops don't just shoot without knowing.

The heads-up display is destroyed. The protection is no longer useful. I rip it off the helmet, and a loose wire dangles to the side.

Calm down. Take a breath. I speak into my mike. "Shield destroyed. I'm blind."

"Drone coming in," Cap replies. "Keep down while we bring it into position.

The slight whirl of blades split the air. A drone hovers over me for a second, dips down and to the right, and then behind the wall.

"Movement. Mie's transponder is moving four floors up, and one without a transponder is running to the middle of the building," a tech's voice sounds in my ear.

"Going in," I say.

Up and over the bricks. Down on one knee. Weapon up and butt tucked into my shoulder. The movement is gone.

"Recon," I say into my mic.

The drone comes into the building. It flies straight ahead in the direction of the retreating figure it saw. I stand with rifle ready and walk forward, trying not to step on any of the bodies.

A gunshot sounds. The drone moves back from an opening at least one-hundred meters. It's past the halfway mark in the building where the boilers and turbines sat a long time ago. A mess of support beams and struts litter the area—perfect places to hide.

I quicken my pace. No backup until Mie gets down here. I'm on my own, just like she is.

Bodies don't litter this area. The firefight happened near the east wall—the one with the hole in it. There's litter spread out. Set designs from TV shows left. Food wrappers from yesteryear lay on the ground from when people flocked to see illegal concerts long ago.

"Mie, get your ass down here. We have someone moving about, and there could be more."

"Clearing," she radios back to me. "Many hidden rooms here. Three more down."

Fuck. That's how they got us. Hidden rooms. Not enough time to find them during the initial search, and they attacked before floodlights could be brought in to aid in the second search.

A bullet ricochets off the pillar just above me. I duck. Too close to the opening of the stairs. They lead down into the darkness that I cannot see past. Need the night vision on the helmet, but it's gone with the faceplate. I'm stuck.

"I'm moving the drone in for a better look. What's your status?" the tech asks.

"Alive," I say. "Get me eyes on who's shooting from below."

"The opening. Side with the stairs. There's someone with a long rifle. Doesn't see me. Going stealth," the tech advises.

The slight noise of the drone disappears into the night. It hovers there, tilting while the small engines adjust to make as little noise as possible but still allows the device to work. A slight dip forward and then down, it goes into the opening.

"One shooter. They have you covered if you stay there. Suggest moving."

"Smartass," I say. But he's right. Need to move somewhere the shooter won't expect. I find a few small rocks. One I toss to the right, away from where I'm heading. It bounces with a clatter.

"That got his attention. The weapon is no longer pointing at you. Target is distracted."

I creep along in an arc. Halfway to the position, I throw another rock out to where the last one landed. This time just one shot is fired at it. The person knows what they're doing. It means they'll move in a second to stay alive.

"Target just moved. They're in a better advantage point for your distraction. Good for you. Their back is to you now."

I pretend to be the drone. Light footsteps. Crouch down. Try to incorporate economy of motion–an approach without being heard or seen.

Gunfire in the distance echoes around me. I freeze. Mie.

"You okay?" I whisper into the mic.

Another shot. Then another.

"Mie! You okay?"

"Yes. Three more down. Weapon empty."

"Grab a clip on your way over, will you? I'm almost dry."

The drone dips into the lower area and is out of sight. I crawl toward the lip of the stairs that lead into the underground chamber.

"You see him, Roberts?" Cap says into my ear.

"No," I whisper.

"We'll light him up."

A pinprick red dot hits the back of the person below me. I aim for it, using the laser on the rifle to match the bead. A squeeze. The rifle barks and jumps in my arms.

"Down. Searching."

The drone's pointer goes off. Mine turns off once my finger leaves the trigger.

"You'll need to light it up a little down there. Remember, I lost my visor."

Our last drone flies by me and into the hole. Light pours out of the opening as it releases flairs before shooting back out with bullets following it.

"Best we could do," Cap says. "If they had night vision, then they'll be sitting ducks for twenty seconds. Get down there."

"And if they don't?" I ask.

"Mie is on her way."

The morbid joke is not lost on me. I'll have to make it up with Cap later on.

Scrambling to my feet, I rush to the stairs and fly down them as fast as possible. The flairs will only last a few minutes, then the darkness will envelop the hole again. At the bottom, I stop by the person I shot and roll the body over—no night vision. The young eyes of a teenager stare back at me. Fuck.

"They have kids down here fighting against us," I say into the mic. "Orders?"

"If they're shooting at you, protect yourself. If you keep any alive, make sure to secure them before moving on."

"Roger."

The bottom is not like the top. Some of the tunnels reach out to the end of the building and others toward the canal. The flairs shot out from the drone give me some illumination, but not much. It's a guess. Where would Wang run to? Safety, I guess. But which way is that?

A door closes. Toward the canal. North from the direction of the sound. He has to have something out there.

I rush toward the noise, feet slamming against the floor in a methodical beat. The light of the flairs is well behind me, but shadows dance against the walls.

A door, like those on old battleships, hangs open before me. The metal bars are extended, unable to get into the corresponding holes to secure it from moving. A gentle push and long dry hinges squeal in protest. I hit the flashlight on the rifle. Bringing up the muzzle, I apply pressure on the trigger. Not enough to fire, but enough to trigger the laser sight to turn on. The room is ghastly. A bed sits in the middle of the floor with a woman on it. She's spread-eagle, legs tied to the sides and arms secured above her head. Bruises color her neck. I drop the light on her face. Pretty and young. Dead for a little while, at least from her coloration.

Two doors. One east and one west. I need to pick one. But which?

I push open the west door. My rifle muzzle penetrates darkness until I turn the light on. The next room was converted into a holding cell. Three women cower in the corner. They whimper as the light touches them.

"Don't worry, I'll get you out." I take three strides to the cage door. It's secured with a simple padlock. I slam the butt of the rifle against it. And again. And again. The lock busts against the rifle's third impact. The women can be freed. A heavy weight lifts from me. One small victory achieved.

"Out, into the next door and to the right tunnel. Follow it to the end and up the stairs." I engage my radio. "Cap, got three captives coming your way."

"You sure they're not part of it?"

One of the girls cries as she enters the other room. Her hysterics remind me of how sheltered today's youth are when it comes to the ugliness of the world.

"Definite," I reply.

There's no exit from the room, just the way I came. Then the east door.

The girls scream again.

I rush out of the jail room in time to see Bojing Wang, arm around the throat of one of the girls, pulling her through the other door.

"Go!" I yell at the two.

The door closes behind Wang, and the wheel starts turning. I leap at it. Both hands grasp. The wheel stops before it hits the lock position. It starts to give way. I leverage myself. Pull. The wheel spins, and I fall back, off-balance.

Standing up quickly, I go to the opposite side of the door and spin the wheel all the way to open. With one foot, I push it in. Nothing. A little farther.

Sounds of struggling and choppy-Chinese. Lights illuminate the hall. Wang is about ten meters down, still struggling to keep the girl with him as he heads toward a right angle in the tunnel.

"Freeze, Wang. There's no way out."

He fires two rounds at me.

I duck behind the door frame as they ricochet. Sounds like a handgun. Glock, maybe a revolver? I can't tell. Didn't get enough time for a good glance. How many rounds has he fired? I keep counting. Two.

Nothing follows up. I look around the door frame, and he's at the turn in the tunnel. Stepping out, rifle up, I rush toward the corner. Twenty meters is not far unless you're running, and someone's life is in the balance. I get to the corner quick and look around.

Wang stands not ten meters away, still pulling the girl with him.

"Enough, Wang. We have shooters surrounding the building."

"We took out all you people," he calls back. "I go free, or woman dies."

He's at another door, and I don't want to lose him. I fire a round into the ground at my feet. Three rapid shots come down the hall. He's panicking. Trapped. Looking for a way out. Five.

"Give it up, Wang. You're dead if you go outside with the girl."

"Fuck you, cop!"

Two more bullets run down the hall. Not a revolver. Seven.

The door down the hall clicks. I sneak a glance around the corner. Wang braces the girl against the wall with his left arm. His right is on the door's wheel. It's not moving as he tries to spin it. Just a muffled click as if something holds it in place. He swears once again in Chinese.

"Fuck, cop! Don't you think I kill her?"

I fire into the wall and duck back. One shot comes down, and then nothing but swearing. He's out of ammo.

Crouching, I step around the corner.

He stands there, gun in one hand, trying to release the clip. The breach of the gun is open. Empty. A madness dances in his eyes. The girl gasps for breath against the crushing effects of his arm.

"You're done, Wang. No bullets in your gun and nowhere to run." I let the rifle drop to my side and draw out Ron's Desert Eagle. My thumb pulls back the hammer.

"You no understand. I have her!" He takes his arm off the girl's throat and spins her in front of him. The tattered clothing barely stays in place as he uses her as a shield.

"We're you going?" I ask, taking a step forward. "There's nowhere to go now. You've reached the end."

"I kill her, cop!" His hand snakes up to the woman's throat. She grabs at it with desperate fingers, but he's too strong. "I swear! She dies!"

I stop, raise the pistol. "I'm a good shot, Wang. You think I can get you from here?"

His head ducks behind hers, and I shuffle closer with him distracted.

"No closer!" he yells. "I kill her!"

"You keep saying that, but what then? You'll lose her as a shield."

His eyes go wide. "It your fault if she die."

"No, it will be your fault. You are the one who will kill her."

Desperation races through his voice. "No more! Back!"

I step closer. "There's no way out for you, Wang. If you get past me, you'll have to deal with Ling. And you know what she thinks of you."

His eyes dart to the girl and then back to me. Sweat beads on his forehead. His grip loosens on the girl's neck. Eyes start to close then go wide.

"I fuck her up!" he says, his hand moving away from her neck and into her tattered top. "She be damaged if I no go free."

The pistol is up. I point it right at his head. Ready to put a bullet into it.

"Yeah, you no want her fucked up. Dead is better," he says.

The woman's eyes are all but whites. He's feeling her up. Hand groping at her breast. She cries the defenseless cry of a captured soul no longer able to fight the evil encompassing it. Tears drop down to her cheeks, leaving trails of clean skin behind.

Wang's got a cigarette in his mouth. A lighter comes up to ignite it. The cocky bastard. It's too much. The bribe, the kidnapping, the assault, the threats. Nothing is sacred to this man–this demon. The world is a better place if he's just covered with dirt in a pine box.

The flame reaches the cigarette. Wang pulls on it until the end lights up.

That's enough. He'll never be civilized. Never rehabilitated. He's an animal.

I pull the trigger.

January 17th, 2033 – Arrest

I carry the woman down the hall and away from the horror. She's lighter than I thought, and my coat doesn't add that much to her weight. At the door to the rape room, I meet Mie. She's breathing heavily and covered in sweat. I didn't know cyborgs could sweat, but then again, I don't think she really is one. Aren't cyborgs controlled in part by their machine parts? Mie lacks in emotional interaction but is one-hundred percent human.

She looks right at me; a question forms in those dark brown eyes. I just nod to the girl in my arms.

"I'm taking her out of here." I walk to the door that leads out of this hell.

"Where Wang?" Mie asks.

I don't turn. There's no real answer to that question. Just time to get this woman the help she'll need to overcome this trauma. Then I can get a hot shower to wash off all the dirt accumulated from this horrid case.

"Roberts! Wang?" Mie asks again.

"Down the hall. Do what you want." I keep walking.

The girl's arms start to loosen their grip around my neck, but her tears still roll out. I hope the other two women made it. If Mie had anything to do with it, they're probably at the command center already. That's why she's so late.

I get to the stairs, arms tired from holding the woman. Carrying her has just about drained me. The strobes of emergency lights dance off the walls as I make my way up the last step and leave the tunnels behind. At the top, I glance at the hole in the wall on the east side of the building. Cap is there, along with multiple paramedics and the area fire department. I head toward them, my legs screaming.

Cap looks up as I'm halfway there and he comes running toward me. The woman squeezes her arms tighter around my shoulders, face buried into my chest. The one side of her head brushes stubble against my chin. There's nothing I can do to make her let go. She's been through hell, and if this makes her able to face life again, who am I to question it.

"Roberts, you okay?" Cap asks.

"Fine." I keep shuffling toward the exit.

"I can take her if you want," he offers.

Her arms tighten. "It's okay. She's not heavy."

I get to the main slaughter area and whisper to the woman, "Keep your eyes closed. Nothing to see here."

Medics come up. One tries to take the woman from me, but she grips my neck like it protects her from the outside world. I have a primal urge to make sure she's safe before I let her go.

"Just show us to a bus," I say.

The medic puts her hand under my arm and guides me to a vehicle. Another medic joins us. He opens the doors to let us in. With their help, I climb in with the woman still clutching me.

I sit on the bench in the bus, gurney not even an arms-length away. Rocking back and forth, I try to calm the woman; tell her she's going to be all right, to let the medics take a look at her. I keep rocking, whispering, and stroking her hair. Thoughts of the torture she endured float into my mind. She didn't deserve it. Finally, she relaxes her grip enough for me to lower her onto the gurney, and one medic takes her vitals. She whispers her name to me. "Gabriella."

"She going to be okay?" I ask.

"Just shock and dehydration," she says, putting in an IV. "We'll get her physically up soon. It's her mind I'd worry about."

I want to strike the side of the bus but hold back the anger. So many of them piling up. There's nothing more I can do, so I stand. The girl looks at me, eyes wide. Lips form the word no.

"You'll be okay. They'll take really good care of you. I'll come and visit soon."

The flashing lights recede into the distance as the bus goes through the parking lot and then behind trees. I just stand there staring after it, hoping pleasant thoughts can once again cloud the woman's nights instead of the nightmares I know will soon haunt her. Maybe she'll be lucky and forget. Maybe she'll be haunted for the rest of her life. I don't know. At least the one who did it paid the ultimate price.

Mie places a hand on my shoulder. Blood covers it. I don't ask. Don't want to know. Just look away and pretend nothing happened.

"You okay?" she asks.

I still watch the distance. The sun lights the horizon and threatens to warm up the world just a little bit before sneaking its way back down. There's no wind anymore. The snow doesn't fall. The sky is clear of clouds. It's going to be a good day. The bad guys are gone. But so are a lot of good guys. And the devil is no longer with us to wiggle free and exert his power against justice.

"Is it worth it?" I ask.

"Worth what?" Mie replies.

"All the pain." I take a deep breath, blow it out. "You went through a lot and survived. Do you ever regret living through it?"

Mie's hand comes off my shoulder. She steps forward to be beside me. The outline of her features takes on a somber mood. But that only lasts a second. "Yes," she says. "And no."

I glance over at her. A tear in her eye threatens to jump before it freezes in the cold winter air.

She lifts a hand to wipe it away, sees the blood, and drops it. "I lived to do this. It drove me. Pushed me. If I not go through it, never would be here. Not help you to stop from happening again. That make it worth living. Saving others."

Mie turns her head toward me. A smile touches her lips but not her eyes. "We do good here. People live because of you and me. The world better we in it."

I nod. It's because of her thoughts and outlook, the simple way of breaking down what we do that makes today more worthwhile. The world does appear to be a better place.

"So, what are you going to do now?" I ask.

She stares into the distance sunrise. "I go home. Hug father."

Julie lingers at the door getting her shoes on when I enter. She drops her bag on the floor at the sight of me and pulls me close. I can get used to this type of reception. It's still early, just after seven, and Sarah is in the bathroom. Probably going to use up the next hour in there.

My shoes are off, and Julie strips away my coat. The rips in the shirt and evidence of the battle that ragged downtown tells her little of what went on. Questions fly at me faster than I can answer them. But when Sarah comes out of the bathroom, she flings her arms around me and hugs as hard as she can. I'm still sore, but who cares about that. If your teenage daughter wants to hug you, let it happen. God knows it's something not usually seen.

The girls have to go, but not because I want them to. Sarah has school, and Julie needs to go to work. At least it's a little safer for them to be out there. Amazing what an overnight assignment can do for your outlook on life.

At least Mie can help me out with the paperwork tomorrow. But now, all I want to is a shower.

The clerk at the desk of the hotel calls me over as I walk in. She's a short woman, maybe 150 cm, but what she lacks in height she makes up for in width. With a smile, she hands an envelope to me with the hotel logo on it. Written on the front is my name, along with Chinese letters.

"What is this?"

She smiles and speaks in a childlike tone. "Our guest, Mie Ling, asked that we keep an eye out for you. Supplied an image and reward if we gave you this before you tried to go up to her room."

"And why would she do that?"

"She checked out this morning. Flight left at one."

I glance at my phone. An hour ago. Why the hell would she leave without saying goodbye?

"You can read it over there if you like." The woman motions to a couch to the side of the lobby.

"Thanks." I step over to it.

The letter is sealed, but it opens easy enough. One sheet of paper rests inside with a flowing handwritten script. It's from Mie.

Detective Bruce Roberts,

I have enjoy work with you over last week. It not intention to have partner during this assignment but could not have more luck with who was given. You actions are credit to integrity and positive reflection on force you belong.

There times when I need take personal to reflect on actions. How I affect people around me, and what they think of me. And even though we start on the wrong shoe, we seem to overcome our difference and close out case efficiently.

If you travels happen to take you to China, please come see me. I be happy to show you around wonderful country. But bring wife and child, for they are good part of you soul. Warn you wife, I make her noodles every day she comes.

I talk with Captain Max about what we been through. I sure he look a little favourable upon your work now. And if no, tell him contact me for correct words.

As I would say in my country, Zhi dao woo men zai jian main - Till we meet again.

Mie

I fold the letter and put it into my pocket.

About the Author

Douglas Owen is a writer, author, editor, and publisher. His love of Science Fiction started at a young age when his Grandmother gave him a copy of Fantastic Tales from the early 1940's. And though she is not with us anymore, her love of "Adult Fairytales" lives on.

Doug lives in Goodwood, Ontario, a hamlet outside of Uxbridge. There he takes care of three cats and brings his wife coffee in the morning (when he remembers).

A technology junky, Doug enjoys working on his computers, servers, and fishing.

Follow Doug on Facebook and watch his website for upcoming books - https://douglasowen.ca

Also by Douglas Owen

The Spear Series

- A New Spear
- A Spear Point
- A Broken Spear
- A Spear for the Realm (Coming 2026)

Inside My Mind

- Volume One
- Volume Two
- Volume Three (coming 2026)

Broken World

- The Hordes
- The Family (Coming 2027)

So You Want To Write A Book

www.ingramcontent.com/pod-product-compliance
Lightning Source LLC
Chambersburg PA
CBHW050341030726
47503CB00008B/2556